Hidden Fede

Federation Trilogy Book Three

Tony Harmsworth

I dedicate this trilogy to Frank Hampson, whose artwork and storylines in the Eagle, inspired my lifelong interest in science fiction

Get Tony Harmsworth's Moonscape Novella FOR FREE

Sign up for the no-spam newsletter and get Moonscape and other exclusive content, all for free.

Details can be found at the end of HIDDEN FEDERATION.

Copyrights and Thanks

Thanks to:

Wendy Harmsworth, Marni Penning and Melanie Underwood

Also, thanks to these VIP Beta Reader Club Members: Annette Burgess, Anne Graham, Jim Hewlett, Dr. H. Craig Holoboski, Dean Howard, Scott Kreisler, Colin Pain, Mike Ramay, Nev Rawlins and Linda Reed

ISBN: 9798654847010

Published by:

Harmsworth.net

Drumnadrochit

Inverness-shire

IV63 6XJ

i) *Federation* Refresher

[Note for non-British readers – Tony writes using UK English spelling, punctuation, and grammar.]

[The Federation Trilogy is a work of speculative science fiction, not a promotion of any particular political system. Enjoy it for what it is – a view into one possible future. If it isn't the particular politics you prefer, please do not allow it to spoil your enjoyment of what is, after all, just an imaginative story. Tony Harmsworth.]

[There is a glossary at https://harmsworth.net/glossary.pdf which you might like to bookmark.]

Author Rummy Blin Breganin, a citizen of the planet Daragnen, wrote his Federation Trilogy when he discovered that Earth had been prohibited from both space flight and all use of quantum technology, the key to interstellar travel.

His first book, written long after the events described in his second book, follows the story of Earth's first contact with the Federation. Rummy wants to point out that this edition often contains Earth measurements and times etc. to save confusion in descriptions of historic alien scenarios.

Initially things seemed to go well, but the Federation's economic system conflicted with that of Western Europe, the United States of America and many other countries. Its similarity to communism immediately caused suspicion and distrust.

The leaders of more than twenty countries were each taken to visit five Federation worlds, including one new member world and the capital of the Federation, Arlucian.

Gradually, President Spence of the USA began to be won over by all of the benefits of membership, but he realised that the Federation's economic system was going to be a hard sell to the wealthy minority who held much of the power in western democracies. They would have to forego their wealth in order to allow the general population to benefit. In other words, there would need to be a modicum of socialism, not a word one would normally associate with America.

The Federation began to make sense to him. Its economic system relied upon automatons. Over several hundred thousand years, the manufacture of robots had been perfected. They could do anything and everything people could ever be asked to do. On Earth in the twenty-first century, we consider that a robot which can pick strawberries is the height of sophistication, but utility robots in the Federation could handle any task. Most were not designed to perform one function well, but to use their AI minds to work out how to do virtually anything, dipping into the Frame (a clean and accurate Federation version of the Internet), if they needed advice or instructions or to manufacture a temporary spare part. If a robot were asked to peel a grape, it would do so perfectly and then go on to prepare a seven-course gourmet meal or strip a jet engine and perform a complete mechanical rebuild, calling in other robots as and when necessary.

Most utility robots could also handle many other jobs from caring for paraplegics and handling all of their hygiene and other needs, to fetching and carrying in homes or industrial workplaces. A domestic robot could be asked to go and do the shopping. It would find out what was needed by examining the contents of the refrigerator, the store cupboards and freezer. Before it left, it would ask if anything special or unusual was required. Saying, 'Yes, get everything for a burger barbecue for eight people this Sunday too,' would not result in a further string of questions other than the obvious request for how many vegans or vegetarians there might be. The robot would then get into the autonomous car which it would ask to take it shopping.

There were, of course, specialist robots which carried out single tasks to perfection – repairing cataracts, or heart valves and so on. Medibots diagnosed and treated all manner of medical problems and some were even more specialised to conduct surgery.

In an industrial or farming setting, robots would carry out all duties ever handled by people, from planting to dealing with cattle insemination programmes. If they ran into problems, they would ask for help – no, not from a person, but from the Frame, an overseer bot or monitoring system. During visits to other worlds by Earth's leaders during the first Federation volume, some bots told the leaders they had not had contact with a living being in hundreds of years of manufacturing.

The upshot of the expertise of robots and other AI systems is that people no longer have anything to do. Profit from all the state-owned businesses throughout the Federation is gathered into a pool and distributed equally so that everyone shares in the wealth of nearly a quarter of a million worlds.

It is easy to imagine how some might view this as being a communist or socialist regime, but it must be remembered that no one had *any* work or any other way to make an income. The galaxy would have been controlled and owned by multi-billionaire owners of key businesses, all staffed by robots. Ex-employees would starve or be supported by the state in some shape or form. There was simply no other alternative.

However, the Federation encouraged people to work about ten per cent of the time on something they would enjoy – rare breed management, teaching, writing, gardening and so on. Inventors suddenly had the time to come up with new ideas and innovations and could get access to the equipment and machine shops or laboratories they might need. This meant that, instead of having to develop their idea themselves, including all of the hassle of raising finance and running the business, they could hand over the idea to robots. Automatons produced the items, keeping in production the successful products, but also stocking more niche items which would never be profitable, but added to the quality of life for people. Inventors also received bonuses as reward for their ideas, but never excessive, perhaps the value of another off-world holiday that year or such like. Crucially, no one could grow to become an oligarch just because they had one good idea or were in the right place at the right time.

The system, of course, would still be seen by some as communism, a reviled system which had reared its head early on twentieth century Earth and persisted for over fifty years in Russia and even longer in China and North Korea. It was so despised that many people were unable to get their heads around the fact that, in a world where not just some, but *all* the work was performed by automatons, some sort of redistribution of wealth was essential. In an automaton economy, a form of socialism was the only solution. It prevented the growth of a system which exploited people, often in other countries, to make others into billionaires. The capitalist system saw wealthy countries ignoring poverty, starvation and disease in poorer countries; and consuming resources and creating pollution, to the serious detriment of the general world population and the environment. It is a fundamental Federation principle that any child born is entitled to an equal share of the resources and wealth of the entire Federation.

In the Federation, the automaton economic system resulted in everyone having a great standard of living, all receiving the same level of medical attention, living anywhere they wished on-world or off-world somewhere else in the galaxy. Poverty is non-existent in the Federation, but so is obscene wealth. Whether it be a person in a rural setting on Veroscando or the Federation president itself (a sexless budding creature), the income was the same. Volunteers who liked action could participate in the Federation rapid-reaction force to deal with natural disasters and unexpected outbreaks of disease. People could do anything they wished to do, as long as it did not hurt others or their planets. If a person had a hankering to do any job which a robot was undertaking, all they had to do was ask the robot to move aside. The robot would continue to observe to ensure quality was up to standard and assist if required. No one was banned from working.

The offer to join the Federation appeared to be a no-brainer and the leaders of most countries saw that if they did not support joining, they would be seen as being more interested in their own greed and selfishness.

Eventually, President Spence achieved some progress with politicians and industrialists, but then there was an unexpected power grab by Vice President Slimbridge who, during just such a meeting, had the president arrested for treason, claiming that he was about to hand over control of the United States to communist aliens.

The president found himself in prison, but the FBI quickly realised that the charges were trumped up and helped him break out with the House minority and majority leaders, the main democratic candidate for president and several of the captains of industry who had been with the president at the time of the arrest and were detained as co-conspirators.

From the outskirts of Washington, they escaped in a Chinook helicopter to New York where they were going to claim diplomatic asylum in the UN complex. However, Vice President Slimbridge, with all the resources of the military, pursued them and had the helicopter shot down as it reached the UN building.

The UN had called a meeting to approve an application for Federation membership and Slimbridge intended to veto the vote despite the other veto-holders, the Security Council, having previously agreed that it would be a free vote. Unknown to Slimbridge, President Spence and most of the other Chinook passengers had been rescued by the Federation from the helicopter an instant before it exploded. UN troops arrested Slimbridge under a warrant from the International Court of Justice in The Hague when he arrived for the debate and entered UN territory.

With Spence back in charge, the meeting was rearranged, and all the leaders of the world met at the UN HQ. In the meantime, elements of the US military sprung Slimbridge and plotted against Spence.

On the day of the vote, Slimbridge had a nuclear bomb detonated under the UN building killing all of the world leaders and the entire Federation diplomatic team. Virtually all of New York was destroyed in the explosion.

A new Federation ambassador was appointed and, after discussing the situation with the Federation Cabinet on Arlucian, it was decided to visit the UK prime minister. The outcome was that Earth was told to clean up its act; that all space research and the use of quantum technology was banned; and there would be no further involvement until Earth decided to contact the Federation to gain membership and that this would not be allowed until all countries in the world were united in that quest.

ii) *Federation and Earth* Refresher

In the second volume we meet the new political characters who will be important. The prime minister of the United Kingdom; the presidents of France, Russia and China plus the new secretary general of the United Nations.

The United States had isolated itself from the rest of the world. President Slimbridge found it difficult to come to terms with the enormity of his actions. He surrounded himself with yes-men. Uprisings were quickly quashed until a group headed by General Beech became organised under the banner of *Free America.*

The Federation remained detached and was playing no part.

Most countries were furious that Slimbridge could have taken such drastic action as to blow up the UN, despite it being against the interests of all other nations.

America became even more isolated. Free America was gaining prestige, acting like a hornet at a barbecue, causing people to swat and miss, but generally have their lives spoiled. Slimbridge was furious.

The United Nations pleaded for help from the Federation and a new plan emerged; one which would allow all countries in the world to join the Federation with the exception of the USA which would keep its independence.

The vote was taken. The United States would retain its independence and the rest of the world would become part of the Federation. It was a unique situation and had never been attempted before in all the hundreds of thousands of years of Federation history.

President Slimbridge soon discovered that remaining independent and sharing the world with the Federation meant that the actions of the USA must not be allowed to harm the planet. Airlines were no longer allowed to fly outside the USA fifty mile coastal limit, and this also applied to US businesses operating cruise liners, fishing and other offshore businesses.

This is when I, Professor Rummy Blin Breganin, the author of this trilogy, arrived on the scene. I watched the effect of partition in the USA, but when I arrived in California, I discovered that the state was considering revolt and had declared a UDI (Unilateral Declaration of Independence). It wanted to break away from the USA and join the Federation.

We pick up the story as I make the decision to flee California. With my one bulging bag, I arrived at Los Angeles airport.

1 LAX

My cab pulled in outside the departures entrance to Los Angeles International Airport.

I alighted, paid the fare, grabbed my bag and tried to find my way through the oppressive throng outside the departures building.

Being of small stature I was buffeted and almost knocked over several times. Most of these inconsiderate people looked around to see what was in their way and, on seeing me, firstly recoiled in horror then, as realisation dawned that I was an alien, they then did their best to ignore me. This was certainly not a pleasant experience and it continued until pressure from behind actually sent me sprawling across the pavement. I was lucky not to be trampled to death.

A kindly individual reached down, grabbed my shoulder and hoisted me to my feet. I thanked him and he said his name was Harry.

'You entering or leaving?' he asked.

'Trying to enter,' I said.

'You speak good English,' he said.

'Thank you.'

'Look. Follow me. Stay close and let's get you inside the building.'

I was grateful for the help. Harry was middle-aged and quite tall and well-built – larger than most humans. It was strange how some humans liked to have large waistlines. He was one of those. I stayed tight by his side and as I looked around, I saw more people pointing at me and shouting 'look' or 'it's one of them' or 'hey, it's an alien' with various levels of incredulity.

Finally, Harry reached the door and we both entered one of the rotating segments. We were trapped, but I guessed Harry knew how these things worked. Eventually, it began to rotate again, and we were able to exit into an even more tightly packed horde.

'Where are you heading to?' asked Harry. 'I'll help you get there.'

'I don't know. I want to leave America and thought London would be a good place to head for,' I said.

Harry looked around, soon saw something which attracted him, and we set off across the concourse. I was still swamped by the crowd and, of course, could see none of the signs or information boards. They were all hidden from me by the melee.

For some ten minutes we scrambled through the crowd, seemingly always fighting against the flow. Suddenly, we were standing by a waist-height desk, so about upper-chest height for me. Above it was a digital sign which announced, 'DEPARTURES TO EUROPE'.

'There's only a robot here,' said Harry. 'I don't know your name.'

'Rummy.'

'Hi, Rummy,' he said, stooping to shake my hand. 'Do you want me to try to find you a real person?'

I think, because of my stature, he was talking to me as if I were a very young person. 'No, no, that won't be necessary. The robot will be fine. Thank you for your help, Yol Harry. I don't know how I'd have made it without you,' I said. 'I take it that the airport is not always this busy.'

'Pleasure's mine,' he said. 'This crowd is very unusual. There must be a lot of people wanting out of California. Mind if I watch you interacting with the bot?'

'No. No problem at all.' I slid my bag around so that it was lying across my feet. I looked up at the bot.

'Good morning, robot. Here's my chip,' I said, holding up my hand.

A laser beam flashed for a second. 'Welcome to LAX, Professor Yol Breganin. My name's Cagert. How can I assist?' said the robot.

'You're a professor?' asked Harry.

'I am. I'm studying Earth's transition,' I said to the human, then to Cagert, 'I'd like to get to London, Cagert.'

'Any particular location?' it asked.

'Somewhere central.'

'There's a shuttle to Hyde Park in seventy-five minutes. Is that central enough?' asked Cagert, displaying a map of London in mid-air with the location of the arrival point flashing.

'That seems central enough, thank you. How much?'

'No charge. All US shuttle departures are free. Lift your hand.' Cagert's laser hit my chip and he passed me a piece of card. 'Your ticket is in your chip and the card is a hard copy.'

[Rummy's note: As part of banning air flights outside of the USA fifty mile coastal waters, the Federation had agreed to provide outward shuttle journeys free of charge in recompense.]

'It cost you nothing?' said Harry.

Cagert replied, 'There is no charge for any shuttles from the USA, sir.'

'What about the return journey?' asked Harry.

'As you don't have a personal chip, I can't send you the details, but you can look up the return prices on the Frame. The address is on this card. Most shuttle journeys would be inexpensive in comparison with the jet flights they replaced,' said Cagert, handing over a printed card about the size of a credit card which showed something similar to a QR code. 'Where do you wish to go?'

'I'm just heading to New Orleans. Don't like the chaos this declaration of independence is causing. I think it could turn nasty,' said Harry.

'Cagert, which way should Yol Harry go for his journey?' I asked.

'Oh, it's okay. I know where to go. Nice to have met you, Rummy. Have a good journey,' said Harry and started heaving his bulk through the crowd to the internal departures gates.

'Where do I go, Cagert?' I asked.

‘Follow this desk to your left and you will find a gateway. Just present your chip and follow the passage.’

‘Thank you, Cagert.’ I kept my right hand on the desktop and walked to the left. People were still jostling me, and I was grateful to reach the gateway.

Once my chip was scanned, I was away from the crowd and made my way down an enclosed glass passageway. One or two humans were also in the passage, looking around themselves at the alien walkway and the mob outside.

I arrived at a waiting area and took a seat. Twenty or so humans and a couple of aliens of unknown species were seated around me. More were arriving all the time. A digital sign told me that boarding would begin in sixty-five minutes.

‘Not travelled in one of these things,’ said a young human woman a couple of seats to my right. ‘What’s it like?’

‘You won’t even know you are moving,’ I said. ‘The door closes and it opens a minute later at your destination.’

‘Hard to believe,’ she said. ‘Where are you from?’

‘Daragnen.’

She stood and moved to the seat next to mine, dragging her hand luggage along the floor. ‘Can’t imagine all the people living on these thousands of worlds. Didn’t believe alien life would ever be discovered. Thought we were alone in the universe.’

‘Most species feel like that before first contact despite the universe having countless billions of worlds,’ I said. ‘We’ve been members for two hundred years, although we did know of another planet in our system which had life for centuries before that. Not intelligent life, though. Finding that life encouraged us to believe that there would be other intelligences elsewhere, but we had no way to travel between the stars.’

‘Two hundred years ago we still drove horses and carriages and were only just beginning to construct railways.’

‘We had spaceflight within our system from about seven hundred years in the past,’ I said. ‘But not interstellar, so many believed we were alone in the universe too.’

‘Did you have as much of a shock as we’ve had when the Federation made contact with you? How did it go on your world? I can’t believe it’s caused such problems in the USA, and now this destructive breakup of the states.’

‘I’ve studied it extensively. Our own membership was quite smoothly enacted. Some independent businesses were unhappy, but they fell into line. I’m planning a book about Federation transition.’

‘That would be fascinating,’ she said. ‘When did it all start?’

‘What, the Federation?’

‘Yes, it must have begun somewhere.’

‘It didn’t begin well,’ I said.

‘Please tell me, they say we have some time to wait before departure.’

‘Well, it’s a long story. I’ll see what I can do.’

‘Thanks, really appreciate it. What’s your name?’

‘Rummy.’

‘Nice to meet you, Rummy. I’m Emily.’

‘Why are you going to London?’ I asked.

‘I have family over there, and, like many people, I’m worried about all of the trouble in the States. Do tell me about the Federation, Rummy.’

‘On the scale of your planet, the Federation is exceedingly old. There were three planets with intelligent lifeforms in the system of Iasuqi approximately six hundred thousand years ago. They loosely traded with each other very much as your countries on Earth used to. There was no faster-than-light travel in those days which meant that journeys between each sometimes took years, depending upon the relative locations of the worlds – and remember, these worlds were all in the same system. Interstellar travel was, to all intents and purposes, impossible. At interplanetary speeds, it would take hundreds of years to even reach the closest star,

'Miift, with two small continents, was the least populated world in the Iasuqi system. Oceans covered eighty per cent of the planet. It was also the place where much of the local space technology was developed. In fact, they provided the ships and space stations for Desfogg and Mepdetvis, the other two worlds with intelligent life in the system. Gradually they increased their influence over the other worlds. You wouldn't call it an empire, but their grip on the economies of the other two became increasingly controlling.

'At this point, a race which had invented a primitive version of the FTL (Faster Than Light) drives we use today arrived in the system and began to trade with the three planets. A result of this was that Desfogg and Mepdetvis were able to obtain better technology from the newcomers than Miift had provided.

'Miift got miffed with the newcomers,' I smiled at my joke, 'and a war began. It was a hopelessly unbalanced event. Miift became a wasteland world and what was left of the population were rescued by Desfogg, who took them in and allowed them to live on part of their world in exile.'

'Who were the newcomers?' the young woman asked.

'They were Arlucians.'

'That sounds familiar,' she said.

'It should do. Arlucian is the capital planet of the Federation,' I told her.

'So, the Federation is actually run by the bad guys?'

'You'd better let me finish,' I said.

We both looked up at the flight sign. I still had plenty of time.

'Arlucian was already visiting and trading with many other planets. There was a loose trading block around one million years ago, that might be the true age of the Federation depending upon your point of view. Do you remember seeing the fishlike ambassador? Yol Hareen Trestogeen?'

'Yes,' Emily said, 'he balanced himself on his tail.'

'That's right. His planet, Pestoch, is a water world in the same system as Arlucian.'

'What, nothing but water?'

'No, it does have land, but it is primarily water and the only intelligent creatures on it lived in the oceans and lakes. They built settlements on land, as you might do in your seas and also developed sophisticated technology, despite their lack of digits.

'However, I digress. Arlucian traded with a few dozen worlds in nearby star systems. There was general condemnation among them when the rumours began about what Arlucian had done to the planet Miift and sanctions were put on them. In effect, none of the known worlds, at that time, would trade with Arlucian at all.

'Factions on Arlucian became aggressive towards X-Jastu, a world in a nearby star system, because it was apparent that they were trying to control the other worlds. A union of planets was formed to enforce sanctions upon Arlucian. A second war took place. The Arlucians had not realised the sophistication of the technology of X-Jastu. Millions of automatons descended on Arlucian and the world became what you would call an occupied police state.'

'Wow!' Emily said.

'How the mighty had fallen,' I said. 'The rule of the Union of Planets over Arlucian continued for more than a generation, relaxation of their control only coming after all of the original ruling classes had died and they felt the punishment could end. X-Jastu called for a meeting of all planets to be held on Arlucian.'

'And the Federation came from that?' asked the young woman.

I looked up and found there was a small audience listening to me. Was it just that I was an alien in their midst? Perhaps. I continued, 'Not quite, Ya Emily, but they decided to share technologies and to ban interplanetary conflict. A committee was created after the Miiftian atrocity, and the trading group became known as the Galactic Empire. Arlucians had always been very capable administrators of whatever they were undertaking, and, as a way of letting the Arlucians know that the failings of their leaders in the past were forgiven, the central administration of the empire was constructed in Oridin. It remains the capital city of Arlucian to this day, six hundred thousand years later.'

'And the Federation arose from that?' asked a man who was standing in the aisle.

'How long ago was this?' asked another.

'Six hundred thousand years although some claim the seeds of the Federation stretch back a million,' I repeated. 'The empire continued to expand. X-Jastu's skills at developing automatons became dispersed among other planets. Some remarkable robots grew out of that combination of original design and new eyes and brains on dozens of planets looked to develop and improve them.

'Gradually, more and more menial tasks were undertaken. With the arrival of intelligent robots came a whole new set of problems.'

My ticket vibrated to advise that the flight was boarding. I noticed, with amusement, that this was an unexpected development for most of the passengers in the waiting area. They all grabbed their pockets and purses, extracting the card version of their tickets and studying them. The sign changed to "boarding" and an orderly queue formed.

With no need for security and no one being able to board unless they were in possession of a valid ticket which was sensed by a gate-bot, the line swiftly vanished into the square-shaped fuselage of an atmospheric shuttle.

The humans sat and began searches for non-existent seat belts. By the time they realised that belts were not provided, the doors opened, and we disembarked onto the roof of what had previously been an office building in the centre of London. We were already there. We exited through glass walkways and boarded a lift to the lower floors. Those with chips in their hands were able to walk straight out into the London sunshine. Two other lines formed to one side. One was for those wishing to become Federation citizens and the other for those who were just visiting.

I decided to stay and watch people interacting with the immigration process.

2 McDonald's

'Emily, it's me,' I said, ducking under a tape barrier to join her in the immigration queue.

'Excuse me, Yol Professor Breganin, you should not be in this line,' said a robot, about the size of a parking meter, which trundled across to intercept me.

'I'm studying Federation integration,' I said. 'I need to see the process.'

'I see,' the robot said, apparently satisfied, and trundled back to its position beside the tape barrier.

'I hope you don't mind me watching your progress through the system,' I said.

'How did it know who you were? Are you famous?' asked Emily.

I laughed and said, 'Not at all. It read my chip.'

'They can do that from a distance? I don't mind you watching,' she said.

'Thank you. They can do it within a certain range. It not only personalises the interaction, but it also gives them a chance to check that you aren't an undesirable,' I explained.

'I'm not sure civil rights organisations would be too happy about that,' she said.

'No, not at first,' I said. 'I'll be speaking to some people to see how their views change over time.'

'You think they'll accept it eventually?'

'This is the beauty of being at this segregated world right from the start. I can learn about how it develops and I'll be putting it in a book, maybe in eight or ten years.' The line shuffled forwards. 'You're next.'

We were now standing at a yellow line on the floor. In front of us were five immigration passages. People had to walk into a space beside the immigration desk, turn and face the desk-bot. An image was taken, records were made of weight and height etc. The person in front passed through and Emily moved into the space.

'Good morning, please give me your name, current address, and date of birth,' said the desk-bot. The voice was disembodied. The bot was built-in to the desk with just a pair of arms emerging from the surface.

Emily spoke the details and was then asked for her current skills, qualifications, bank account and other information.

'Can I confirm that you wish to enter to become a Federation resident? Answer yes or no.'

'Yes,' she said, then hurriedly added, 'but I might want to go back in the future.'

'Of course, but you wish to enter to live here rather than as a tourist?'

'Yes.'

'Please extend your less favoured hand, palm down, onto the blue panel set into the desk,' said the bot.

Emily extended her left hand and laid it squarely where required.

'You might feel a slight sting,' said the bot.

The left mechanical hand took Emily's, moved her thumb to one side and held it firmly in place. The other hand reached into a container beside the desk, and removed what appeared to be a pair of forceps, similar to long-nosed pliers. They briefly gripped the fold of flesh between her finger and thumb and withdrew.

'Your chip is installed. It has a full record of your details, and you can now use it to access your bank to pay for any purchases. Your American dollars have been converted to Federation afeds at the current exchange rate, which is one to one. I also injected some nanobots which will ensure no infection or rejection occurs. They will leave your body in two weeks. Your monthly income will appear in your bank account during the last week of the month. Do you understand?'

'I think so,' said Emily.

'Any Federation infobot can explain anything which requires clarification. You should also, when you have time but within a month, contact an infobot to answer a more detailed questionnaire so that your record can be more comprehensive. Welcome to the Federation. You are now a Federation citizen. Congratulations.'

'That was easy,' she said to me, picking up her bag, while examining her left hand. There was a small red mark, but the chip itself was too tiny to be visible.

'They often put chips in shoulders at birth, but the hand is easier for adults and is becoming the most common location. I'm really grateful for being able to watch that. I'm sure you'll enjoy Federation life,' I said, shaking her hand.

'You don't get away as easily as that, Rummy. Can I buy you lunch? I want more of the story.'

I was taken aback. This was the first time anyone on Earth had suggested eating together. I said yes and we left the arrivals building onto a busy highway near Marble Arch. Emily took me into a McDonalds restaurant facing the monument. I'd seen these all over the United States, but never entered one.

'What would you like?' she asked as we stood in line, looking up at the illustrated menu. 'Gosh, they're all robots.'

This wasn't unusual to me, of course, but I could imagine how it might look to her. 'The business seems to have transitioned,' I said. 'There are unlikely to be any humans involved now.'

'Amazing,' she said as a six-armed automaton served the customer in front of us and we moved forward.

'What would you like, Emily, and you Rummy?' asked the robot.

'Gosh, it knows our names,' she said. 'A Big Mac with fries and lemonade for me, please. I'm paying for both.'

'The same,' I said, not really knowing what else to choose.

'No, sir. They've already said they will not enter the US now that the independence is signed and sealed. We'll be on our own,' said Bernie.

'Okay, let's leave,' said the governor.

'My place first. Isobel will help us disguise,' said Mark.

The governor pulled a pistol from his desk drawer, stuck it into his waistband and the three men left the office.

Our meals were provided and we climbed the stairs and sat in a quiet corner.

'Well? What happened to the empire?' she asked.

I took a bite of the burger. It was lovely, but probably too full of calories for its size. The gherkin was a rather weird flavour, but very enjoyable.

'What is the green thing?' I asked.

'Gherkins or sometimes just called pickles.'

'Odd.'

'Acquired taste,' she said and laughed.

Once I'd swallowed, I said, 'Automatons continued to become more sophisticated. Intelligent utility robots could do anything a living creature could do, faster, more accurately and in a greater variety of situations. You could ask your domestic bot to peel the skin off a soft fruit or build a wall in your garden. Once they reached that skill level problems arose. The companies that made the automatons were becoming exceedingly rich, while they employed fewer and fewer living creatures. Those creatures lost their jobs and, depending upon which world they lived on or political system, some had to fall back on state support while others, quite literally, starved. Something had to be done.'

'I suppose that is like word processing software reducing the need for typing pools,' she said.

'Typing pool?' I asked.

'Rooms of people, usually women, who did nothing but type letters dictated by others. Tens of thousands of those jobs disappeared in the last century.'

'Typing?'

'A typewriter was a machine for writing letters. Keys were hit the same as with a computer, but the impression on paper was made by a metal hammer with a reverse of the letter required. It hit the paper through an inked ribbon to leave the letter on the page. Variations had the type on a golf ball which spun around depending upon which key you typed. My father still has one of those.'

'Sounds dreadfully complicated. Must have taken ages to make a whole letter,' I said.

'Well, no actually. A good typist could achieve at least seventy-five words per minute or more.'

'Extraordinary. What happened to the people who lost their jobs as typists?' I asked.

'They were out of work and had to find something else to do to earn a living.'

'And did they?'

'Oh, yes. In fact, we never really heard anything again about all those lost typists' jobs. They must have just done something else.'

'Yes, that is what happened on most worlds as computers and robots arrived. Initially, it seems to be a similar situation, but with the increasing sophistication of the automatons it was more serious as there were no other jobs to do. Automatons could do everything and anything. All that was needed was to produce more of them until they undertook everything a being could do,' I said.

'So, what happened?' Emily asked.

'Economies started to fail. Large proportions of populations could find no way to earn money. Most societies had some sort of safety net, a bare bones weekly payment, but it hardly covered their living costs. There was no way to buy luxuries. Even in socialist systems on some worlds, the payments were not sufficient. Automatons could make things exceedingly cheaply, but there were still fewer people capable of buying them. Owners and shareholders of the automaton companies were living in splendid, unbelievable luxury, yet continually complained about their sales and profits falling. It was the beginning of an enormous galaxy-wide economic depression. Something had to give.'

'What?' she asked.

‘Revolution and terrorism. Violent protests, damage to buildings and robots.’

‘Shocking.’

‘Yes, but the news spread, and similar terrorist acts took place throughout the empire. So many were involved that, even when they were caught, the authorities found themselves under attack and had to release their prisoners. The failing economies of the empire’s planets dipped from poor to non-existent.’

‘How did they stop it?’ she asked.

‘They didn’t. That is when the Federation charter was created,’ I said, finishing my fries and taking a last draught from my lemonade.

‘And that was it?’

‘Yes.’

‘Where can I see the charter?’ she asked.

‘On the Frame.’

‘Frame?’ she asked.

‘You call it the Internet, but it is sanitised to warn of articles which might mislead and factually erroneous material is automatically removed. It’s very carefully policed to ensure no abuse of freedom of speech et cetera.’

‘Thank you, Rummy. That was fascinating.’

‘And thank you for, what was it, the Big Mac? Delicious. Really odd having those gherkin things with bread, cheese, salad and meat. Thanks.’

‘My pleasure,’ said Emily.

‘Now,’ I said. ‘I must go. I’m hoping to see Earth’s newly appointed administrator.’

‘Oh, and who is that?’

‘Lara Horvat. She used to be the secretary general of what you called the United Nations. I understand she was offered the role of administrator and accepted.’

‘Why don’t robots do those jobs, then?’

'Ya Horvat's appointment is not an unusual situation. In fact, planetary governance is always undertaken by living beings from that world. The administrator is Earth's senior official. Federation ambassadors are biological entities too, but always alien to the world for which they are ambassadors.'

'If robots are intelligent, why don't they want to take up ruling positions? Surely they'd do it better than us.'

'Yes, they probably would and they are used as advisors. When the Federation was first formed, a part of a robot's control chip was to prevent such a desire arising. It's very sophisticated and the security as near infallible as it is possible to be. You'd need to talk to a cybernetics engineer to have it explained properly,' I said.

'Lovely meeting you,' said Emily.

'My pleasure,' I said, then had a thought. 'Can I recommend that you go to an esponging centre. Learn Galactic Standard – takes less than an hour then ask for a course on primitive Iasuqi. Once you've done that, try a course on primitive X-Jastu or the Union of Planets.'

'Iasuqi was the system with Miift in it?' she asked. 'Is esponging expensive?'

'No. It's education. In the Federation, education is always free. I am still having trouble understanding why the USA, and some of the rest of the pre-Federation world, had universities and schools which charge fees. What a crazy system – putting a price on education. Yes, Iasuqi is the system in which Miift exists. That course will elaborate upon what I've been telling you, but makes you also feel part of the action. You'll be given a POV (Point of View) option. Choose Debruek. He's fascinating. Then do one on Arlucian's interaction with Miift. I produced that second one. My favourite POV is Heldrian,' I said.

'Oh. You've really studied it?'

'Yes, although today I am more interested in recent Federation history. I must go. Pleasure meeting you, Emily.'

'Goodbye,' she said, and I headed out into the sunshine.

3 Permissions

Marcia Gray, a tall, slim, white, brunette, knocked on the door and entered Lara Horvat's office in the old ministry of defence building. 'There's a small alien asking to see you,' she said.

'Oh, who is it?'

'His name is Professor Breganin. He says it will only take a minute or two.'

'Okay. Show him in.'

I sat in the reception area, flicking through magazines, waiting patiently.

Ya Gray emerged through some double doors and beckoned me. We followed a long corridor, turned into an outer office where there were a couple of humans and some bots working and then through a stunning polished mahogany door.

I'd seen Ya Horvat in the media and immediately recognised her. She was a diminutive person, not much taller than me, with the slightly swarthy skin tone of those from the east of Europe from where she originated. Her hair was such a dark brown as to be virtually black. I guessed that she was about forty Earth years old.

She stood, walked around her desk, shook my hand and said, in Galactic Standard, 'Pleased to meet you, Yol Professor Breganin. How can I be of help?'

'The honour is mine,' I said.

She waved me to a seat and returned to her own.

'I'm a Professor at Dinbelay University on Daragnen. I'm a Federation historian and I would like to study the transition of Earth. It is unusual in that there has never been a segregated membership – the United States remaining independent and the rest of the world joining.'

'Yes, I suppose it is… different,' said the administrator.

'I've just arrived from the United States and would like a letter of introduction which I can show to the administrators around the world so that they will cooperate with me. Could you provide one?'

'I don't see why not,' she said and pressed a button on her desk. 'Marcia, when the professor leaves, he'll dictate a letter. When it's done, bring it in for my signature.'

I heard an affirmative reply come over the handsfree system.

'That's kind of you, Ya Horvat. Can I ask you a few questions before I leave?'

'Please do.'

'Has there been any change in relations between the Federation and the United States? I've just arrived from California and it was all rather chaotic.'

'No, professor. If anything, things are worse. President Slimbridge didn't fully understand what independence meant in the context of sharing the planet with the Federation,' said Lara.

'How do you mean?' I asked.

'Take air travel. It was agreed that the Federation would provide free transport for all people leaving the States. The details were in the document he signed, but he hadn't thought about the repercussions and still wanted aircraft to be flying to and from the USA. The Federation doesn't allow commercial jet or propeller aeroplanes owing to the pollution they cause. This meant that no flights outside the USA were permitted for anything except light aircraft.'

'Did that cause a problem?'

'Only to the president's battered ego,' said Lara. 'The same applied to shipping. Federation ships use electric motors. Although they are currently powered by land-based generators, gradually the power will be beamed direct to the ships from solar reflectors in orbit. In effect, this means that all the older generation of cruise ships and freighters are restricted to US coastal waters. Again, this was clearly laid out in the agreement, but the implications passed him by. Americans can still take cruises around the world, but they must be on Federation ships. He was very upset over that and there were a few incidents.'

'Incidents?'

'On two occasions, cruise ships set off from Florida to visit the Caribbean islands. This is a very popular destination for US tourists. The first ship set off on its route as if nothing had changed. Cruising, of course, is one of the most polluting forms of travel. A large cruise ship uses eighty thousand gallons of highly polluting diesel fuel, every single day. That, per passenger, produces almost twice the carbon footprint of flying.'

'That's huge. I didn't know. Explains the CO_2 concerns I'd heard the Federation had about Earth,' I said.

'Yes. The planet was reaching a tipping point but is now receding from it.'

'What, even in these few weeks?'

'Yes. The global CO_2 levels are measured in Hawaii and the last I saw, they had dropped to 410 parts per million.'

'What's the target?'

'A long way to go but 325 parts per million. However, the drastic reduction in production of CO_2 outside of America could see the target achieved in just a few years.'

'Anyway, Ya Horvat, the incidents. You were saying…'

'The first ship set off as normal and two Federation Enforcement ships came alongside and told the captain to return to US coastal waters. The captain complied.

'A few days later, a second ship left Miami accompanied by two US navy ships – a cruiser and destroyer. A couple of hours after they left US coastal waters, the Federation ships approached and asked the captains to return to US waters. The destroyer captain replied, saying that they had no intention of changing course. The Federation applied some sort of forcefield and slowed the cruise liner to stationary in only ten minutes. The destroyer told the Federation to release the cruise ship or it would take action. The Federation Enforcement ships refused to release the cruise liner and the destroyer fired a shot across their bow.

'Because the destroyer had just threatened to fire on the Federation ships, action was inevitable. A huge starship appeared above them. The navy ships were physically turned around and the forcefield pushed them back to US waters at more than fifty knots, throwing up huge bow waves. The captain of the cruise ship was told to turn and return to coastal waters, which he duly did.'

'Fascinating, thanks. And the other incident?' I asked.

'Very similar, but it was a large private yacht. A belligerent individual on board, probably the owner, refused to return to San Francisco and, once more, the Federation ships used their forcefields to turn it and propel it back to the Californian coast.'

'Were there any repercussions?'

'Oh, yes. Ambassador Yol Lorel Distern was called to the White House and castigated by the president. It ended up as a one-way shouting match, but eventually, President Slimbridge stormed out of the oval office and Matthew Brown, his chief advisor, calmed things down and there have not been further incidents since. I think the president was actually quite frightened of the sheer power of the Federation's forcefields. The arrival of the starship to resolve the Caribbean Sea incident was, I think, a real shock to him.'

'He is indeed a strange character,' I said. 'I've been reading about the American presidents and their constitution. Slimbridge seems most unlike the cool, clear-thinking leaders they had in the past.'

'It is no secret that I would like to see him gone. You know he is also a murderer. He blew up the United Nations building in New York to try to stop Federation membership.'

'Yes, I'd heard. I intend to write about that too,' I said. 'I've just sent my contact details to your computer. Please pass them on to anyone who might be able to help me – people involved in the thick of it, I think that's the expression.'

'With pleasure. Lovely to meet you, Professor.'

'My pleasure, Ya Horvat.'

She stood and took me out to her assistant's office where Ya Marcia Gray produced the letter of authority on official paper.

Now, where to start.

ooooooooooooo

Armed with my letter of introduction from the Earth's administrator, I could begin my research. Firstly, I needed to catch up. I contacted Miles DeVere, a journalist from *The Times* who majored in reporting on crime stories. We met up in a very comfortable lounge of a central London hotel.

'So, you're Professor Breganin,' he said. 'Pleased to meet you. Call me Miles.'

'I'm Rummy. Thanks for seeing me, Miles.'

'First alien I've met.'

'Now you're members, you'll soon see more, especially in tourist centres like London,' I said.

'What would you like to know? Why me?'

'I wanted to speak to someone who knew the crime scene really well,' I said. 'I'm studying transition. It is now many weeks since you became part of the Federation and I'd like to know how that affected criminals. Your reputation is the best. What happened in those first few days?'

'A lot. A huge and spectacular change.'

'I assume you were flooded with police bots and nano-crime-sensors?' I asked.

'Yes. The sheer number of them was staggering. There seemed to be a police bot on every street corner.

'At first,' he continued, 'the gangs and criminals didn't realise what it would be like. Of course, the Home Office had warned everyone that crime would no longer be tolerated, but most petty criminals didn't think it would stop them buying or selling weed or be able to stop their handbag and mobile phone thefts. Particularly those perpetrated from scooters and motorbikes.'

'Yes, I can imagine,' I said.

'I couldn't believe the efficiency of the nanobots. They detected illegal substances within a hundred metres, police bots were called, and arrests made.'

'Yes,' I said. 'Once a drug or substance is declared illegal – it can be different in some regions – the information is kept in a regional file. Nanobots in the Iran administrative region, for instance, have alcohol set as illegal. It works well. On Daragnen, and a growing number of other worlds, tobacco is illegal.'

'And crime stopping, Rummy, I actually watched a handbag theft in progress in Regent Street. It was grabbed by scooter thieves. They slowed down, the passenger grabbed the bag and the driver accelerated away. One of the most difficult crimes to prevent.'

'And…?'

'The scooter travelled about ten metres and stopped dead, the two thieves were thrown off the bike and instantly paralysed.'

'Yes, stasis.'

'Two police bots were on the scene in seconds. The bag was recovered and returned to the woman, the two perpetrators were stood against a blank area of wall and put into an hour's stasis. Their scooter was parked beside them. I heard the police bot say, "You are guilty of petty theft. Punishment is one hour stasis. You are now on the register and if you commit a second crime, the punishment will be one day's stasis. These are the details of your crime." It hung a lanyard around each of their necks with something the size of a credit card attached.'

'Pretty standard,' I said. 'The card would show them their crime and punishment and it would also be stored on their chips.'

'Ah, I think one of them wasn't chipped. Another robot arrived and chipped him.'

'Okay.'

'I didn't get to see what happened with drug deals, but one of my friends, a guy called Keith, who has a cocaine habit filled me in.'

‘What did he say?’ I asked.

‘He told me he’d gone to his local pub, where he usually bought his coke. Outside there were two of his usual suppliers in stasis. He entered and bought a drink. Another supplier came in via the fire exit. Keith offered a twenty pound note and a packet was passed over. Instantly a police bot entered. They were both taken outside. The supplier was given an hour’s stasis and Keith got ten minutes. When the stasis ended he examined his lanyard. It had a QR type code. He scanned it with his phone and was provided with an appointment at a clinic which he could attend if he was addicted.’

‘Did he go?’

‘No and he was picked up a second time and given an hour’s stasis. He hasn’t used cocaine since.’

‘And what sort of effect has this had on petty criminals?’ I asked.

‘Well, it’s stopped, completely. Detection seems to be very close to one hundred per cent and the stasis sentences increased each time the same person was captured. Now everyone had a decent income, almost £5,000 per month, and there was guaranteed punishment if you committed crimes, it stopped petty theft almost overnight. The gang bosses were livid. They had masses of illegal drugs and couldn’t distribute them. Their millionaire lifestyles encouraged them to try to outsmart the bots, but, so far as I’m aware, the streets of London are clear of drugs. It’s extraordinary.

‘The gang bosses found that having any drugs in their homes or business premises resulted in stasis sentences. I was surprised that they started at just an hour, but I do know of one who was caught six times. He was given six months in a prison where he was forced to read books. I’ll be interested to see if he reoffends. If you know you are going to be caught, it seems pointless. Mind you, civil rights groups are up in arms about the chips and the nanobots.’

'Yes, I intend to look at that soon. What else have you seen during these early days of the Federation?' I asked.

'Sex trafficking. I was aware of one or two Eastern European gangs who brought young girls to the UK to be provided for sex. The prettiest were kept for themselves or charged at a premium. Nasty people.'

'What sort of ages?' I asked.

'Usually late teens, but there was also a huge market for girls, and boys, thirteen and up. It's a horrible life. They are imprisoned in flats, usually, just a squalid room in large Victorian houses. They're never allowed out and forced to perform every sex act you can imagine and many you can't. The gangs kept the money, of course.'

'Difficult to imagine how it got detected if they couldn't cry out for help,' I said.

'The nanobots. I heard from another criminal source that a nanobot tracking a drug dealer, followed him into one of the brothels where it stopped him from having sex with a barely teenaged girl. Within hours it was shut down and lengthy stasis sentences were given to the gang leaders who were pursued across Europe. Once they knew about it, the nanobots went out specifically to find similar places and a surprising number of houses were shut down pretty quickly. The girls, and some young men, found themselves free and with plenty of money to live normally. Children were returned to their homes.'

'Must have been wonderful for them,' I said.

'Indeed, although I understand many are in ongoing counselling.'

'Yes. I guess they would need help. Any other areas I should know about?'

'There is no longer anything for me to write about, that's for sure,' he said and laughed. 'The Federation's wrecked my career.'

'I'm sorry,' I said.

‘Oh, don’t be. There’s a lot to do. I’m sketching out a book on the masterminds behind drug dealing and sex trafficking. If there’s no current crime to write about, I can dig into history. I’ll keep notes for you if there is anything unusual.’

‘There must still be some crime.’

‘Yes. A murder two nights ago. Bots can’t spot and stop someone who is going to kill someone else. Especially a domestic murder as this one appears to be. There is also still domestic violence and youth violence, the odd bar brawl and such like. Frankly, I’m not interested in writing about such things. It was diamond heists, drug hauls, sex traffickers and gang murders which interested me… and they seem to be gone,’ he said in a wistful tone of voice.

4 Lost Cause

Arnold Pattison, governor of California, sat with his head in his hands. Two of his advisors stood by the window looking out over the bay.

'So, what support do we have left?' asked the governor, finally looking up from his desk.

Bernie Laker, turned to face him. 'We have the Marines we recruited at the beginning. They're prepared to hold firm. All of the others withdrew support when Slimbridge sent the troops to capture you.'

'They all backed down?'

'Yes, every base. Now they're being deployed on the streets throughout the state except here,' said Bernie Laker. 'Slimbridge has a force of six thousand just outside the city. They're awaiting your answer to the offer of a peaceful surrender.'

'It'll be a bloodbath if we try to fight, sir,' said the other adviser, Mark Lock, 'if you don't surrender.'

'Okay, Mark. Get the word out that it is all over and the troops should return to their bases. You two leave too. No point in all of us being caught,' said the governor.

'I'm staying, sir,' said Bernie Laker.

'We'll likely be executed,' said the governor.

'Rather that than live under Slimbridge, sir.'

Mark Lock returned his phone to his pocket. 'It's done. General Booth says he'll be making a break for it.'

'You go, Mark.'

'If you're prepared to head for Mexico, I'll come with you, sir. If we're quick we could rig some disguises and make our way down the state,' said Mark.

'Shame we're so damn far north,' said the governor. 'You think we could make it? Would the Fed come and get us, do you think?'

5 Kenya

The next morning, I took a shuttle to Kenya. The journalist at *The Times* had told me that an acquaintance of his was a political journalist in Nairobi. The perfect contact for my needs.

The shuttle opened its doors into an airconditioned building which used to be a terminal of Jomo Kenyatta International Airport. Gone were the days when the airport was busy with hourly flights arriving and departing. Federation shuttles were rapidly replacing aircraft.

I walked through to the arrivals area and a tall, black, thirty-something, grinning man with dark glasses and a broad-brimmed hat, was holding a board which said "PROFESSOR BREGANIN".

He laughed, then said, 'Guess I should have realised you'd stand out in the crowd. Miles didn't give me a description, just said, "he's not of this world".'

I was the only alien in the shuttle. The journalist seemed very pleasant and I shook his hand. All around us, curious spectators were staring at me. A child ran up and tapped me on the arm and asked, 'You an allenan?'

'Yes, I am. I'm a Daragnen,' I replied. 'Are you an Earthling?'

He laughed and ran away, but I was certainly becoming quite a local attraction.

'Now, how can I help you, Professor?'

'Just call me Rummy, please,' I said, turning back to my host.

'I'm Joseph,' he said. 'Joseph Ingaro.'

'Thanks for seeing me at such short notice, Joseph.'

'Come. Let's find a quiet area. There's a table over there, in the corner,' he said. 'Fancy a coffee?'

'No, I'm not keen on fancy coffees. A fruit juice would be fine,' I said.

I sat at the table, looking out at the almost deserted apron. A light aircraft was taxiing towards a runway. I watched as it gained speed and rose into the air. Joseph returned with a huge fruit juice and equally large milky latte.

'Miles said that I might be able to assist you,' Joseph said.

'Yes. Miles told me that you are the best political journalist in the whole of Africa,' I said, and explained about my book project. 'So, I want to know how it has affected this part of Africa from top to bottom.'

'Well, bottom up,' he said and laughed at what he'd said. 'Those at the bottom cannot believe it. Suddenly they have money, man. They able to buy things, such luxuries as they never dreamed of. Can you imagine living most of your life on two or three dollars a day and then finding you had seemingly bottomless pockets? It's as if the whole country has won the lottery.'

'The effect was positive, then?'

'Mostly,' he said, taking a drink from his coffee and eating a Danish pastry.

He'd brought one for me too. I don't like sugary food, but decided I'd better honour the gesture.

'Not totally?'

He finished his mouthful and said, 'No. People will be people. In the first few days, the local traders put their prices up. If people had money then they could pay much more for their daily shopping, so why not charge more. There was an instant inflation. I saw vegetables increase tenfold in a few days.'

'This is before the trading bots arrived?'

'Oh, yes,' he continued. 'We didn't see any of those for almost a week. In my neighbourhood, the first trade to be taken over was a bakery.' He laughed at the thought. 'Suddenly everyone flocked to the robot bakery as it was selling at normal prices. Gradually, other retail outlets were taken over and it had the same effect on vegetables, plantain and other fruit, meat et cetera. This meant that people had too much money again. It took a while before they realised that they could use it to improve their homes, their methods of transport. Rickety bicycles were replaced by mopeds, mopeds by cars. The way of life during transition was changing extremely rapidly.'

He finished his Danish and I did likewise.

'Hey! Want to visit a village?' he asked.

'I'd love to,' I said.

We left the air conditioned futuristic airport building and emerged into the sun and roasting heat. Joseph hired a cab and we set off into the countryside.

'Hot here,' I said.

'Yes. Driver. Turn up the aircon, please,' said Joseph.

'Turning up the aircon, Joseph,' said the driver.

'I still can't get used to this,' Joseph said, tapping the armrest. 'Being driven by a robot. It's like magic, and they all know my name!'

'Soon you won't even see the robot. These old cars will be replaced by autonomous vehicles which have the robot built into the structure.'

'Amazing,' he said.

'What are we going to see?' I asked, looking out at the dusty street with its strange assortment of decrepit shacks lining each side, sometimes interspersed with others which had been painted bright lemon, sky blue, chartreuse green, tangerine and magenta. Strangely beautiful. 'These are homes?'

'Yes. Most families in this area have a single room. Two if they have more cash, but, of course, all of that is changing. The demand for new homes is escalating. Driver, slow down.'

'Slowing down, Joseph.'

'If you look closely, you'll see that many of these shacks have sprouted extensions. Most are crudely built, but that will change as they realise that the money is not going to dry up. Also, men who had to work ten hours a day for a pittance, now have free time and money. They are wanting to improve their homes. Not all, of course.'

'Not all?'

'Some get rolling drunk every day, stupidly trying to turn their newfound paradise into a worse form of hell than they lived in originally. However, the fact that income is paid equally to each member of a family means that wives are not left destitute by these husbands. Also, their children's money is allowed to be used only in prescribed ways. You can buy food, medicines and other products, but not gamble with it or buy Kenya Cane.'

'What's that?'

'A potent white rum. How do they stop a child's income being used for certain items? It seems a great idea.'

'I don't know the actual mechanics, but, presumably, they put a tag on each afed issued to someone under the age you are able to purchase alcohol and then don't allow it to be transferred,' I explained.

'But it could be done through a third party. Pay for some vegetables but be given alcohol.'

'That would be illegal so both parties would be risking stasis if the transaction were observed or tracked and nanobots would certainly notice it. I guess it would work that way,' I said.

'Well, there were lots of people in stasis in the streets in the first week, but it is remarkable how quickly that has stopped.'

'Is it so remarkable? If you have a good income, why risk your freedom by abusing it,' I said.

'Some clearly do,' said Joseph.

'They'll learn. What about corruption? Miles said Kenya is a hotbed of corruption.'

'Driver. Stop the car,' said Joseph. 'Rummy, do you see those two cops leaning against the fence over there?'

'Yes.'

'Normally, they'd be looking for people breaking the law – not just the legal law, but anything they thought could or should be against the law, like minding your own business,' Joseph said, and laughed. 'Well, they would normally wait for someone to come along on foot or in a vehicle and they'd stop them and make life so difficult that the person would give them some cash or produce in order to get by.' The car drove on.

'I saw lots of police in the streets in stasis the first week or so. Now they're being replaced by cop-bots. Bots are incorruptible. Seeing live cops like that is increasingly rare. Presumably they are just honest cops who want to keep working or carrying out their community service.'

'What about corruption at higher levels?'

'Wonderful. It has been totally stamped out. Under threat of severe stasis sentences, most government officials have now given up working and live off their monthly payments. Stopping the accumulation of wealth has taken away the desire to enter politics. Sad, isn't it? The only reason to become a politician in our country was to get rich through dodgy deals or bribes. Our president vamoosed during the first week.'

'Vamoosed?'

'It means, scarpered or fled. Nanobots have stopped the corruption and accumulation of wealth of any description.'

'What do you mean by any description?' I asked.

'Oh, you know, jewellery, precious metals. One of the ministers thought he could get away with his fortune by buying gold or diamonds, but I'm told they will soon be valueless.'

'Yes, diamonds lie around on the surface of Endareen. Still need cutting and polishing, of course.'

'Didn't know the name of the place. The price of gold is now no more than any other attractive metal. Gold and diamonds still have an intrinsic value, but only a handful of cents. The village I wanted to show you is just ahead, but there seems to be a bottleneck.'

We were stuck in a traffic jam. A robot resurfacing machine ahead of us was creating a new road surface.

Joseph said, 'These outlying streets had just been dirt tracks with more potholes than flat surfaces.'

The resurfacing-bot pulled over and let the queue of traffic pass. What a difference between the old road surface and the new one we'd been travelling on.

The village comprised maybe two or three hundred shacks, around most of which there was feverish building activity as lean-tos and extensions were being added by building bots or the owners themselves. On our right was a large, modern-looking structure, quite clearly a supermarket. It was busy.

We both got out of the vehicle and I was immediately the magnet for forty or fifty children aged between toddlers and teenagers. All were amazed at seeing "an alien".

I let them touch my hands and watched some younger ones who did it as a dare, briefly touching a finger or arm then running off to hide.

'Am I safe?' I asked.

'Yes. They're just curious. Come into the store,' said Joseph.

I fought my way free of the goggling mob and followed him. A woman emerged from the door, carrying three bulging bags of produce. Inside, the aisles were heaving with people who'd come from far and wide to the new shop where miraculous gadgets and utensils flew off the shelves.

'See what it means to them,' said Joseph. 'They're thrilled to be able to buy things they might've only seen or been told about. You see that woman with an electric kettle in her trolley?' I nodded. 'If we followed her home, we'd probably find that she has no electricity supply. We might even find the husband getting back from Nairobi with a generator so that they can use the kettle! It is miraculous, and this is just the first few weeks.'

'Yes. I can see what you mean. I'd like to talk to some people,' I said.

I approached a young woman, twenty-something, wearing a brightly coloured print dress. It had vibrant lime and moss grasses with crimson blooms and black outlined coral butterflies.

She wore a matching headscarf. Amazing colours. 'Excuse me,' I said. She looked around then looked me up and down. 'Can I ask you a few questions for a book I'm writing?'

She stared at me as if I was mad, then looked up at Joseph. 'He's an alien,' she said to him, as if Joseph could somehow transmute me into a human.

'I am,' I said. 'From a world a long way from here. I'm a university professor researching the transitioning Earth.'

'*The transitioning Earth?* what's that there then?' she said and tossed her head as if it was unimportant.

'Your world is moving from being independent into a member or the Federation. I'm writing a book about it,' I said.

'I know that, my man,' she said, then laughed, 'but you is not a man. What you need to know from me?'

'What did you do before the transition date? Did you have a job?'

'I did. I was servant to the Okanga family. Now one of you does their servanting.'

'You mean an alien or a robot?'

'Yes, not alive. But it more like a man than you is,' she said, and laughed again.

'What will you do now, without your job?' I asked.

'Ha. What I won't do is fetching and carrying for thems anymore.'

'But what will you do instead?'

She looked puzzled. 'I dunno. I ask my friend Mora if I wanna know future. I can't tell fortunes. Right nows I'm having a rest from the work.'

'What would you like to do, if you could do anything you wanted?'

She thought for a moment. 'School finished with me when I was ten. Maybe I go back to de school, if theys let someone my age come back to schooling.'

‘What would you like to learn?’ I asked.

‘I liked the numbers. I was good at it too. Theys wouldn’t let me stay to learn more.’

‘Who wouldn’t?’

‘My ma and da. They needed me to work the fields until I could get a proper job, like the servanting. Me knowing numbers was no help to my da. He had all the numbers he ever needed.’

‘And what would you do with the numbers, once you had them?’

‘I seen people working in shops and offices. They had to have numbers. I could do that. Get a better job.’

‘All those jobs are gone too,’ I said, ‘or they soon will be.’

This fact seemed to have passed her by. She looked puzzled, then said, ‘Then I dunno. I could travel.’

‘You’d like to see other places?’

‘Yes. Never been beyond Nairobi. All my life, nor my ma and da.’

‘What would you do in other places?’

‘Look at green parks and skyscrapers and things. Could go see a red bus in London.’

‘What about other worlds? Would you like to go to the moon or another planet?’

‘I dunno, my man. Moon don’t seem very ‘ospitable. All grey. See that on Okanga’s telly once. Don’t like idea of that, sir. What’s your world like then?’

‘Very rural, it grows food. We have two suns in our sky and a huge moon which fills half the sky. We have giant butterflies, too, a metre wingspan. People come from all over the galaxy to see them,’ I said.

‘Well, well. That interests me plenty. Maybe you see me in your village shop one day, but spose I never have nuff money for dat.’

‘The journey to Daragnen, my planet, is five hundred afeds.’

'Hey, man. That's only haff of what I got last Friday. You seryuss. I could fly to your Darenan planet for jess five hunderd?' She looked hard at Joseph. 'Hey, you. Is this man thing spoofing me?'

'No, if he says five hundred then it's five hundred,' said Joseph.

'I dunno,' she said. 'Guess the worl has changed complete for sure.'

'Thank you for answering my questions,' I said.

We wandered around the small township and I managed to talk to eight people. Many of them were in the same situation as the woman. They hadn't yet adjusted to the new order and were still in a phase where they were enjoying relative riches.

'Not very inspiring,' said Joseph as we got back into the taxi and asked it to take me back to the airport.

'No. It's fascinating. It'll change, Joseph. If I may, I'll come back to you in six months and see what these people are doing then. Is that okay with you?' I asked.

'Well, if I'm still here. The Federation has killed corruption in government stone dead. My life has been spent in trying to expose it. I'll need to find a new angle, I suppose. If I'm still here in six months, by all means look me up.'

'I will, Joseph. So many thanks for your help.'

'Good luck with the book. I might write my own book,' Joseph said.

'Yes. There should be a record of how the world changed with the coming of the Federation. It will be different in each region.'

'Yes. Hadn't thought about that. The old Kenyan guard is gone. Politics will never be the same again here. People used to go into it to see how much they could make, now the new administrators are people genuinely interested in helping others. Virtually the entire government has disappeared, no doubt trying to make the most of ill-gotten gains.'

‘They won’t get away with it. In a year or two, their surpluses will be collected.’

‘Could be cash or gold,’ said Joseph.

‘Cash would be of no use and the mines on the moon of Jerodonia are full of precious metals. Gold will plummet in value.’

‘Seriously?’

‘Yes, once the people of Earth realise that they can buy a kilo of gold for a few afeds values will certainly disappear.’

‘They’ll be finding ways to transfer their wealth to afeds, then.’

‘Can’t do it. Every afed has a history trail. They’ll be caught.’

‘Would be interesting to see how many ways they find to try to circumnavigate the Federation exchequer.’

‘There you go,’ I said, ‘you have your subject matter.’

‘Thanks, Rummy. I think I might just do that.’

At the airport, I caught a shuttle back to London. Miles had happily been enlisted to assist me. There were many areas where an alien professor could not gain trust, but a British journalist could. Now I’d find out how he’d got on.

6 Esponging Centre

A few weeks after arriving in the province of England, Emily had visited her relations, then, having nothing better to occupy her, she returned to the esponging centre in London to find out more about the early history of the Federation. She'd already learned Galactic Standard which was compulsory for all immigrants to Federation territories. It took little more than half an hour and the knowledge of the language was as if it had been learned from birth.

The esponging centre was a large four-storey glass monstrosity off the Bayswater Road. It had once been a government department dealing with pensions, so was now defunct. A door-bot opened the double doors to let Emily in, welcomed her by name, checked she wasn't a current student and directed her to the reception area.

'Good morning, Emily Fraser. How can I assist?' asked a spindly robot, which appeared to be sitting behind the reception desk, but was actually an integral part of it.

'I was told to ask for a course on Primitive Iasuqi,' she said.

'You understand that this is an immersive course?' asked the bot.

'Yes, but I'd like to know more.'

'Immersive courses take over your mind and insert you into the scenarios as a character. You cannot change what the character does as this is a history course, but you will feel the character's reasoning and thought processes. The Iasuqi course comprises four scenarios. You should be aware that the first scenario lasts approximately one hour, but it will feel to you as if you have been immersed for whatever length of time the scenario requires. You can extract yourself at any time by using the safe word "END COURSE". You will be able to pick up where you left off at a future time.'

'Am I in any danger in the course? I didn't expect to need a safe word.'

'Although you might appear to be in danger, you can come to no harm. In certain circumstances the danger might appear to be acute or involve painful situations, hence a method of quick release.'

'Okay. Where do I go?'

'You understand the process and the safe word?'

'I do,' Emily said.

'Repeat the safe word.'

'End course.'

'That is correct. Go to booth one seventy-four. That is the first floor and the seventy-fourth booth. I sense an American accent so please note that the Federation uses the terminology that the lowest floor of a building is the ground floor, not the first floor, although it is not important unless you are using stairs,' said the bot. 'Your key to start the course is now loaded onto your chip.'

'What was the charge?'

'It is education. There is no charge,' said the bot.

That's what Rummy had told her, but she felt the need to check. 'Thank you,' Emily said, and made her way to the lifts.

The steel doors opened as she approached, and she entered the elevator and looked around for the floor buttons.

'There are no buttons,' she murmured to herself.

'Mind the doors,' said the lift and began to rise.

She wondered if the lift was just a recorded voice or an actual bot. 'Why are there no buttons?' she asked.

'I know your destination from your chip, Emily,' the lift said, 'but you can see the floor number on the display above the door.'

She exited into a long corridor which stretched both ways. A flashing arrow indicated she should head right.

About twenty-five metres along the corridor, another flashing arrow indicated that she should turn left. She opened a door marked 1-74, and it led into a small room, maybe three metres by eight metres. A door on the right was open. It was a bathroom with toilet and wash hand basin.

The walls were pastel green. There was no window, but the end wall had a very large television monitor which was currently showing views of the English countryside.

'Good day, Emily. Please help yourself to tea, coffee or other beverages, and biscuits from the counter on your right. Use the bathroom facilities if you have a need, and when you are ready to begin, sit in the chair and say, "BEGIN",' said the room-bot.

Emily poured a coffee from the dispenser and looked around. This was all very civilised. The pastel walls were relaxing as was the pageant of stunning views blending into each other on the television. The chair was extremely luxurious, padded with what appeared to be leather. She sank into it and watched a series of chocolate box country cottages drift by on the screen, plucked up courage, and said, 'Begin.'

'A list of characters is on the screen. Choose your character by saying the number,' said the room-bot.

Emily looked down the list for the name Rummy had given her. She hadn't been expecting to see so many names. This was obviously an amazing system, allowing the student to experience the historical situation through the eyes of dozens of individuals.

There it was. 'Debruek. Number twenty-two,' she said.

'Please put the eye mask on,' said the room-bot.

One of the Federation's non-plastic, biodegradable transparent bags emerged from a slot in front of her. It contained a standard blindfold, similar to the one she'd had to wear to learn Galactic Standard.

Emily extracted it and fastened it around her head.

'Scenario one of four will begin shortly,' said the room-bot.

Dim light had been reaching her eyes around the edges of the soft eye mask. Now it was dimming further, and Emily found herself in the blackest of blacks.

Almost imperceptibly, a background hum grew louder until it sounded like the faint whine of a washing machine on spin cycle in some other room. Emily began to see images.

In front of her was a metal framework. It supported windows which curved over her head. Beneath the framework was a double console. Two creatures were sitting at controls. Even from behind, these were clearly aliens. Their heads rose from their shoulders and widened, like fleshy inverted pyramids atop their stubby necks.

As the scene became clearer, Emily could see stars in the sky through the windows. She was in a spaceship. A beautiful planet with land of lilac and peanut and seas of lapis and cobalt came into view on the left and began to fill the scene.

'In orbit around Mepdetvis, sire,' said a voice off to one side.

Emily looked and saw that it was another of the aliens, but in what was obviously a commander's uniform, bedecked with medals and with gold braid snaking around his neck and down his arms, with knots on his shoulders and chest. More crested his peaked cap.

Suddenly, someone was using her lips and she said, 'Very good, admiral. How long before we can descend? I want my arrival to surprise President Jovak. You're sure he doesn't know I'm on board.'

'As sure as we can be, sire,' said the admiral.

How had the esponger done this, made her actually voice the character she was playing? Did the admiral hear the male voice of Debruek, or was he hearing her voice? Did it matter? She was, to all intents and purposes, on board a Miift ship approaching the world of Mepdetvis. Somewhere, in the same planetary system, must be the other world, Desfogg.

She thought back to Rummy's story about the three worlds. He had told her that Miift had become dominant until the newcomers, Arlucians, had arrived with faster-than-light technology and spoiled their party. She wondered what stage things were at. Had Arlucians already arrived or was this before, when Miift was still ruling the roost?

'The shuttle will depart in about an hour, sire,' said the admiral. 'We'll arrive in the capital early in the morning, when it is awake and beginning its day.'

'I'm leaving the bridge. I'll be in my stateroom with my chancellor,' Emily heard herself saying, and she, or rather, Debruek, turned and marched out of the starship bridge and into a long, dismal corridor.

Having passed several saluting or bowing members of the crew and open doorways, Debruek entered a plush, carpeted and draped area where another of the aliens was sitting in a luxurious armchair. It jumped to its feet on Debruek's entry.

'Sire?'

'Bek. You're ready? We descend in an hour,' said Debruek. He looked towards what seemed to be a younger alien standing to attention against the wall. 'Boy, get me a latril.' The young alien bowed and rushed through a partition between the drapes.

Debruek sat in an even more luxurious seat, waved Bek to sit and, in short measure, a steaming gold mug was brought to him. The "boy" bowed again and returned to his position beside the wall. Emily could even smell the "latril". It had hints of cinnamon and nutmeg.

'Yes, ready, sire,' said Chancellor Bek.

∞∞∞∞∞∞∞

Emily watched as the scene faded to black, momentarily held the stasis then brightened again. She was now seated at the centre of one of the longer sides of a six metre oval table, the inner area inlaid with something which looked like crocodile skin, but heavier duty and with raised spiny points, similar to sharpened fingernails. This skin would not be something one would want to brush against in the wild.

She looked to her right and saw the chancellor and a couple more of her species. The other way, were two or three more. Opposite was a similar delegation, but of a different species. The dress of the central individual was very elaborate. A face observed her from a hole in the top of the tunic which allowed two close-set eyes to see out, but little else. She assumed that this was President Jovak.

'To what do we owe this honour, King Debruek?' said the president, the sound emanating through a hole which opened above his eyes. Gosh, she was a king, thought Emily.

'I hear you are cancelling long term construction contracts for ships, armaments and other technologies. Why is that?' Emily heard herself saying in an aggressive, punchy manner.

'We got a better deal.'

'From where?'

'From the Arlucians. Not only is their technology more effective, but it is also considerably cheaper. Their ships can move between our planets faster. You should try them, Debruek.'

'You cannot break contracts for work in progress. If you don't want to buy more, that is up to you, but you cannot break contracts which are nearing completion. We have had thousands of workers trying to meet your deadlines. You can't just cancel, out of hand.'

'Don't lecture me on business etiquette. Your ships are now obsolete. Who would want a six month journey time between our worlds when it can be done in minutes? You had our deposits when the contracts began. You'll get no more now. They are worthless junk.'

The room fell into silence for a minute.

Debruek stood up, causing all of his party to leap to their feet instantly. 'Jovak – there will be consequences for this!'

Emily saw the scene fade and turn to black once more.

All of a sudden, she was in an ornate room. Palatial, with golden decorations and she was looking down the length of it. Miiftians lined both sides stretching away from her, their backs to the windows where a strong bluish sunlight drenched the room in unearthly brightness.

Doors at the opposite end opened and an usher, dressed in ornate navy and fern coloured breeches and jacket with tails, entered. He bowed to King Debruek, and said, 'Your Highness, the Arlucian ambassador and his assistants.'

Emily looked up and watched five distinctly humanoid aliens enter the room. Arlucians were pale looking with rounded facial features and short legs for their body height. Their clothing was very formal and beautifully tailored.

The delegation arrived at the foot of Debruek's raised dais. The lead Arlucian said, 'I bring greetings from the president of Arlucian to Debruek, the king of the Miiftians.'

'Arrest them and impound their ships!' Debruek commanded.

The Arlucians were clearly shocked, but unable to resist the pouncing of two dozen armed soldiers who had been lining the sides of the hallway. There was a brief struggle, but the Arlucians were no match for the number of Miiftians.

Debruek stood, turned right and walked off through a door to the right of the throne. Several individuals followed him, including the chancellor.

The scene faded and she found herself in a new location.

They were now in a luxurious lounge. The king was sitting in the most ornate chair and waved the others to the various seats facing towards him.

'Your Highness, I think this will bring trouble,' said one of the older courtiers.

'Trouble for them. Have you impounded their ships, Zeloll?'

Zeloll held a gadget to his ear. 'Yes, Your Highness. All but one which vanished from orbit. It will no doubt report back to Arlucian.'

'Let them,' Debruek said. 'Erind, how are our reinforcements coming along?'

‘We now have sixteen armed ships in orbit, sire. Two of those are the new battlecruiser class and will be virtually invincible. Three more will be ready for launch in a few weeks as will fifteen more light cruisers,’ said the person called Erind.

‘Sire,’ the older courtier said, ‘I fear we are underestimating the opposition. My brother-in-law has been examining one of their ships. It has a drive based on quantum mechanics. We’ve never seen technology like it. They could be back faster than we might expect.’

‘Nonsense, Betron. With a force such as ours awaiting them, speed will not matter. When they appear in orbit, you are to give the order to open fire immediately,’ Emily heard herself saying. It didn’t seem wise to her, but despite her being as if within the king, she had no influence over the arguments or decisions he was making. He seemed to be drunk with his power.

‘We should not be so confident, sire,’ said the old Miiftian.

‘Betron, I’m not interested in your tantrums or those of your brother-in-law. Leave us!’

The old Miiftian stood, bowed to the king, said, ‘Your Highness,’ and left the room.

A glugging sound filled the room and Erind put his device to his ear. The noise stopped. Shock crossed his face. He looked up towards the king.

‘What is it, Erind?’ asked Debruek.

‘Sire,’ he stuttered, ‘ten Arlucian ships have just appeared in orbit near station one.’

‘How close is that to our battlecruisers?’

‘Two are right beside it, Your Highness.’

‘Tell them to open fire.’

The scene faded and Emily found herself in pitch black once more. Slowly the black became speckled with bright spots. Stars. She was in space, in an Arlucian ship. Beneath her was Miift and a space station comprising balls and tubes linked together like a laboratory model construction of a molecule. Two ships, which dwarfed the space station opened fire on the Arlucian ship. She watched flashes of red, yellow and magenta as projectiles were hurled towards them. The ship disintegrated around her and she found herself floating in space, gasping to breathe. The struggle ended and as whoever was hosting her died, she watched her limbs hanging limply in the cosmos, spinning gradually away from the scene of the carnage as her life was extinguished.

Once more, her vision faded through black and she was again in the royal palace lounge. Erind was listening intently to his gadget.

'Sire, all ten of their ships have been totally destroyed.'

'Any damage to ours?' Debruek asked.

'None, sire.'

'That's the way to deal with these upstarts. How dare they destroy our trade and standing in the Iasuqi system. Well done, Erind.'

The room faded away and the room-bot was speaking. 'You have experienced scenario one of the Iasuqi history vista. You may remove your eye mask. Ninety-five minutes have elapsed.'

Emily eased the blindfold upwards and the screen was showing fields of wheat, barley, lavender, hills of heather and swathes of sunflowers. She was surprised she'd been in the scenario for over an hour and a half. It only seemed like ten minutes.

'It is suggested that you remain seated for five minutes to allow any disorientation to settle,' said the room-bot. 'You must wait at least forty-eight hours before returning for scenario two.'

7 Redundant

One of the most criticised aspects of changing to the Federation's sociological behaviour was the effect upon innovative and entrepreneurial individuals. How would people react who had suddenly found they were no longer needed; that a robot was capable of doing everything they did, but faster, better and more accurately? Instead of a blessing, could it become a nightmare?

Miles had agreed to delve into these aspects for me by surreptitiously quizzing friends and acquaintances "down the pub" or in other watering holes.

We met at his apartment at the Hyde Park end of the Edgeware Road. He delighted in telling me that you could actually see Marble Arch if you leaned out of his window.

A jug of freshly squeezed orange sat on his glass coffee table and we both sipped the golden nectar. I'd become a fan. It was like no other fruit juice I'd ever encountered. It wouldn't take long for the juice growing automatons to discover its popularity and the whole galaxy would benefit.

'So, Miles, how did you get on?' I asked.

'The hardest part was getting them to continue talking when they realised that I was working on a project and not just interested in them as friends or casual acquaintances,' he said.

'Yes, I can imagine.'

He pressed a remote control and a giant television monitor sprang into life. 'You have to ignore the filming, Rummy. The camera was poking out of my top pocket. It was the sound I was interested in,' he said hurriedly as the scene showed his hand pushing a part-glazed door open as he entered the noisy environment of The Rose and Crown as the engraving said on the door.

Several people turned to see who'd entered and a couple shouted, 'Hiya Miles,' over the din.

‘Whatcha having?’ asked a tall, well-built individual sitting on a tall stool and leaning on the bar, waving Miles over with his jug of dark beer.

‘Pint of Bishop’s Tipple would go down well, Ron,’ Miles replied.

Ron caught the bartender’s eye and the said beer was delivered in a straight pint glass. Ron shuffled over to the next stool and Miles joined him at the bar, taking time to allow the camera to get a pretty good view of his friend.

Ron was around his mid-thirties, white, dark-haired with bushy eyebrows. ‘How’ve you been?’ he asked.

‘Not bad,’ said Miles. ‘You?’

‘Feel like a spare bulb for a string of Christmas tree lights.’

‘Really? Why’s that?’

‘Can’t get used to all this leisure time. Feel as if my life has been taken away from me. I’m better off but miss the cut and thrust of my job.’

‘Plumber, weren’t you?’ Miles asked.

‘Well, heating and gas too.’

‘Can’t you ask to go back to work? They made a big thing about no one having to give up work if they didn’t want to.’

‘I did,’ said Ron. ‘I went back, and they let me go on house calls. My “mate” was a robot. It was meant to assist me, but it was clearly a far better engineer than I was. I did one day then gave up. The last call was a house where a joint had a drip between floors. I was about to start taking up carpets and floorboards and the robot stopped me. It said it might be easier if it did this one. It then took up one corner of the carpet, lifted a single floorboard section and extended its telescopic arms into the space. In less than fifteen minutes, without being able to see the problem, it had replaced the joint and had everything back in place. It was then that I realised that I truly *was* redundant.’

‘I can see why that would be depressing. What about golf? You loved golf.’

'Yes. I was playing every day at first, but you can only enjoy so much golf. Fifteen rounds in three weeks. God, Miles, I don't want to play fucking golf every day for the rest of my life.'

'No.'

'Federation councillor suggested I spend a day writing down things I'd like to do,' said Ron. 'I did that.'

'What came up?'

'Fucking train driver!' he said and burst into laughter.

Miles laughed too and the picture wobbled up and down. 'There must have been something else on the list,' Miles said.

'Footballer, but I'm too old. Cricketer. Tropical fish – I'm working on that. Set up a tank last week. Joined an aquarist club on Tuesday night. Made me realise I had a lot to learn.'

'What did the Fed councillor say after you showed him the list?' Miles asked.

'Wasn't a him. It was an it! A robot. Just came from its office half an hour ago. Decided to get pissed,' said Ron, looking at Miles' almost full glass and ordering a refill for himself.'

'I'll get that,' Miles said, holding his left hand out for the barman to scan. 'Charlie seems happy enough.'

'Well, he can keep his job and all the social stuff that goes with it. He's only just come back as barman last week. Prior to that we had a tin man for several weeks. Told good jokes, mind you, better than Charlie's, but not the same as a person. Charlie said he couldn't not be behind a bar,' said Ron. 'The tin man does all the collecting and washing of glasses and prepares the food with another in the kitchen. Great food, mind you. Charlie tells him to leave the tables sometimes and goes around collecting glasses himself. Think he gets a buzz from talking to the people at the tables. Perfect for him really.'

'Yes, I can see that,' Miles said as the camera recorded Charlie bending over a table in the bay window, taking five glasses in one hand and wiping the table with the other, while laughing and exchanging banter with some husbands and wives who were regulars.

'Fed councillor gave me this,' said Ron, handing Miles an open envelope from which he extracted a piece of A4 paper.

Miles read the sheet, but it was too dim for the camera to pick up the detail. 'Some good ideas here, Ron,' Miles said.

'S'pose so. I'm going to try the coaching tomorrow. Four 'til six for the under sixteens.'

'You were a good schoolboy player, weren't you?' Miles asked.

'Yeah, not bad. Did a trial for Brentford, but my parents wanted me to take an apprenticeship. That knocked it on the head,' said Ron.

'Well, good luck with that, Ron,' Miles said.

Another man walked over and tapped Ron on the shoulder. 'You're on, mate.'

'I'm on the pool table rota. Wanna game?'

Miles nodded and the camera followed Ron over to the pool table. Fingers appeared in front of the lens and the image went black.

'I'll ask him how it's going in a week or two,' said Miles. 'Want another?'

'Yes. That one was disappointing,' I said.

'It's fairly general. This one is more positive. I'd spoken to her in the swimming pool and she was happy for me to come back to her place to interview her. I won't tell Ron he was part of a project though, until he's settled, anyway,' Miles said and began another sequence of video.

'You don't mind me filming,' Miles asked.

'No, as long as it's not used publicly,' the female voice said.

An image flared on the screen and settled into good quality. Miles had put the camera on a side table. His right arm was visible and a thirty-something, mixed-race woman was relaxed on a sofa opposite. Her face had that rather lovely toast skin-colour of people of mixed Caucasian and Caribbean parents, her hair very Afro, but lips and bone structure more European.

'Elena, how are you getting on now that your job has gone? Can I get you to describe it, and your situation?' asked Miles.

'Yes, sure. My name is Elena Caswell, I'm thirty-eight. Until Federation Day, I was senior quality control engineer at BAC Systems (British Aerospace). I'd been there since graduating. I'd worked my way up the organisation, starting as a hardware then software engineer on electronic systems for jet fighters,' she said.

'So, very well paid? Were you earning more than the new standard?' asked Miles.

'No, actually. As you know, they increased the standard to fifty-seven thousand afeds once they realised that Earth was way behind the rest of the Federation. With the pound/afed rate at more or less one to one and my BAC salary only fifty-two thousand pounds, I'm marginally better off. My husband, Eric, was only earning forty thousand. Our joint income of one hundred and fourteen thousand afeds is quite a big jump. You're sure this won't be seen by the public?'

'I promise. It is just for a friend who's writing a book on the transition, Elena,' said Miles. 'You both adjusted well, then?'

'Well, money is one thing, being at a loose end is quite another. Eric threw himself into sports. He's older than me, as you know, but he's swiftly becoming extra-fit. Plays walking football, bowls, ten-pin bowling, darts and he's now training for a marathon. That all seems to keep him happy.'

'How about you?'

'Not so good at first,' she said. Something amused her and she laughed. 'You won't believe this, but I gave the entire house a deep spring clean. Then watched a lot of daytime television, but I was bored, and I felt I was slipping into some sort of mild depression. Eric saved the day,' she said.

'How's that?'

'He bought me an easel and the most magnificent artist's kit. Come see,' she said.

Suddenly, her head was out of shot. Miles picked up the camera and followed her through the house to a room overlooking the garden. She opened the door and Miles slowly panned around the room, eventually zooming in on a canvas on the easel. 'Wow!' he said. 'All this in just a few weeks.'

'Yes. He bought me watercolours and pastels and I did a few paintings. I was always good at art at school. My teachers wanted me to study art, but the careers' master insisted I should do physics and maths at uni. Look at this one,' she said, pointing at a beautiful oil painting of a rural scene.

Miles moved the camera towards it and then took some close-ups of the brushwork. 'It's incredible, Elena.'

'Yes. Didn't realise I had the talent and, as you can see, I'm quite prolific. What do you think of the bust of Eric?' she said, carefully removing a damp cloth from a clay sculpture.

'Amazing,' Miles said. 'You've really caught his likeness. Well done.'

'We had a Federation councillor come to visit us last week and it was gushing over my artwork and Eric's interest in sport. It suggested I hold an exhibition in the town hall.'

'You going to?'

'It's free in a couple of months for a week and I've made a provisional booking.'

'It has all worked out well for you, then? Discovering that talent.'

'Yes, and I've met some other artists. They're nowhere near as good as me, but they get a lot out of it too and I've been helping them. We book a room at the theatre each Friday and I help them with composition, light and shade and so on. We all get a huge amount out of it.'

'Sounds good.'

'Miles, it's changed my life and some of theirs too,' she said with glee.

'You wouldn't go back then?'

'Not a chance.'

Miles cut the video.

I asked, 'How many of these have you done, Miles?'

'Six so far,' he said. 'The real test will be in a few months, I suppose.'

'Are you happy to keep doing this for me,' I asked.

'No problem, Rummy. Really enjoying it. Some are not so good. There are more who are unhappy than happy, so how that changes over time will be really interesting. I think older people are struggling. Retirement always had its cost in terms of depression and lack of self-worth, but now it is happening to younger people it will certainly have a cost. I'll try to get a couple of recordings for you.'

∞∞∞∞∞∞∞

My next appointment was with a certain Bernard Crocket, the leader of a group of civil rights protestors. I arrived at a café just off Regent Street. When he saw me enter, he jumped to his feet, came over and shook my hand.

'I know you said I would recognise you, but I hadn't realised you were an alien,' he said, looking me up and down. 'Come over here. My name's Bernie.'

I followed him to a table in the corner where another man stood to meet me. 'I'm Rummy.'

'This is Geoffrey,' said Bernie. 'Would you like a coffee? Or tea?'

'Fresh orange juice if they have it please. I'm becoming rather addicted to it,' I said.

'So, how can we help you? What's this project you're working on?' asked Geoffrey.

'I'm writing a book on Earth's transition and I'd heard that you and your group are most unhappy and regularly protesting,' I said.

'That's right,' said Bernie. 'You've put chips into most of us. Our group have removed them. The chips track us everywhere we go and contain all sorts of details about us – where we live, how much we have in the bank, what our expertise is. It is totally oppressive and we strongly object.'

'What reaction have you had?'

'None. That's the odd thing. No one seems to care that we're not complying,' said Geoffrey.

'Why would they?' I asked.

'Well, what's the pointing chipping us if they're not going to control us?' asked Geoffrey.

'It isn't to control individuals,' I said. 'It's to control society.'

'Well, we're protesting on society's behalf,' said Bernie.

'You don't think the benefits outweigh your worries? Virtually all crime has stopped. If you get hurt in an accident, your chip contains all the information about your body including allergies to drugs, blood type, previous medical history and so on,' I said.

'Yes, but how do we know we're not going to be challenged for our political views or our religion?' asked Bernie. 'And we don't want to be tracked.'

'If you do nothing against society, then why would they want to track you?' I asked. I'd heard similar arguments on other transitioning worlds.

'That is not the point. We want to be free. We don't want to be tracked or observed. Our right to freedom is in jeopardy,' said Geoffrey.

'Since Federation Day,' I said, 'drugs have disappeared from the streets, gang violence has vanished, crimes have been stopped, corruption has ended. Do you not agree that is a good thing?'

‘Yes,’ said Bernie, ‘but it goes too far. We are prisoners.’

‘But you’ve removed your chips, and no one has stopped you. You haven’t had them forcibly re-inserted. What’s the problem?’

‘We want to free everyone. It’s not just us, it is the millions of people who have been chipped without realising the implications,’ said Geoffrey.

‘So, you would rather have all the crime back, the burglaries, the assaults, the corruption? That would surely be the result. You’d be back where you were before the Federation.’

‘No, but we’d like it done in a way that doesn’t require us all to be tracked by computers,’ said Bernie.

I finished my orange juice. ‘Thanks for your help,’ I said. ‘Most useful, and thanks for the drink too. Can I come back to talk to you in a few months’ time?’

‘Of course. No problem. Here’s my card,’ said Bernie.

‘Ah, yes. I can’t locate you via your chip. Thanks,’ I said, tucking it into my pocket and leaving the café.

I didn’t think I’d learned much from these two. The arguments were the same I’d read about on many worlds. There are always some people who would suffer all sorts of hardships in order to retain some sort of freedom from the state. It would never change.

8 War

Emily's second trip to the esponging centre was the following Monday.

Reception gave her a different booth this time but it was identical to the original. She made herself a mug of green tea, retrieved some digestive biscuits from the biscuit barrel, and sat in the luxuriously padded chair. The scenes on the screen this time were rugged cliffs and seascapes, waves crashing against the rock and spume flying in the wind.

Emily listened to the instructions and said, 'Begin.'

'A list of characters is on the screen. Choose your character by saying the number,' said the room-bot.

Emily looked down the list for Debruek. There were dozens this time and Debruek wasn't on his own. The screen showed "Debruek/Erind". Its number was forty-seven. She presumed these were the correct characters to choose. She remembered Erind as one of Debruek's advisors. Military, she thought.

'Number forty-seven,' she said.

'This scenario contains scenes which some students might find distressing. Are you sure you wish to proceed?' said the room-bot.

'Yes. Please proceed,' she said.

'Please put the eye mask on.'

The biodegradable bag appeared from the desk and she slid the blindfold over her head.

'Scenario two of four will begin shortly,' said the room-bot.

Emily was back in the same palatial room she had been in when scenario one had ended. This time, however, she, or rather, Debruek, was sitting at a long dining table, consuming a multicoloured dish which could have passed for pasta. Within it were red and rust meat-like slivers. It was really tasty. The meat was slightly gamey, but not overly so and the pasta-like material quite firm, like underdone dry pasta, but less chewy.

Erind sat on his right, without food, sipping from a golden metal challis. On his left were two young Miiftians, possibly the king's children, and a female of the species. Emily guessed at female. She had no knowledge of the sexes of this species, but she had less rugged features to her pyramidal head and sported more colourful clothing.

King Debruek finished his dish and spoke, 'Etolda, take the children from the room. I have matters of state to discuss with Erind.'

Etolda did not reply. She tapped the children on their backs and signalled for them to follow her. They disappeared through one of the doors.

'Boy, bring me some wine,' said Debruek and a servant jumped into action, pouring from a large, ornate and bejewelled flask into a goblet similar to that which Erind was using. 'Do you need more?' Debruek asked his guest.

'No, sire. Thank you.'

Debruek rose from the table and meandered over to the same luxurious seat Emily remembered from the last scenario. Erind followed and sat in one of the simpler chairs facing the king.

'So, Erind, no sign of the Arlucians? I said we'd see them off.'

'Yes, sire. So far, so good, but it has only been a week.'

'We know they can travel extremely quickly. If they were going to return, they'd have been here within a day or two.'

'We can hope, sire. Another battlecruiser entered orbit yesterday, Your Highness and is being fitted out as we speak,' said Erind.

'So, we're ready for anything?'

'We're ready for some things, but I fear their technology, sire. If their weapons are as advanced as their ships, we could still face trouble.'

A warbling sound could be heard and Erind took a small, flat device, like a cell phone, from his tunic pocket. 'Excuse me, sire.

I should answer this.' Debruek waved impatiently for him to go ahead.

Erind listened. His eyes widened and, despite his features being alien to Emily, she felt she was witnessing absolute shock and horror passing across his face.

'Sire,' he said, but almost immediately a siren blasted out through every room of the palace.

'What is it?' shouted the king above the din.

'We're under attack, sire! A fleet of Arlucian ships.'

'Deal with them!' commanded the king.

'Too many,' said Erind.

'How many?'

'Hundreds, sire!'

From somewhere outside the palace came a huge explosion. The windows blew inwards and the whole building shook. Parts of the ceiling collapsed, and Emily saw Erind thrown across the room as a second shockwave from another explosion tore through the building.

All of a sudden, Emily felt disorientated and instead of looking through Debruek's eyes, she was now seeing the scene from the other side of the room through the eyes of Erind.

She coughed, or rather Erind did, as dust filled the room and slowly began to settle. Her hip hurt, or rather Erind's hip hurt, but she could feel real pain. Everything was covered in a coat of dismal, greyish powder. Erind could see the "boy" dusting himself off and looking towards the king. Erind turned over, let out a yell as he discovered his wrist had broken, and tried to sit up, despite the nausea which flooded through his, and Emily's, being. Emily felt as if she was close to passing out. *Should she end the course now?*

Where was the king? A scree of rubble was piled, almost the height of the room, over the place where King Debruek's seat had been.

‘Quick, get help, boy,’ Erind shouted as he struggled to his feet, yelping in pain as his wrist fell limply to his side. Emily felt the pain. *My God, it was so real!* She wanted to know what was going to happen.

The boy ran from the room.

Erind limped over to the pile of masonry where the king had been sitting. No sign of him.

A dozen men ran into the room, led by the boy, rushed to Erind’s side, and began to pick at the stone, tossing lumps to each side as they tried to reach the king. For a moment, Erind wondered if one of the alabaster statues had fallen into this melee of broken rock, but no – it was the king’s arm, lying there, lifeless, poking out of the rubble.

The helpers redoubled their efforts to uncover the monarch, but Erind knew he was dead. He turned and staggered to a break in the wall.

The palace sat on a knoll overlooking the great eastern ocean of Miift, which covered a third of the world. Emily, and therefore Erind, stared into the distance. Giant waves crashed onto the shore. The streets were wet with saline incursions. Bombs must have landed in the sea too, creating enormous tsunamis which would have carried away anyone unfortunate enough to have been in the streets below. He looked at the central market square. Its rag, tag and bobtail of coloured canopies was gone. What remained were a few remnants of said canopies, lying tangled and shredded at exits from the market as evidence that the square had been flooded and all had been pulled along by the retreating deluge.

He could do no more in the palace. He needed to get to the defence ministry. His communicator worked no longer. No signal. The power must have failed. He could hardly see a single building which remained standing. What had the Arlucians hit them with?

Unsteady and in fear of further hurting his wrist and hip, he climbed clumsily down the rubble and onto a pathway which circled the palace. It was blocked by further falls of masonry in many places, but slowly he was able to climb over them or around them to progress towards street level.

What was this in the street? Rounded shapes like sacks of old clothes lay here and there. He used his boot to upturn one. Emily gasped with Erind as they saw the burned and crushed face of a young Miiftian girl. What had caused the burning?

His progress was slow, and he didn't encounter another living person. A scoggle dashed out of the ruin of a building on the right. Its fur had been burned almost clean away. It tried to bite Erind's leg, but he managed to kick it, causing more pain to his damaged hip. The animal slunk away, whining, into the hole in a wall from which it had emerged.

No straight route was available to him and his wrist hurt with every step he took. The hospital was beside the defence building. Continuing that way was the best he could do. Smoke rose to the left, right, ahead and behind him. He coughed to clear the acrid dust from his throat, which had begun to hurt. Now his other hand bothered him. It felt hot, as if the air was scalding him, but only his exposed skin. The backs of his hands were becoming red, and marks, like the blisters of some contagious disease were appearing. Small at first but growing into painful welts. Emily didn't know if she could stand this scenario any longer for she too, felt Erind's pain. His walking slowed still further. Could he even make it to the ministry? What was attacking his skin?

He upturned another body. It's skin was also red raw.

Erind unclipped his communicator, pressed a couple of buttons as he rested it in the crook of his bad hand, and swiped the screen. He lifted it with his good hand, although both were now equally painful, and waved it in the air. He stopped and looked at the screen. Emily saw pulsing red stars on the screen with the figures 153 flashing among them. She was thankful for Erind's soliloquy which followed, or she might not have realised what was happening.

'One fifty-three,' Erind whispered to himself. 'It must have been a nuclear bomb. The bastards nuked us.'

Emily felt nausea rising and then she was vomiting into the street. It wasn't actually her, of course, it was Erind, but she felt the heaving and tasted the burning acrid mess as her stomach contents headed streetwise. Radiation was killing him. She was desperately close to crying "end course" but tried to hold on.

He, Erind, with Emily, tumbled forward and the connection was broken. Erind had parted company with Emily and with life itself. She didn't quite see him make his final fall into the gutter for he was dead before he hit the ground.

The room faded away and the room-bot was speaking.

'You have experienced scenario two of the Iasuqi history vista. You may remove your eye mask.'

Emily ripped it from her head and examined her hands, expecting to see blistering and peeling skin. The projection had been so realistic. The screen was once again portraying cliffs and waves crashing into them, plus inland shots of the rolling hills of what looked like English countryside.

'You might feel unwell after that scenario, Emily,' said the room-bot.

She still felt sick, but gradually the natural scenes dragged her back from the edge. In a minute she thought she'd recovered, but suddenly had to rush into the tiny toilet where she delivered up her breakfast. She struggled back to the seat.

'It is suggested that you remain seated for at least five minutes to allow any disorientation to settle,' said the room-bot. 'You must wait at least forty-eight hours before returning for scenario three.'

It was closer to fifteen minutes before she felt well enough to face the streets of London once more. She didn't think she'd ever return for the rest of the course. Erind's death had been all too real.

9 Crossing Borders

General Dick Beech and Colonel Mike Henderson, both in jeans and sweatshirts, watched as the Buick slowed to a halt on US 7, just south of the border with Canada. A man dressed in tan trousers, white shirt and brown leather jacket, emerged from the driver's door, walked around to the front of the car and lifted the hood.

Dick and Mike had been walking cross-country through the light woodland until they reached the highway. Next, they followed it south until they saw a wooden post with its top half painted bright green. They moved back into the woodland to keep out of sight of any traffic until the Buick arrived.

The driver leaned into the engine compartment, then walked to the rear of the vehicle and lifted the trunk. That was the signal.

Dick and Mike looked both ways along the highway. One car was heading in their direction from the north. They watched and waited.

The red Ford shot past the Buick, continued into the distance and eventually was lost to view.

The two men ran out of the woods, threw a couple of bulging backpacks into the trunk, jumped into the back seat and waited.

The driver looked up and down the highway, scanned the nearby woods, closed the trunk and hood, climbed back into the driver's seat and headed south, keeping strictly within the speed limit.

ꝏꝏꝏꝏꝏꝏꝏ

Governor Arnold Pattison, Mark Lock and Bernie Laker had reached Los Angeles. Mark had a cousin who lived in Buena Park. Their nondescript Chrysler pulled up four houses down the street. They got out and walked to number twenty-two.

'Mark,' said a tall brunette woman in her thirties rushing into his arms. 'We've been so worried. Isobel said you were heading this way, but there has been a real hue and cry out for you. You've been on every television channel.'

'Guessed that, Diane. We've been keeping our heads down and using side roads,' said Mark, extracting himself from the hug and introducing Governor Pattison and Bernie Laker. 'Where's Leon?'

'At the store. He'll be back shortly,' Diane said.

'We parked down the road. The car needs to be moved away from the area,' said Bernie.

'Right,' she said, and called into the house, 'Roger, are you there?'

A young lad, well over six feet tall, with a spotty complexion and mop of curly hair, appeared from somewhere in the hallway. 'Mom?'

'Give me the keys,' Diane said to Bernie who handed them over complete with the Avis tag. 'Roger, take this car to the mall and park it in a crowded car park.' She looked back at the three men. 'Anything in it you need?'

'Yes, a holdall and two backpacks,' said Mark.

'Roger, go find your brothers and fetch the luggage, then get rid of the car,' said Diane.

'Right, Mom,' the youth said, then called his brothers to help him with the bags.

'Come on in, let me get you some coffee or tea. Which would you prefer?'

They'd only just got their coffee and biscuits when the sitting room door opened and in marched Mark's cousin, Leon. Introductions were made all round.

'What's your plan, Governor?' asked Leon.

'We've decided to get out of the country and try to work against Slimbridge from Federation territory,' said Arnold. 'What do you think is the best way over the border?'

'I'm told there are no checks going out,' said Leon. 'If I drive, we should be able to get straight through. I'll leave you once you are in Federation Mexico and come straight back. Already done that a few times for others. You'll need to register as visitors to the Federation or residents but that's all done well over the border. You'll be in the clear by then.'

'You'll be safe too?' asked Mark.

'Yes. No bother. If there are police watching for you, we'll return when they're gone. Frankly, I think Slimbridge is so glad to have prevented California joining the Federation, that he's really not too bothered about a few people heading over the border. From his point of view, it is the potential troublemakers who are leaving. Suits him fine.'

∞∞∞∞∞∞∞∞

Peter Stone, the Internet billionaire who was now a Federation citizen living in Canada, had been a key player in the successful operations of the Free America group. He was finding it very frustrating that he was unable to make use of Federation technology to assist further. Today he travelled to Moscow, trying to follow up a lead to obtain, of all things, a starship.

After checking-in to his hotel, he walked a few hundred metres and entered Red Square. On the left was the enormous department store, GUM. Inside, he entered the coffee shop near the fountain and ordered a light breakfast. He sat and placed his trilby on the table to one side and his camera and phone to the other.

Ten minutes later, a plump, middle-aged Russian woman sat down opposite him.

'You having a good breakfast?' she asked.

'I am. Excellent.'

'Peter Stone?'

'The same. Are you Olga?'

'I am,' she said.

'Are you able to help me?'

'Indeed. Pay for your breakfast and come with me, I'll be in the doorway,' she said, standing and leaving the eatery.

Peter flashed his chip at the device on the table, rose, and ambled towards the entrance.

'Come,' Olga said.

They made an odd couple, walking through Red Square, dodging its hordes of tourists, until they reached a parking area outside the main square. They climbed four steps and entered the back of a box van.

Inside, there was a red circle painted on the floor.

'Stand within the circle,' Olga said.

Peter entered the circle and turned to face his host. All of a sudden, neither she nor the van were there. He'd arrived in the comfortable lounge area of a Federation starship.

An Arlucian walked over to him, looking slightly comic with its short legs and long torso. 'Yol Peter Stone, yes?'

'Indeed. Are you Yol Twedin?'

'I am, welcome to the Golden Orne starship. Come over here, we'll have some privacy.' The Arlucian led Peter over to a sitting area beside a large window, through which most of Africa could be seen.

'Coffee?' asked Yol Twedin.

'Please.'

'You want a starship? To buy or hire?' asked the alien, as he signalled a robot to take the order.

'I'd like to buy one. It must be equipped with beaming technology and will need a crew.'

'Small starships can be hired for a few thousand afeds, but it is rare to actually own one. They start at about a hundred thousand without QE drives. They would be fine for getting to and from your moon. To buy one of those, a large number of you would have to club together.'

'That doesn't suit me, Yol Twedin. I could arrange payment in US dollars, by setting up accounts for you and the crew, but I'd require a full starship with an on-board meeting room and two separate holding areas,' said Peter.

'My goodness, Yol Stone. It sounds as if you are planning something illegal. You sound as if you need a seventy metre ship, which would need a skipper, crewman and a few robots. That would cost in the region of six million American dollars. I could be the captain. How would this work?'

Peter leaned forward and spoke quietly. 'That sort of money is no problem and can be deposited in a US bank for you. An additional one hundred thousand dollars would be deposited in American bank accounts for each of the crew. How does that sound?'

'Who would be the owner? It is illegal to sell technology to the United States.'

'I'd be the nominal owner, but the money would come from a corporate body in Seattle. Can you work with that?'

'Yol Stone, you are risking a lengthy stasis if you are caught doing this, so will any crew and, unfortunately, myself. What's it for?'

'Sorry, Yol Twedin, that's not something I am going to divulge.'

The Arlucian looked hard at the Internet guru. 'Not enough,' he said.

'Name your price, but take into account, that when we finish with the starship, you will have it back and can sell it to someone else.'

'Okay,' he said and continued to think. 'Ten million for the ship, five million for me and two crew at five hundred thousand dollars each, and you have a deal.'

'You drive a hard bargain, Yol Twedin,' said Peter. 'You have your deal. I'll tell you when we want it and for how long. Probably only a week or two. I will require a room on board set out like page one in this folder and two holding areas for male and female humans in a separate area. You are to change the ship's name to "Spangled Banner". Is that all clear and agreed?'

'I want my five million paid in advance before I start work,' said the alien.

'One million. How do I contact you with the bank details et cetera?'

'Okay. One million up front, non-refundable. You can message me on this address. I've just posted it to your cell phone.'

Peter Stone stood and offered his hand to confirm the deal. Thirty seconds later he was climbing down the steps of the van in the Moscow car park. He was quite content. He'd been prepared to go as high as a billion.

10 Fallout

Emily vomited. She flushed the toilet and washed her face, sitting on the side of the bath to recover her composure. Eventually she stood, drank some cold water and went through to her hotel bedroom. She sat on the only easy chair provided and looked out of the window at the scene across Hyde Park.

Occasionally she felt disorientated and once more she rushed back into the bathroom, but her unproductive retching eventually stopped,

She'd left the esponging centre just a couple of hours previously and was shocked at the effect the story of Miift had had upon her.

For two days, she just relaxed in the hotel, interspersing reading with visits to the British Museum of Natural History and the neighbouring Science Museum. A whole section of the Science Museum had been closed off. She asked about it and was told that it was being updated with new knowledge about the worlds of the Federation. How, she wondered, could any museum cover the science of nearly a quarter of a million worlds?

Almost a week later, she'd been walking back across Hyde Park to her hotel and could see the glass walls of the esponging centre over to her right.

She'd made a resolution never to return to it after the experience of Erind dying. The system had given her all of Erind's feelings and thoughts as he stumbled onwards, coming to realise that he was not going to survive. The anguish and physical pain of the blistering had been real. It had not *felt* real – to her, it *was* a real experience!

Yet, behind it all, there was a desperate need to know what happened next. It grew to be almost an addiction reminiscent of wishing to watch a soap opera which you'd resolved never to waste any more time upon.

Emily stood, stock still, on the path, looking at the windows of the building which she could see through the magnificent sycamores which lined the Bayswater Road.

Her disgust at the Arlucians using nuclear weapons on the people of the planet Miift had stopped her following up on the rest of the story. She must find out what happened next. Rummy had given her a broad outline, but she wanted more. She returned to her hotel, resolved to head to the esponging centre after lunch, but was also determined to use the safe word next time, if the immersion was becoming too distressing. She wasn't going to leave it so late if it happened again.

ꝏꝏꝏꝏꝏꝏ

'A list of characters is on the screen. Choose your character by saying the number,' said the room-bot.

'I don't know whose perspective I would like. Can you provide an indication of who the individuals are, please?' she said.

'Most of these characters are Desfoggians or Miiftians. You might find the story told from Hel Joreen's perspective to be most useful first as it contains more of an overview,' said the room-bot.

'Okay. Number fifty-eight, Joreen,' said Emily.

'I could also add Golda Verdon to the scenario. Her viewpoint will intersperse with that of Hel Joreen,' said the room-bot. This scenario contains scenes which some students might find distressing. Are you sure you wish to proceed?' said the room-bot.

Oh dear. Should she continue? Her memory of the previous scenario flooded back. It is, after all, just a scenario, she told herself. Surely, she could blank out the bad bits.

'Do you wish to proceed?' asked the room-bot again.

'Yes. Please proceed and please add Golda Verdon,' she said.

'Please put the eye mask on.'

The transparent bag appeared from the desk and she slid the blindfold over her head as before.

'Scenario three of four will begin shortly,' said the room-bot.

The darkness intensified, then the buzz of conversation and electronic noises entered her consciousness. There was a smell reminiscent of curry, garam masala, perhaps. It was on her breath.

A wardroom came into focus. A throbbing vibration told her that she was on board a large ship, but was it on the sea or in space? That she couldn't tell. The walls were made of metal. It looked like steel but had a slightly purple hint to its sheen. Tables were made of the same material and benches lined up either side of each. There must have been thirty or forty beings seated, eating their meal with its curry odour. The chatter was mainly sombre from the words she heard.

'If it's radiation poisoning, we won't be able to do a great deal,' said the person sitting on her right.

She laid her cutlery down on the plate, noticing her grey, three-fingered hands, which gave her a warning that she was about to look at yet another alien. She glanced at the speaker.

His face and neck were the same grey colour which bore wrinkles in places and the odd darker blemish. With no chin, the bottom lip of its ample mouth hung slightly open. The lip itself was almost black with the interior of the mouth a shocking pink, contrasting with the dull-coloured skin. She could see no teeth, but a large rough-textured tongue. Emily couldn't help herself trying to feel if she too, lacked teeth. It appeared so.

Above the alien's black top lip, four holes might have been nostrils, but were set flat into the face. Either side were the eyes. They were oval in appearance with lids which flicked up from beneath when they blinked. The moist eyeballs were white, but the irises were the most beautiful golden colour, streaked with dark lines leading from the outer rim to a black pupil. They reminded Emily of a fanciful dragon's eye.

The alien's face was framed by a tight tangle of what might be hair but looked less flexible. Any ears were hidden from view by knots of the bristles.

Emily felt herself speaking through Joreen, 'We'll do what we can.'

'What on Desfogg brought it on? What did Debruek do to deserve this?' the speaker asked.

'The captain was telling me that Debruek imprisoned the entire Arlucian delegation, then destroyed all of their ships. There were many deaths, Mes,' Joreen said.

'But to bomb Miift with nukes seems an overreaction,' said Mes. 'How much of the planet is damaged?'

'A lot. The captain tells me the radiation is in the general atmosphere. We might have to evacuate survivors.'

'Really? How? There are billions of them.'

'But fewer every day, Mes. Fewer every day.'

'Now hear this,' came over a loudspeaker. 'Now hear this. This is the captain We are approaching Miift. All of our normal landing areas are within a badly irradiated quadrant of the planet. We are heading to the north, to a land called Vona and will make base there. Landing in three hours. That is all.'

'I think I'd like to see the approach, sir. Are you coming?' asked Mes.

'No rush. Must finish this excellent stew. We don't know how often we'll be getting a solid meal once we get to the surface,' said Joreen.

'True,' said Mes, sitting down again and continuing to eat.

Emily enjoyed the meal. The smell and flavours were good. It reminded her of a well-made, genuine tandoori, although some of the larger pieces were a little unpleasant to swallow. The rasping nature of Joreen's tongue did a good job of mastication but would never be as effective as teeth.

Once they'd finished dining, the two Desfoggians got to their feet and exited the wardroom into a long corridor. Emily couldn't tell how big the Desfoggians were, as she had nothing for comparison, but they were a little cumbersome, with two hefty legs, enormous feet and their bodies tended to lean forward as if suffering from stenosis.

Eventually, they arrived at a sliding door. Joreen opened it and they entered an observation room. Disorientation immediately overcame Emily as she saw that everything was upside down. The Desfoggians launched themselves, immediately far more graceful than when they were walking, towards a window which ran the full length of the wall. They somersaulted and the planet outside the ship disconcertingly rotated so that they were looking down upon it rather than up. Now in freefall, they gripped a handrail and peered at the planet Miift below. Emily experienced a brief wave of nausea, but it quickly passed. Joreen wasn't affected apparently.

The ocean and sea areas looked as pristine as ever, but as they dropped through the atmosphere and flew over the main continent, the destruction wrought by the bombs became increasingly obvious.

'Isn't that peninsula where the capital stands?' Mes asked, looking down at a diminutive Florida-like area of land.

'Stood! Yes, it appears dead,' Joreen said.

The ship continued its descent and the two medical officers' horror at the devastation grew. There were ten huge impact craters and nothing lived within thirty miles of each. The residential areas were no more than crumbling, blackened buildings. The agricultural land was discoloured too. Towns which were intact, could now be seen in great detail. An enormous tide of sentient creatures and livestock was moving north, away from the capital. They used cars, buses, trucks and even animal-drawn vehicles had been pressed into service. A growing number were on foot, carrying whatever they were able to salvage from their homes and herding their animals before them.

'They're still trying to get away from the bombsites,' Mes said.

'They are. But why? They must know that the destruction is over,' said Joreen.

'Maybe the radiation is being blown by the wind,' said Mes. 'Computer, which way is the wind blowing on the continent beneath us?'

'The wind on the large continent is blowing from the south-east,' said the computer.

'There, see,' said Mes. 'They're running from the radiation.'

'Could be,' Emily heard herself saying. 'There's Vona appearing over the horizon. We'll be down soon.'

'Don't know much about Vona,' said Mes.

'No, but there is a big city towards the west of it. Gusv Xommoen, I believe,' said Joreen.

The landscape below them became clearer as the ship lost altitude. An armada of small vessels were crossing the sea, escaping from the main continent.

The starship crossed the narrow sea between the large continent and Vona and was now flying at just a few thousand metres. The ports in the southeast were full of boats and the same panicked migration of people could be seen progressing inland, still in a north-westerly direction, but it became less obvious as they neared the province of which Gusv Xommoen was the main city. Here, life appeared to be continuing as normal. People could be seen in the fields, in the shopping streets and milling around the city centre.

'Now hear this. Landing in three minutes. That is all,' said the captain over the loudspeaker.

'Come on,' Joreen said. 'We'd better get ready.'

The two Desfoggians left the observation deck. Emily was out of breath as they progressed swiftly towards the rear of the starship. She suddenly felt as if she was losing her grip on reality. It was as if Joreen was trying to shrug off his or her unknown companion.

The corridor became less distinct and faded to black.

11 Earth's Administrator

This time, I made an appointment to see Earth's administrator. I arrived on time and sat in her assistant, Marcia Gray's office. We chatted for a while and I managed to get an insight into how her life had changed since joining the Federation.

'Did you always work for the government?' I asked.

'No, Professor. After I got my degree, I entered a law firm, but sadly, it bored the pants off me,' she said.

'That's a new one on me, Ya Gray. What does "bored the pants off" mean? Is underwear involved?'

She laughed loudly, 'No, it's just an expression of how boring something might be. Anyway, I got a job as a clerk in the Ministry Of Defence and worked my way up to be an assistant to a junior minister.'

'How did you end up here then?'

'Ms Horvat was looking for a small team to work with her when she became administrator. The Defence Ministry was closing down, so I jumped in,' said Marcia.

'But you needn't have done anything,' I said.

'Now that really *would* have bored the pants off me!' she said and laughed.

'Ah. I see.' I laughed too. 'And are you enjoying it?'

'Oh, yes. Lara's a terrific boss, I meet lots of important people and aliens and the whole department is absolutely fascinating to be part of,' she said enthusiastically.

A buzzer sounded.

'You can enter now,' said Ya Gray.

I made my way along the long corridor and into Ya Horvat's office.

'Yol Breganin, how lovely to see you again,' said the administrator, walking around her desk to shake my hand. 'How is your book progressing? Take a seat.'

I sat in one of her visitor's chairs. 'Slow, Ya Horvat. I am finding it more difficult to obtain information than I imagined. Part of that is because I am an alien. People are either reticent to talk or gushing with useless information. I've found one or two good sources, though.'

'I see. How can I help?'

'If it is not too much of a burden, I'd like an appointment to interview you about the changes from your perspective. Could we do that?'

'How long would you need, Professor?'

'I think a couple of hours would be sufficient, perhaps less,' I said.

Lara Horvat looked at her computer screen. 'I could do tomorrow at ten if that were suitable to you.'

'Oh, yes. Ideal. Ya Horvat, there's something else.'

She looked at me quizzically.

'Paula Wilson. How much contact do you have with her?'

'I see her from time to time. She's writing my biography.'

'Ah,' I said. 'I'm sure she'll make a great job of it. I've read her biography of Ya Perfect Okafor. There was an unpublished copy in Ambassador Yol Hareen Trestogeen's personal study.'

'We both attended his spawning,' said Lara.

'Truly? How honoured you must have been. I've only seen documentaries of the spawnings on Pestoch.'

'Yes, but so sad, for such a clever and intelligent person to end his life in such a way.'

'It is unusual, indeed, but many species have unusual cultural or religious celebrations,' I said. 'I'd like to meet Ya Wilson. Could you give me her contact details?

'I'd need to ask her permission, Professor. Give your current contact information to Marcia on the way out and I'll get her to pass it to Paula. I'm sure she'll be delighted to meet you,' said the administrator.

'Thank you. I'll let her scan my chip.'

'Yes, of course. Such things are so much easier now, I'll see you tomorrow,' she said.

12 Evacuation

A new scene burst into existence. Emily was in the yard of a home looking upwards as a giant starship descended towards the apron of the airport which lay alongside the house. How exciting to see.

'Golda! Come see!' a voice shouted from inside.

'No. You come see this, Rebor! There's an Arlucian starship coming down at the airport, but it's decorated in Desfoggian colours. What does it mean?'

Emily realised she was now in Golda Verdon and was a Miiftian. Who was she shouting at?

Emily, or rather, Golda looked around and another Miiftian, with two pyramidal heads was coming out of the house. Two heads? Surely not. One was smaller than the other. Oh, no! It was a child clinging on to its father's back and looking over his shoulder.

'See!' said Golda, pointing at the starship, the lower part of which was now disappearing behind trees as it settled onto the apron.

'It's Desfoggian,' said Rebor.

'Definitely an Arlucian-made ship. I thought we were going to get bombed until I saw the Desfoggian crest on the hull,' said Golda.

'It's what all this war was over. Desfogg and Mepdetvis have been buying new ships from Arlucian and cancelling contracts with us,' said Rebor, returning to the house. 'There's an urgent news bulletin. I've got it on freeze Frame.'

Golda took a last look at the top part of the starship. It was now stationary, then she turned and followed her husband inside.

The living area was like any other. Seats, flooring, decorative pictures and ornaments, giant visiscreen, one or two toys on the floor, incidental tables and miscellaneous books and magazines on shelves or scattered on the tables.

‘Ready? Here, I’ll run it back to the beginning,’ said Rebor, manipulating a remote control device.

Golda sat beside two more young Miiftians, perhaps older children. The newscaster began to speak.

‘This is a worldwide broadcast,’ she said. ‘Hindit Ottery is making a broadcast from Gusv Xommoen which is now the Miiftian capital city. He has grave and distressing news for you.’

The television scene switched to a comfortable sitting room and the camera zoomed slowly in to a serious looking Miiftian, relaxed in a leather easy chair with a scoggle sitting at his right hand, which petted the animal, stroking it from brow to shoulder. It emitted a continual, pleasurable, low droning moan. Behind were bookshelves filled with political hardbacks peppered with odd natural history works. A photographic family portrait sat on a table in the corner.

‘Good afternoon, people of Miiftian. I regret that I am bringing sad tidings and an even worse prognosis.

‘Arlucians, the people from the other star system, have taken revenge for King Debruek’s attack on their fleet of ships. The rights and wrongs of that may never be known, but they sent an armada of starships in retaliation. The king is dead. In fact, a nuclear bombardment of the other continent killed millions of people, and not just instantly. The major killer is the lethal radiation, created during the explosions. Everyone within ten miles of the bombs died within an hour. The radiation is now spreading on the wind. It is moving north-west towards us.

‘As the radiation advanced, the population of the other continent began a migration ahead of the radiation cloud. It can be outrun, but it is coming relentlessly, killing all it encounters – people, animals, trees and crops.

‘A few of us were able to send hyperspace messages to Desfogg and Mepdetvis. The latter did not respond, but the Desfoggians have reacted to our cry for help. Ships will be landing in the northeast of Vona. They will evacuate as many as possible.

'You might be wondering why we need to evacuate Vona. Tragically, I must tell you that you cannot outrun the radiation forever. The other continent will be uninhabitable within two days and the radiation will be blown by the wind, across the straits of Zendo and onwards over Vona. I have just come from a meeting with scientists who say that everything on Vona will be dead within a week, perhaps sooner.

'After that, the only safe place will be the southern icy continent and the radiation will reach it too, eventually. It is not a safe haven and, as you know, it suffers temperatures far below freezing, year round. Nothing can live there in those conditions, except research teams on the ice shelf.'

Hindit Ottery sat back in his chair and wiped tears from his eyes.

'The Desfoggians will send as many ships as they can. Each ship can carry varying numbers, but a few thousand is the limit. Those of you in the city might have seen one of the ships touch down at the airport a few minutes ago. If you are under the age of forty, please take your passport and make your way to the airport. I regret that no one older than forty will be taken aboard.'

Rebor and Golda sat silently when the broadcast ended. The eldest child said, 'Da, what does it mean?'

Rebor seemed to be in a trance and Golda answered, 'Nothing, child. It means we must go on a trip. Get your coats and shoes on, quickly.'

She turned to Rebor, slapped him on the shoulder, 'Snap out of it. We must go!'

Emily found herself immersed in the blackest of black before the bridge of the starship materialised around her. She was back inside the Desfoggian medical officer, Hel Joreen.

'Sir, you must recall the crew and close the hatches. The air here is deadly,' Joreen said, speaking to a uniformed person seated in the centre of the bridge. 'Some of these people will not survive.'

The captain looked at him sharply. 'Already?'

Joreen continued, 'The air, even this far from the bombing, is contaminated. Breathing it in for more than an hour, possibly less, is a death sentence.'

'What are you telling me, Hel?' asked the captain.

'We must leave here now, sir. Stop the embarkation and move to the far north western tip of Vona. Some there will not yet be affected,' replied Joreen.

'What? Abandon those boarding now?'

'Yes. They won't live. This is the worst form of radiation. It is in the form of a microscopic dust and embeds itself in the lungs. It is not treatable, and you must recall all our crew immediately, sir, or they most certainly will die.'

'Security, hear this,' said the captain, speaking into a microphone. 'All crew return to the ship and immediately close the airlocks. Repeat – all crew return to the ship immediately and close the airlocks. No more Miiftians to be boarded.'

He looked at a panel before him. Eleven of twelve lights showed green and the other red. 'Airlock four. Close now!'

'Sir,' a tiny radio voice said, 'Bromin here. People have rushed the guard.'

The captain looked at Emily and said, 'Hel, you are certain about the danger.'

'Certain, sir,' said Joreen.

The captain depressed the transmit switch on the microphone, 'Bromin, open fire. You *must* shut that airlock immediately. It is life or death. We are lifting off.'

'Sir, really?' said Bromin.

'Do it *now*!' the captain shouted.

We heard the rattle of gunfire. The light turned green.

'Helm, raise us twenty metres,' said the captain.

Emily felt the floor move beneath her as the ship rose from the ground.

'Grendor, translate this, over the external speaker system,' said the captain, passing a different microphone to another Desfoggian crew member.

'People of Miiftian. This transport is full. We suggest you make your way northwest. More of our ships will be arriving there,' said the captain.

Grendor repeated the message in Miiftian and, although I understood it when I was seeing the world through Golda's eyes, it was now just a garble of foreign words. This must be long before Galactic Standard had been invented.

The ship began to rise faster and headed northwest.

'Hel,' said the captain. 'Check the passengers. Any dead should be thrown off when we land. We can't afford to be carrying dead people.'

'Yes, sir,' Emily heard Joreen saying, before turning to rush off the ship's bridge.

Once more, black of black descended.

'Why's it going?' said Rebor.

'Don't know. Maybe it's full,' Emily heard herself saying as Golda.

The ship rose further into the air as the badly translated message came over the ship's speakers and enlightened them.

'Come,' said Rebor, 'let's head homeward. We can get the pickup.'

Of course, after the message, the entire heaving mass, comprising everyone who had come to the starship in the hope of salvation, turned as one and followed the main thoroughfare away from the airport.

Golda and her family turned the other way, returning home to pack some possessions and travel north-east in their ground vehicle.

As they entered the house, Emily could feel Golda's hands and face beginning to sting. She looked at her skin. Blisters, exactly as had occurred to Erind during the previous scenario.

Did she really want to stay with this family until the end came. She looked at the others. The face of the baby in Rebor's backpack looked red. Golda touched its skin. That was enough for Emily.

She bellowed, '*End course*!'

The scene vanished instantly, and she pulled the blindfold away. The room was as it always was, and lovely scenic views were following each other on the giant television monitor.

'Emily,' said the room-bot. 'You ended the scenario early.'

'It is too depressing. I don't want to watch that family die.'

'You could continue the scenario as Hel Joreen. There is one more section to take place,' said the room-bot.

'Okay. I'm going to make a coffee first.'

'As you wish, Emily. Just say "Begin" to watch the rest of the scenario as Hel Joreen. I've removed the sections on Golda Verdon.'

'I assume they did die,' said Emily.

'They did,' said the room-bot.

Emily made her coffee and sat back in the luxurious chair. The television was now depicting scenes of sports arenas taken from artistic perspectives.

'Room-bot, how many of these courses and scenarios are there?' Emily asked.

'The number is in the millions, but in reference to a human lifetime, if you experienced a new scenario every forty-eight hours, for the rest of your life, you would only have reached a sixtieth of the timescale between where you are now and the modern Federation.'

'I feared as much.'

'You need to be selective. I have loaded a prospectus onto your chip. Take a look at it after the fourth scenario of this course. You might wish to follow it to get a broad understanding of the Federation's development.'

'Thank you,' said Emily, then, 'begin.'

‘Please put the eye mask on.’

She picked up the discarded blindfold and covered her eyes.

‘Scenario three of four will continue shortly,’ said the room-bot.

Darkness descended briefly, then was replaced by the most brilliant sunshine, as Emily stepped from the ramp of the starship onto the soil of the planet Miift. She looked around, or rather, Hel Joreen took in the scene.

A few hundred metres before her, was the ocean. Gentle breakers cascaded onto a golden beach. As a beach-loving Californian, Emily loved surfing but hadn’t had too much opportunity of late. This was the perfect surf for a relaxing day’s fun. Not large enough to satisfy the experts, but not too taxing for the beginners either. Perfect for an intermediate like her.

But this surf was stripped of play, the beach was filling with people who were being herded into more organised lines on their approach to the ship.

Joreen walked into a nearby tent. ‘What’s it looking like, Mes?’ he asked his junior colleague.

‘Not good. We’re already reading eight. Ten minutes breathing at level twenty would be a death sentence,’ said Mes.

‘How fast is it increasing?’

‘When I set up last night, it was four. If the wind doesn’t change direction, we will reach fifteen late this afternoon and will have to stop the embarkation and leave. When is the Garincha due?’

Joreen turned and looked to the heavens. ‘Any minute, actually. There’s no point in the Breadona coming. The captain says it won’t be here for twenty-four hours.’

Joreen removed a communicator from his pocket and called the captain. ‘Sir, radiation is building faster than we expected. Ensign Risteroid has just advised me that it will be too dangerous to stay beyond mid-afternoon.’

Emily heard the reply, 'I'll tell the Garincha and Breadona. Is there any point in the Breadona coming? There would seem no reason if all they can take away is dying people.'

'The wind direction might change,' said Joreen.

'Yes. We can hope,' said the captain. 'Nothing lost if they arrive and it is too late, but much to gain if there is still a chance for the fittest Miiftians to board. How is boarding?'

'We have four thousand on board, sir. There's space for another two which we should achieve well before the radiation becomes dangerous.'

'I'll call Colonel Tederon and tell him to ensure every crew member outside the ship is wearing full protective gear.'

'Thank you, sir. We'll shut down this medical centre at lunchtime and bring our staff aboard,' said Joreen.

'Someone will answer for this,' said the captain, and Emily heard his voice breaking with emotion. 'It is just so dreadful.'

'Yes, sir,' said Joreen. 'I'll let you know when we're back aboard.'

Hel Joreen and Mes Risteroid stepped out of the tent into the sunshine. The day looked just perfect. The grass verdant, trees and shrubs with blossom in bloom, the sand golden and the azure sea broken only by white horses crashing onto the beach. The tide of Miiftian people was enormous, tens of thousands in the temporarily fenced funnel leading to the ship. Emily tried to count two thousand. Twenty blocks of a hundred leading away from the boarding ramp. Everyone beyond that would be turned away.

'Here's the Garincha,' said Mes, pointing at a huge grey shape in the sky, making its way groundward.

Joreen called Colonel Tederon on his communicator. 'Colonel, Joreen here. Get your troops to cut off at eighteen hundred from now.'

'Right, Joreen. We'll create a barrier and tell the remainder to head to the Garincha. How many will she hold?'

'More than us, but the radiation might have exceeded limits before they are full.'

'Okay, Joreen. See you later,' said the colonel.

Joreen cut the call and turned towards his colleague. 'I'll leave you to break down the medical tent after lunch, Mes. Call me if you need me.'

Emily wanted to stay and watch, but Joreen turned and headed up the ramp. The scene faded to black.

Emily knew exactly where she was when the pitch black relented and allowed a new location to come into her mind. She could see Joreen's hands on a rail in front of him and the observation window of the starship allowed her/him to look down on the continent of Vona. Mes stood alongside Joreen. He passed a steaming mug to Joreen and sipped his own. Emily smelled a not unattractive aroma like some herbal teas she'd had in the past. The taste was less pleasant, but her host seemed to enjoy it.

The ship swung out over the ocean to the northwest of Vona. To the right, the Garincha stood in fields. Leading from its two ramps were funnels of people trying to get on board. The people continued as far as the eye could see in both directions. Literally millions upon millions.

Joreen looked at his timepiece. 'That's it,' he said. 'Anyone boarding the Garincha now is a dead person walking.'

'Why are they still boarding?' asked Mes.

'I should imagine they'll stop soon.'

Emily lost sight of the Garincha as the starship banked left. Dozens of boats were fleeing Vona, but they had nowhere to go. The main continent was already dead. Miift only had three land masses. Both of the main continents would become permanent cemeteries in hours. The only remaining land was a research outpost on the southern pole. The Breadona had agreed to divert there to pick up the final Miiftians to be living on their own world. Probably only a few dozen.

The starship had completed its turn and was now heading south-east across Vona. Millions were still racing to get to the coast. Word of the huge transport ship, the Garincha, had given false hope. Our starship moved slowly over the hordes of travellers, but after just fifty miles, the numbers were dribs and drabs. On the ground and in the fields, lying on the streets and sheltering under trees were the dead and the dying. Fifty miles further and there was no longer movement. Another fifty miles and the ground cover, trees and shrubs were losing their leaves and gradually blending into a dead land of blacks and greys.

'Will it ever be inhabited again?' asked Mes.

'Not in our lifetimes,' Joreen said. 'We have witnessed the end of a world.'

'How many have been saved?'

'A few hundred in their own ships. We have six thousand. The Garincha could carry ten thousand, but I doubt if more than five will survive.'

'Awful,' said Mes.

'To paraphrase the captain, someone really *must* answer for this.'

Emily was crying. Real tears for all of the dead and sick people experiencing the hope that the giant ships portrayed, only to die as they abandoned them to the radiation.

The room faded away and the room-bot was speaking.

'You have experienced scenario three of the Iasuqi history vista. You may remove your eye mask. Please take time to recover. You must not return for scenario four for at least forty-eight hours.'

Emily wiped away her tears. 'Room-bot. What will I learn in scenario four? I don't want another depressing experience like the last one.'

'Scenario four of the Iasuqi system history does not contain similar imagery,' said the room-bot.

'Thank you,' Emily said.

It was over an hour and another coffee later that she finally managed to leave the booth and get out into the sunshine of Hyde Park.

Esponging, this wonderful educational tool, was obviously a double-edged sword.

13 Washington

The front doorbell rang.

Charles Mayne, once Democratic congressman, and later a traitor in President Slimbridge's opinion, grabbed his wig from the hall stand, checked his appearance in the mirror, mussing and pulling the long hair over his ears and collar, and walked to the door.

He opened it.

Outside stood a bearded unkempt individual carrying a small red bucket portraying the name SAFEGUARD, a charity for the homeless.

'I'll get something,' said Charles, about to turn from the door.

'Take a closer look, Congressman,' said the bearded man.

At the word "Congressman", Charles Mayne froze. He was exposed. Someone knew who he was. The impulse to fight or flee, coursed through his blood as his stomach felt as if it had fallen through the floor. Was this one of Slimbridge's secret service?

He looked hard at the gaunt, bearded face. There was something familiar, but what?

'Sorry to give you a fright, Charles. It's Bob.'

'Good God, Bob Nixon,' said Charles, looking up and down the street for anything suspicious. 'Bob, come on in.'

The two men walked through the hallway and into a large modern kitchen. An attractive fifty-ish woman was preparing food at one of the kitchen units.

'This is my wife, Carol. Don't think you ever met her,' said Charles.

'Ah, you're wrong there, Charles. We met at a charity fundraiser about three years ago.'

'That's right,' said Carol. 'I remember. Excuse me not shaking hands. They're covered in onion.'

'No problem,' said Bob.

'Would you join us? I'm just making a salad for lunch,' said Carol.

'I'd be delighted.'

'Come over here,' said Charles and he led the man to the dining table which sat in a bay window, overlooking an extensive garden. 'So, to what do I owe this shock? My heart fell through my boots when you recognised me.'

'Yes, sorry,' said the bearded man, sitting opposite the congressman. 'Do you still entertain political ambitions?'

'Of course, but I can't do anything without revealing that I'm back in the United States. Slimbridge still has an arrest warrant out for me… and you, I presume.'

'True, but Free America, although fragmented, is gathering its resources again. I'm here to feel out your sentiments.'

'But why me? I'm a Democrat, Bob.'

'You said you'd be prepared to be the figurehead and would call an election after we'd overthrown Slimbridge. Is that still the case?'

'Yes. I'd given up hope though. Thought Free America had died when the Federation rescued us from execution,' said Charles.

Carol arrived at the table with three plates of salad with cheese, ham and pineapple. She passed two to the others and sat at the head of the table. 'You conspirators don't mind me listening in?'

'No, not at all, Carol,' said Bob.

'Right. Spill it, Bob.'

'It has been a year. Rumours are rife about how much better life is in Canada and Mexico. There is a slow, but sure emigration in progress. We know Slimbridge is worried about it and is about to move to seal the borders,' said Bob.

'He's going to ban emigration?' asked Carol.

'Legal emigration, yes. The Federation will accept any willing immigrant, so if you can get over the border, you're welcomed with open arms. Poverty isn't helping. Unemployment has grown to almost thirteen per cent and benefits have been cut as government debt has grown. Slimbridge knows he's in trouble. It isn't just poverty; it's the growing inequality.'

'Slimbridge still has a forty per cent approval rating,' said Charles.

'We're not sure where that comes from. We had survey teams out and people are really polarised. Around half think he can do no wrong and the other half think he is a disaster zone. That means that half of Americans are open to be swayed.'

'Those polarised people, how does the split work?' asked Charles.

'As you might imagine,' Bob said, 'the unemployed and disadvantaged are against him and the wealthy and privileged are for him. Among the others, some are stoically accepting that the Slimbridge way is the American way and the others love the country and their homes and are prepared to put up with almost anything in order to stay both free and where they are. It is this group who are expressing the most dissatisfaction with Slimbridge, but not enough to protest.'

'Because protests are put down,' said Carol.

'Exactly!' said Bob.

'So, you must have some sort of plan, or you wouldn't be here,' said Charles.

'We have,' said Bob, 'but we need to know that you are on board and will stand as an interim leader before a full election is called.'

There was silence.

'Well?' asked Bob.

'Yes, but there is a problem.'

'Spit it out, Charles,' said Bob.

'I have become a fan of the Federation. Those eight months we lived in Spain had a big effect on us, didn't they?'

'Yes, life was brilliant,' said Carol.

‘You’re not alone in feeling like that. Why is it a problem?’ asked Bob.

‘I would want not just an election for a new leader, but a properly informed referendum on joining the Federation too.’

‘I think that would be acceptable. You’d need to stand on that ticket in the election you call after taking power. We think you might be up against Matthew Brown,’ said Bob.

‘But he’s just an economist, not a politician,’ said Charles.

‘We’ve been watching him. He’s the man who is holding Slimbridge’s administration together. We’ve had people feeling out his views. He’s a Republican through and through, and very much against everything the Federation stands for. Mind you, much of that is a lack of understanding.’

‘Okay, so how does the plan work?’ asked Charles.

‘Now we know you are “in”, we will set up for you to meet the others.’

‘Who are the others?’

‘You’ll know some. General Dick Beech, Colonel Mike Henderson and, with you on board, we know Jim Collins will come back from Canada.’

‘And how many foot soldiers?’

‘That’s Dick’s concern. You can bet he’s got it covered,’ said Bob.

14 Interstellar Conference

It took Emily almost a week before she felt ready to return to the esponging centre, but at least she had the room-bot's assurance that the last scenario wouldn't show the dreadful scenes of death and destruction she'd previously seen on Miift. She spent a while on the Frame, studying more about the Iasuqi system and discovered that some Miiftians were returning to the planet after some six hundred thousand years in exile. The radiation was still there, but robots had spent several decades scraping the surface and burying the radioactive soil. Plants were beginning to gain a foothold and Miiftian scientists living on Desfogg, were cloning some of the original wildlife from the best preserved remains brought back by recent expeditions. It worked with some creatures, but not all. The oceans had survived the catastrophe and were teaming with life, providing the early settlers with a good source of protein. It would be a long time indeed before the planet would be home to anything like the original population.

'A list of characters is on the screen. Choose your character by saying the number,' said the room-bot.

There were eight names and Emily only recognised one of them, President Gareel Jovak, and she thought he'd been rather selfish and arrogant in his dealings with King Debruek of Miift in the earlier scenario. It was cancelling all of their Miiftian orders which resulted in the war.

On the list were President Gedor Nesofin of Desfogg; Prime Minister Delika Ostroy who was the leader of the Miiftians in exile; President Gareel Jovak of Mepdetvis; President Boronic Feredic of a planet called X-Jastu; First Minister Korodin Eveskreen of Pestoch – Emily knew this was the water world in the same system as Arlucian; the others were from planets she hadn't heard of at all – President Coll Svertich of Opwispitt; President Jek Prodiv of Iyivis; and President Kil Trovver of Garnth.

Who should she choose? She knew that Pestochians were important in the later Federation, but this was still six hundred thousand years ago. Allegiances could change given the periods involved. She chose one she knew nothing about – President Kil Trovver. 'Number eight,' she said.

'Please put the eye mask on,' said the room-bot. 'Scenario four of four will begin shortly.'

Slowly, the scene materialised. She was sitting at a large circular table in a plush room with windows along one side. Outside, trees filled most of the view, with staggeringly high mountains in the far distance; Himalayan in scale. In the room, Emily could see that she was one of eight aliens sitting around the table. Emily immediately recognised President Jovak, almost opposite and the fishy personality of the Pestochian First Minister. She looked down at a document. The others were all reading it too.

'This report is damning of all concerned,' said President Nesofin.

'So, let me get this straight, I'll summarise, tell me if I'm misunderstanding anything,' said First Minister Eveskreen. 'Desfogg, Mepdetvis and Miift had an insular trading relationship which had continued for many decades. Miiftian people were the innovators.'

President Jovak jumped in, 'Our people are innovative too, it's just that Miift had the monopoly on materials needed for flight between the planets. They were undoubtedly skilled, but each planet had its own specialities. We were the breadbasket of the Iasuqi system.'

'Don't speak of us as if we are not at this table,' said Prime Minister Ostroy.

'No offence intended, Delika, but your people were dominating interplanetary trade.'

'Please, please,' said the Pestochian First Minister, 'let me summarise.'

Emily saw the others relax a little.

'To continue – the Arlucians arrived in your system and began trading with all three planets, particularly selling quantum drive ships which could move between the planets faster than light.' The first minister looked up and each of the Iasuqi representatives nodded or gave some other confirmation that they agreed. 'Suddenly, Desfogg and Mepdetvis stopped buying Miiftian technology because, compared with Arlucian's it was outdated and slow. Yes?'

'Yes,' said Prime Minister Ostroy. 'But it—'

'Please, Delika, let me finish what the report summarises,' said the Pestochian. 'This did not become a problem until Miift discovered that work in progress on ships and other space technology was being cancelled by Desfogg and Mepdetvis.' He waved the prime minister down again.

'King Debruek travelled to Mepdetvis to find out what was going on, and you,' he said, pointing at President Jovak, 'told them that you were no longer buying any technology from them, despite the fact that they had shipyards full of part-finished ships you had ordered.'

'They were no longer any use to us,' said President Jovak.

'Please, Gareel. All the reasoning is in the report. We'll be here all day if you keep interrupting. You've all signed off the accuracy of the report. Now, if we are going to understand and help, we must work from the facts.'

'Sorry,' said President Jovak. 'Please continue.'

'At this point, we know that King Debruek stormed out of the meeting. In a stroke, Mepdetvis and Desfogg had destroyed Miift's economy.'

'We didn't cancel our orders, Korodin,' said President Nesofin. 'Desfoggians honour their contracts.'

President Jovak jumped up and faced President Nesofin, 'Why, you condescending restgard[1], how dare you criticise us. We had dozens of ships on order. You had only two or three.'

'For galaxy's sake, stop it!' Emily heard her character saying. He was furious. She felt the heat in his face. 'We've agreed to meet here, arranged an independent report and you two are acting like a couple of schoolkids. Please, Korodin, continue.'

'Whatever the rights and wrongs of cancelling or not cancelling orders,' said First Minister Eveskreen, 'King Debruek seems to have decided to put the blame on Arlucian. He summoned an Arlucian delegation and, without warning, imprisoned them and destroyed their ships.'

Prime Minister Ostroy looked down at the table. He made no attempt to counter the claim.

'We should note that the Miiftians in exile have not tried to defend the rash actions of their king. The Arlucians sent a small fleet which arrived in orbit around Miift. King Debruek had them all destroyed on arrival without any negotiation or discussion.' First Minister Eveskreen laid the report on the table in front of him and looked up at the other members of the group. 'What happened next is the most disgraceful piece of overreaction any of us will ever have encountered. The Arlucians attacked Miift with extremely dirty, nuclear devices. The intention was clear – they intended to wipe out the entire planet. If it hadn't been for the swift actions of the Desfoggian people, the Miiftians would now be extinct, or as good as.

'That is the summary. Now we, as a group of like-minded intelligent species, must decide what action to take.' First

---

[1] Mepdetvisian sewer dwelling invertebrate.

Minister Korodin leaned back. 'Let each of you provide your opinions. Gedor, you befriended Miift in its hour of need. You first.'

'Firstly, I must condemn the Miiftian government, although I fear it was primarily King Debruek at fault. Their unprovoked assault on the visiting Arlucian delegation was unforgiveable. However, it is clear that Arlucian overreacted. Wiping out an entire species in revenge is not the behaviour of a civilised race. They may be technologically advanced, but their actions were intolerable. I don't know how to punish them though,' said the President of Desfogg.

'Gareel – your views.'

'Mepdetvis was the first planet in this system which the Arlucians visited. We got on well with them and once we discovered the quality of their ships and the fact that FTL travel could be used within the Iasuqi system, we did rather jump at the opportunity. We treated Miift badly, cancelling legally binding contracts, but Debruek and his minions had been taking advantage of us, and the Desfoggians for many decades.' He looked across at President Gedor Nesofin, who nodded agreement. 'We should have provided help to Miift and didn't. I regret that, but the Arlucians were completely out of order in their actions.'

'Coll. What do you think?'

The president of Opwispitt leaned forwards in his seat. He said, 'Arlucian's behaviour is unacceptable. We didn't know any species from the system of Iasuqi until this awful event, and in less than a year, it is difficult to assess any new friends. I see our meeting today as an opportunity to create a cohesive confederation of planets. If we are to do that, then we must be sure that we condemn any world which steps over the line. We have had a long relationship with Arlucian, but I have seen them take similar, though less drastic action in the past. We must be wise and thoughtful about this.'

'Yes, well said, Coll. And you, Jek, what's your view?'

President Jek Prodiv, a chameleon-like creature, had so blended into his seat as to appear to be an empty chair. The space the Iyivisian occupied rippled and his shape became clearer to the others in the room. All of a sudden, colours undulated across his body. He was speaking. An electronic gadget on the table before him produced the words, 'We too, have long traded with the Arlucians and have had no problems with them, although they have tended to act as if they are superior to us and other species we know. We cannot allow such behaviour to continue. Let me throw the word "isolation" onto the table.' He blended back into his seat.

'Kil, we've known each other for a long time, what do you think?' said the Pestochian, spraying himself with a fine mist of water.

'Thank you, Korodin,' said President Trovver. 'I suppose our worlds have had more interaction with Arlucian than any others. Pestoch and Garnth are both in the same system, with Arlucian almost midway between us. We've been trading for almost four hundred thousand years. When Arlucian came up with FLT quantum travel, it changed the balance of interplanetary economics. They certainly took a more dominant role in the planetary system. Jek suggests isolation. That would be difficult for us. Our economies are quite integrated. Surely it would also damage Pestoch, Korodin?'

'It would, but I too, agree something must be done. How about you, Boronic? X-Jastu is the most technologically advanced of all the worlds we know, including Arlucian. What's your opinion?'

Boronic's body swelled as he began to speak, 'It is true that our technology is at a high level. It was, of course, us who arrived in your system, Korodin, and introduced quantum travel to all three of you. Arlucian conveniently forgets that. We must take action.' Boronic's body shrank down to a single ball then inflated anew. 'I would also like to remind everyone here that we have all emerged from solitary planets which once had individual countries or states which warred with each other. We had one national leader who tried to murder every person who smelled different to his own countrymen. He almost succeeded, but the other countries eventually stood against him. Millions of our people died in a horrendous conflict.'

'Boronic,' said Korodin, 'what has this to do with the matter at hand?'

'What I am saying is that none of our planets became civilised until we were able to throw off national boundaries and work together with free movement of people worldwide and tolerance of different beliefs. Now we find ourselves, like individual countries, but in the vastness of space. We are finding new intelligent species as we travel outwards. Until we learn to work together, we will always be susceptible to tyrannical leaders like King Debruek and arrogant administrations like the Arlucians. We should turn this disaster into an opportunity. President Svertich suggested a confederation. It could be an empire or whatever we want to call it, but this should see the beginnings of it and it must take action to condemn Arlucian.'

'Well said,' said the president of Mepdetvis.

'Delika,' said Korodin, 'you represent the Miiftians in exile on Desfogg. Let us know what you would consider a fair retribution.'

Prime Minister Ostroy got to his feet and wandered over to the window and looked towards the trees and distant mountains. 'The Desfoggians have been good to us. They've given us a small section of their world to call our own. In fact, many of us have tried to integrate with the native people and, I must say, that is going well.

'An expedition back to our world has studied the damage caused by the radiation. The Arlucians could have used a "clean" bomb, if ever a bomb can be called clean, but they chose to use the dirtiest bomb they could possibly manufacture. They were not taking revenge for the destruction of their ships and diplomatic team – they were intent on the complete annihilation of our species. They knew the radiation would make Miift uninhabitable. Our scientists tell us that it will remain so forever, or half a million years which is almost the same. There must be an adequate punishment.'

'Thank you, Delika. As the first minister of Pestoch, I too have an opinion. Isolating Arlucian would hurt our economy, as well as that of Garnth, but I do agree that some form of isolation is likely to be both fair and justified.'

'In that case,' said Boronic of X-Jastu, 'I propose that we form a loose empire of planets, of which we are the rule-making committee, and we ban Arlucian from interplanetary trade for a period of ten years. How does that sound?'

There was a mumble of agreement around the room as it disappeared into a swirling mist of blackness.

'You have experienced scenario four of the Iasuqi history vista. You may remove your eye mask.'

Emily eased the blindfold upwards and the screen was again showing fields of wheat, barley, lavender, hills of heather and swathes of sunflowers.

'It is suggested that you remain seated for five minutes to allow any disorientation to settle,' said the room-bot. 'You must wait at least forty-eight hours before returning.'

'How can I find out what happens next?' said Emily. 'I want to see how Arlucian deals with its isolation and how things progress.'

'I would recommend X-Jastu course six. It follows on from what you have been learning so far, but you must leave forty-eight hours before returning,' said the room-bot.

'Why is there this forty-eight hour rule?'

'Esponging causes heightened interaction between the mind's synapses. They must be allowed to return to normal activity before the synapses are artificially excited again,' said the room-bot.

'Thank you,' Emily said, then made herself a cup of tea and enjoyed it while watching the giant television portraying underwater life on the Red Sea reefs.

15 Mafia

Carlo shouted out Sofia's name as he found his release, his hands pulling her tightly to him as her naked body collapsed forward upon his bare chest. She smiled into his flushed face as he gasped for breath. God, it was good with him.

His hands gripped her hips fiercely as he tried to stop the motions she still needed. Eventually she enjoyed her own ecstasy and stilled. His arms circled her back, holding her tightly against him as he whispered, 'Sofia, Sofia, oh God, Sofia.'

Their stillness held for a long while, then he relaxed, freeing her to roll to one side where she stared at the room's ornate plasterwork, its colourful ceiling rose, and pink glass chandelier.

His hand snaked its way over to her hip and caressed it. With him it was welcome, with others it was just business. She wondered if he felt about her as she did about him.

She liked Carlo but this Federation thing was changing everything. The battle to invest her earnings no longer mattered. With no need for wealth, why let someone abuse your body. She wanted out.

'Can only give you three hundred this time,' he said apologetically.

'I don't want it, Carlo. You can have me free anytime.'

'I don't like to not pay.'

'It really isn't important. I mean it. I love these little trysts with you.'

His hand fell from her hip and their fingers met and clasped each other like real lovers.

'God, that was good, Sofia,' he said quietly, his breathing returning to normal.

'For me too, Carlo.'

'Really?'

'Absolutely.'

'I might love you, girl,' he whispered.

'Could be mutual.'

'You mean that?'

'Yes,' she said, rolling right and kissing his cheek, admiring his suntanned complexion and designer stubble. Her left arm and leg climbed over him lovingly.

'That's so good, Sofia.'

'Yes, lovely,' she agreed.

Then he ruined the spell by saying, 'Roberto says you're not answering his calls. He's becoming, let's say, *concerned.*'

'I'm avoiding him,' she said, a frown spoiling the soft lines of her forehead, and her arm and leg leaving him as she rolled onto her back once more. Why did he have to ruin their closeness? 'It's not the same now.'

'How's that?' he asked, but Sofia knew he already had the answer.

'It was different before. I was building up a fortune. Twelve hundred and fifty euros for an hour with him and he rarely lasted ten minutes!' she said, laughing.

'He'll find a way around these restrictions, you'll see.'

'But wealth is nothing. I had a fortune put away for when I decided to retire from this game. Now it'll be taken away in tax. I get a good income from the state. Much more than I imagined. I don't like him, Carlo, and he hurts me sometimes. I don't like the way he paid me last time either. He gave me eight hundred afeds and I told him it wasn't enough, so a case of champagne arrived at my flat and offers of food and clothes from some of the local shops. I hate his ability to coerce people and they must know why they're having to be nice to me. I don't like it. When I walk through the village, I'm sure they're all looking at me and telling their friends I'm the godfather's whore. They must despise me.'

'He still has power. Don't upset him, Sofia. And if you get free food, dresses and other goodies, isn't that compensation enough.'

‘Gerado’s bakery is already taken over. They’ll be free of him soon.’

‘He’ll threaten them and their families until they give him their money,’ said Carlo. ‘They’ll never be free of him.’

‘What? He’s still charging protection, even when they no longer have businesses? I heard Martino reported him and had his face slashed. The police got the culprit, but we all know it was Roberto who ordered it.’

‘They’ll never catch him, Sofia. Be good to him… it would ensure your wellbeing,’ said Carlo more seriously.

‘I know, but I want more from life. I want to dance, sing and try acting. I like you enough to settle down.’

‘Really? I’ll protect you if I can, but don’t push it, Sofia. He’s a frightening man when he gets crossed.’

‘What about those Federation information booths? Do you think they are worth visiting?’ Sofia asked.

Carlo propped himself up on one arm and looked at her seriously. ‘If you do, don’t let anyone see you. *No one.* Understand?’

‘I’ll take care,’ she said, sitting on the edge of the bed and slipping into her shoes. She covered her nakedness with a skimpy summer dress. The tryst was over, and she took just ten afeds from the brass plate. That would cover her taxis and the wine she’d brought.

∞∞∞∞∞∞∞∞

Over the eight weeks since Federation Day, millions of information booths had been set up in towns and cities. By the time of Sofia’s tryst with Carlo, one had also been installed in Olzai. She’d heard that it was small, just three confidential booths where you could speak to a Federation representative in absolute confidentiality. Would that mean Mafia bosses like Roberto Giordano would not discover what was said about them? How could she be sure? Roberto had ears and eyes everywhere.

Sofia dressed conservatively for her visit, wearing a calf-length brown skirt, hiding her undoubtedly beautiful legs. A soft suede jacket and flimsy yellow blouse concealed her bust, while flat shoes added a dowdiness which might make her less noticeable as she walked into the small town. She carried a little handbag and a large supermarket-branded hessian shopping bag. A headscarf covered most of her hair and added yet more anonymity and not a little severity.

She meandered through the compact shopping area, stopping to buy one or two items to prepare for a meal, made a brief visit to the pharmacy then walked casually past the booth. It was set in what had once been a baker's shop, which the Federation closed when they shifted most of Olzai's bread production to the larger of the four bakeries in the village. It was all run by robots now.

Beyond the booth, Sofia visited a haberdashery and bought some seafoam coloured ribbons. As she emerged, she stood in the shop frontage, as if looking at the ribbon colours in natural daylight, judging if the shade of light green was vibrant enough. Surreptitiously, she looked up and down the street. An old woman was entering a butcher's shop and a man went by on a bicycle. Sofia could see no one looking at the street from the shops and upper floors. No movement of lace curtains with betraying eyes behind. Another cyclist passed by leaving the sound of a rusty chain on cogs in his wake. She marked time until he disappeared from view. The street was now deserted.

She tucked the ribbons back into the candy-striped paper bag, strode hurriedly to the booth, glanced around herself one final time to ensure that she wasn't being observed and promptly entered.

'Good afternoon, Sofia. Please enter one of the three booths,' said a disembodied voice.

Hearing her name gave her a shock, her heart skipping a beat. Then she remembered that your name could be read from the chip in your left hand.

She looked back at the street. The dark glass hid her from the view of anyone passing by. The road was still quiet. She turned and entered the left of the three open-doored cubicles. Each was about four metres square, large enough for a small group or family to enter.

'Please take a seat, Sofia,' said a different voice. It was the head and shoulders of a mannikin-like robot, seated behind a curved desk.

Sofia selected the nearest seat to the centre of the front row.

'I want to talk to someone,' she said nervously.

'Sofia, before we speak, might one of my assistants show you something of interest?'

What the hell did this mean? 'Why?' she asked, nervous of anything out of the ordinary.

'You will see. It will do you no harm.'

'You *are* from the Federation?' she asked, wondering if the *family* had infiltrated the booths and set it up as a fake.

'Yes, this is an official Federation booth.'

'Okay, what do you want to show me?'

'Place your handbag on the desk.'

This was puzzling. She put her shopping bag on the floor beside her and laid the handbag on the desk.

'My assistant is a small robot. He will not harm you or your property.'

'Okay,' Sofia said apprehensively.

A section of the right end of the desk opened and a mechanical device arose from the hole. It was no bigger than an anniversary clock, made of a silvery metal and had all sorts of arms plus four legs. It scuttled across the desk to the handbag, carefully unzipped the purse section and removed a small medallion.

'My Saint Christopher,' said Sofia. 'It protects travellers. It was given to me by a boyfriend.'

'I'm sorry, Sofia, but this St Christopher is concealing something from you. May my assistant open it?'

'It doesn't open,' Sofia said confidently.

'Oh, but it does,' said the mannikin.

Sofia leaned forward to watch as the tiny robot brought out a tool which shone a bright light onto the surface. It was like an X-ray and, inside the medallion, Sofia could see electronic components.

She put her hand to her mouth in shock. 'What is it?'

'It is a microphone and movement tracker,' said a tinny voice from the small metal bot.

Sofia gasped. 'Someone knows I am here then?'

'No. It stopped transmitting when you approached within a hundred metres of the booth, but I thought you should be aware of it. My assistant can stop it working permanently if you wish,' said the mannikin.

'Yes, yes. Please do.' She felt horrified that she'd been tracked.

The tiny bot irradiated the medallion again and then returned it to her purse.

'There's nothing else, is there?' she asked in trepidation.

'No, you are now clear of surveillance devices,' said the mannikin as the tiny bot tumbled through the hole in the desk which then re-sealed itself as if it had never been there. 'Now, Sofia, why did you want to talk to me?'

How should she say this? She felt ashamed. Just get it over and done with. 'I sell my body for sex,' she blurted out. 'What is the Federation's view on that?'

'It is your body, Sofia. The Federation has no regulation about what your planet refers to as prostitution.'

'I don't always take money, and don't like that word for it. Sometimes I do it because I want to.'

'That is your right.'

‘There is a man, a very powerful man who hurts me and wants me to continue to give him sex for money, but with my Federation income I don’t need to do this anymore.’

‘Then don’t do it,’ said the mannikin.

‘It isn’t that easy. If I don’t do it, he will hurt me or send someone else to hurt me.’

‘That is against the law.’

‘I know that, but it is too late once he has already had my face slashed with a razor or worse.’

‘We can stop that.’

‘How?’

‘Don’t worry, Sofia. I’ll explain. You definitely want it to stop?’

‘Absolutely, but I don’t want to end up in more trouble or more danger. They could even harm my parents, cousins and other relations to get at me,’ she said, becoming more flustered.

‘There is nothing for you or your parents to fear. We will put you into special shielding.’

‘No. I don’t want to look out of the ordinary,’ she protested.

‘Shielding isn’t like that, Sofia. Shielding is conducted by nanobots. No one, not even you, will ever see them. Let me explain how this will work.’

16 Union of Planets

Emily sat back, asked the course to begin and the light, creeping around the edges of the blindfold, faded to black.

A scene developed. She was on board the graceful X-Jastuvian starship, Orman, as it dropped out of hyperspace and sat in orbit around the lightly ringed world of Arlucian. It was unusual in that, like Earth, it also had a large moon.

Communication passed to and from the ship. Emily realised that she was seeing the scenario from the viewpoint of President Boronic Feredic of X-Jastu. It was the strangest sensation. Boronic's body was no more than a bag of watery material. It moved about, making him taller, fatter, thinner, stockier and it was all most disconcerting. Emily wondered if she might be able to stop the course and re-start in a different character.

The diplomacy between ship and land was slow and ponderous. Emily got the distinct impression that Arlucian was being deliberately obstructive. Pestoch, Garnth and X-Jastu had embassies on Arlucian, but this was an unprecedented request. Three planetary leaders all arriving on the same ship and wanting to visit the Arlucian president at the same time, without having previously made an appointment.

Arlucian knew it was in trouble, or, at least, it had a communal guilty conscience over the one-sided war with the planet Miift. A communal "it" knew what it had done, although the news of the complete devastation of Miift was only just beginning to leak out to the general populace. President Duf of Arlucian was a ruthless individual and he had no intention of giving ground to his opposition who were calling for his resignation. Out on the streets, posters began to appear, saying that the genocidal attack on Miift was not done in their name.

Eventually, permission was granted for the leaders to descend to the surface and a meeting room was set up for the conference.

The X-Jastuvian starship slid out of orbit and made its way towards the capital of Arlucian, the city of Oridin.

Presidents Boronic Feredic, Kil Trovver and First Minister Korodin Eveskreen were shown into a stateroom lined with Arlucian teak in the presidential palace and sat at an ornate table. The wood was an almost iridescent golden colour with very subtle highlighted grain. They awaited President Drow Duf of Arlucian. And they waited.

After some fifty minutes, the three leaders were becoming unsettled by the delay. First Minister Eveskreen, who knew President Duf better than the others, left the room. He returned and said that he was told the president would be here shortly.

'Where is he? Dammit, this is insulting,' said President Trovver.

Emily watched as her host materialised an arm and hand out of his fluid shape and lifted a communicator from his carrycase. 'Yes, Captain,' he said.

President Feredic listened, then put the communicator down. 'My captain reports that a fleet of Arlucian ships are creating a formation in orbit and two of them have descended and are sitting either side of the Orman.'

'This is an aggressive move,' said President Trovver.

'Posturing, only, I'd wager,' said First Minister Eveskreen. 'Drow wants us to know that he's got the upper hand before he arrives. One deret gets you ten that he'll walk through that door within two minutes.'

Almost immediately, the door opened and the Arlucian leader walked into the room, accompanied by a squad of six fully-armed soldiers who stood with their backs to the wall.

'Kil, Korodin, so sorry to keep you waiting and, oh, President Boronic Feredic. Didn't expect you to be here,' said President Duf.

'That is surprising, as it is my flagship you are surrounding and my flagship in whose launch orbit you have positioned a fleet of your ships,' said President Feredic.

'What is the issue? Why are you here?' asked the Arlucian president, dismissing the X-Jastuvian's concerns as not warranting a response.

Emily felt her globular shape puffing itself up in size. 'We have some information for you.'

'Let's have it, Boronic.'

'Sixteen planets including the two remaining planets in the Iasuqi system have formed a planetary group called the Union of Planets. X-Jastu has been elected as the prime planet for eight years and that makes me the acting union general secretary,' said the globular being, its shape moving in tune with the sentiments of the information.

'And why were we not involved in this so-called planetary union?'

'We would very much like you to be part of the Union, Drow, but before you join, your actions at Miift need to be dealt with,' said President Feredic.

'We attacked Miift in self-defence. They imprisoned our diplomatic team and destroyed a fleet of ten ships we sent to investigate.'

'But, Drow, your retaliation was genocide! You wiped out their entire planet and all the people except for a few rescued by the Mepdetvisians. It will be uninhabitable for over half a million years,' said First Minister Eveskreen.

'Whatever you say, President Duf, the Union of Planets has decided that Arlucian must be sanctioned as your action involved unreasonable aggressive behaviour,' said President Feredic.

'Don't be ridiculous!'

'From today,' said President Feredic, taking pleasure in ignoring Drow's outburst and swelling up almost to the point of explosion. 'You will not be allowed to trade with any of the Union's planets except for altruistic provisions or other welfare aid. The sanctions will apply for ten years.'

'And how do you intend to enforce that?'

‘Break the sanctions and you will find out, President Duf,’ said President Feredic. ‘I suggest you do not test our resolve.’

‘And you two agree with this?’ he asked, looking at the Pestochian and Garnthian leaders.

‘We do,’ they said, almost simultaneously.

‘All sixteen planets in the Union have agreed with this course of action,’ said President Trovver.

‘Get off my planet, now! The lot of you. Go!’ he shouted. ‘Captain of the guard, escort these aliens to their ship.’

The scene faded to black and the room-bot was speaking again. ‘That is the end of part one of the X-Jastuvian course. You must allow forty-eight hours before returning for part two.

Emily tried to stand up and promptly fell over. She realised that she was trying to move by making herself flow across the floor in the manner of President Boronic Feredic. She made her way back to her feet then stumbled against the cupboard in front of her and fell to the floor a second time. The carpet was spongy, and all the surfaces were padded. She was unhurt. She’d always wondered why there were no hard surfaces in these booths. Now she understood. It took more than fifteen minutes and plenty of concentration to be able to leave the esponging centre without lurching from handhold to handhold.

17 Rehabilitation

Miles put Rummy in touch with a volunteer worker at the Kensington Habit Centre, not a stone's throw from Harrods department store. Her name was Aileen Walker.

'First time I've met an alien,' she said, when I sat opposite her in the lounge area of the Golden Fleece bar.

'Am I what you expected?'

'Your skin is drier than I thought it might be from your picture and it makes me feel like hunching, the way your head sits so low on your shoulders. You're short too. It's nice to be able to understand everyone these days, though,' she said, looking deeply into my eyes and studying what she could see of me above the table.

'Galactic Standard?' I asked.

'Yes. I deal with all sorts of nationalities with this being London and it's lovely not having to listen to someone in Polish and then tell some Spaniard what he said using my pidgin Spanish. Everyone speaks GS now and it makes it so much easier.'

'How long have you been at the rehabilitation centre?'

'Over six months now.'

'And how's it going, or should I ask, how has it changed?'

'I've been working closely with Carol Hedges who looked after the addicts for years before I came to help. The first week after Federation Day was sheer chaos.'

'Please elaborate,' I said, sipping my glass of red wine and eating some of the crunchy things from the dish in the centre of the table. Humans had strange customs. Eating while social drinking. Weird. On Daragnen we usually ate before drinking.

'Suddenly all drugs were banned. The first day saw prices go through the roof with all sorts of fights and victimisation breaking out. The centre was littered with people with broken noses, slashed faces and other injuries. On the streets it was even more serious. So many of them were suffering from withdrawal symptoms and none of them believed us when we told them that the Federation alternative meds would help them.'

'But they did in the end?' I asked.

'Yes, but there were repercussions. The drug barons started trying to victimise us, telling us we were destroying their businesses. Cop-bots were regularly appearing and putting them into stasis. My God, that's an effective punishment!'

'Yes. They wouldn't like that.'

'No,' she continued, 'the pushers were all high on their stashes of drugs for resale and the stasis had them climbing the walls as the drugs left their systems. You've never seen such manic expressions on people as we saw that first week. We were in danger too, from the suppliers, barons and pushers.'

'I can imagine. What happened to you?'

'We didn't know we were being protected until someone grabbed me and was about to cut my throat. We were both frozen into stasis and a cop-bot arrived, unfroze me and extricated me from the perp's arms. I'm afraid I ended up in a panic attack and another different bot arrived to calm me down.'

'You're okay now?' She nodded in reply. 'How long did it take to settle down?' I asked.

'Surprisingly quickly, really, but we had lots of people still arriving who'd been eking out their supply of drugs and finally having no option but to come to us for help. That's when Carol left.'

'Where did she go?'

'She told me she wanted to visit Arlucian and its moon.'

'Really?'

'Yes. There was a documentary about the moon being a luxurious retreat. That was it. She upped and went!'

'I've heard it is good, but never been myself,' I said.

'So that left the centre in the hands of us volunteers, but by then we were pretty good at it. Almost all visits were by addicts who had run out of their particular nectar and wanted to get off the stuff. Fairly standard really. I must say, though, that there could have been a bit more leniency in those first few days. We felt it was a bit heavy handed – the Federation rules.'

'I'll be sure to make a note of that opinion in my book. Do you like volunteering?'

'Oh, yes, Professor, especially with the robots clearing up any mess and keeping the place tidy. It was such a relief to know we were under permanent observation to prevent us being hurt. Before Federation Day, I was a clerk in an anonymous office in the financial quarter. Boring, boring, boring. Now I was earning more than ever before and doing something really worthwhile. In fact, our work will soon be done. The numbers entering the centre for help now are just dribs and drabs. Two or three a day, usually. I have a hankering for a beach holiday, so I'm tempted to go off to Bali.'

'Good for you,' I said.

'Do you need to know anything else?' she asked me.

'No. That's it. Just trying to get a general picture of how things are changing. Would you go back to your pre-Federation life?'

'Not a chance,' she said adamantly.

18 Sanction Busting

The resolve of the Union of Planets did not take long to be tested as Emily discovered on her next visit to the esponging centre. X-Jastu part two of five was soon underway.

Emily had chosen First Minister Eveskreen for her character in the second scenario of the X-Jastuvian course. It was odd having both eyes on one side of her face and difficult to move around on land with a tail which was not best adapted for the purpose. She'd read up on Pestoch before coming for this second scenario and had learned that between those early years of the Federation and today, the Pestochians had evolved stronger fins containing fleshy elements and this also strengthened their tails today, but in this event, taking place six hundred thousand years earlier, her host did not have the benefit of those improvements,

She, or rather Korodin Eveskreen, was on a video call with her previous host, President Boronic Feredic of X-Jastu.

'We were definitely offered produce by an Arlucian envoy,' said Korodin.

'And you turned it down?'

'Of course, but here's the rub, the ship did not return to Arlucian, but left a hyperspace signature that it was heading to Mepdetvis.'

'Perhaps they're just testing our resolve. I'm sure that Gareel's people will also turn it down,' said Boronic.

'We have an embassy there, Boronic, and we know for a fact that the transport landed at a place called Camkoob.'

'That's not good,' said Boronic. 'We must be able to trust each other not to break the sanctions.'

'What should we do?' Korodin asked.

'Get your ambassador to pay a visit to President Gareel Jovak and gently challenge him. Maybe that part of Mepdetvis isn't aware they are breaking sanctions.'

'I'll be surprised if any regional governor would go against Gareel's regulations,' said Korodin. 'He's quite authoritarian.'

'Okay, Korodin, but try anyway. I'd rather not go in heavy-handed on this. We must make this Union of Planets work.'

Emily's scenario faded through black and she rematerialised in another Pestochian who was being shown into a luxurious office in the capital city of Mepdetvis.

A Mepdetvisian opened the door for her and announced, 'Ambassador Yonkresteen, sir.'

Gareel was quickly to his feet and greeted the ambassador. 'Lucelle, how nice to see you.' He took the female ambassador's fin and shook it gently. 'Come in, take a seat. How can I help?'

'Thank you, Yol President. It is good to meet you too, sir,' Emily heard herself saying as she struggled to fit into a rather unhelpfully shaped, albeit luxurious chair. 'I have something to report to you. I hope it doesn't get one of your local administrators into trouble.'

'What is it, Lucelle. How would he or she be in trouble?'

'Well, information came into my possession that an Arlucian transport landed in Camkoob, against sanctions.' Emily watched President Jovak's expression harden. 'I guessed that you didn't know and wanted to bring it to your attention.'

'Thank you, Lucelle. Very good of you to come to me with this information. I shall get straight onto the governor and get him to investigate. Who else knows about his indiscretion?'

'Our first minister and, I believe, President Feredic,' said Lucelle. 'It might be a good diplomatic move for you to speak to them direct rather than tell me what action you're taking.'

'Yes. I can see how that might look better. Thank you so much, Lucelle. Now, would you like to join me for a beverage before you dash back to the embassy?'

'That would be most pleasant, Yol President.'

The scene faded and Emily was asked to choose a follow-on character. She removed the blindfold and was faced with a screen full of names.

'Room-bot,' she said, 'this is a huge list of alien names. I am not studying this subject except through this course. Please select appropriate characters for me.'

'Certainly, Emily. Put on your blindfold. The next character is Arlucian freighter captain, Bral Destrom. Say begin when you are ready,' said the room-bot.

'Begin,' she said.

She was being led along a wooden panelled corridor and up a ramp. A Desfoggian held one arm and an X-Jastuvian, who had materialised a limb from his globular body was holding the other. Its grip was squishy.

She emerged into a courtroom. Although it was alien, it was immediately recognisable. She was contained within a glazed-panel cubicle. A large desk to her right was clearly a judge's bench. In front of her, an assortment of aliens, many she recognised from the interstellar conference, sat at tables. On the right, was a spectators' gallery filled mostly with X-Jastuvians, but there were also some Arlucians. She looked at her own limbs and realised she too, was from Arlucian. She could see her reflection in the glass. She was an Arlucian in a uniform.

'The court is in session,' said an Opwispittian, probably the clerk, passing papers up to the judge. 'Judge Corole Inesteen presiding.' She was a Pestochian.

'Read the charges,' said the judge.

The clerk read from a document. 'It is charged that on the two hundred and sixth day of the hundred and forty six thousand, three hundred and twenty-fourth new era year, you, Captain Bral Destrom, did knowingly land on the planet Mepdetvis with a cargo of trunpis and sabcagbe, breaking the sanctions imposed upon the planet Arlucian. How do you plead?'

'Not guilty. Arlucian recognises no such sanction,' Emily heard herself saying, defiantly.

The judge spoke softly, 'That you do not recognise the crime is not relevant here. The Union of Planets has determined that Arlucian is not permitted to trade with any of the Union planets except with cargoes which could be described as altruist or otherwise serving welfare needs. Trunpis and sabcagbe are neither.'

An Arlucian at one of the benches facing the judge's bench, spoke, 'Our planet does not recognise the sanctions, therefore Captain Destrom cannot possibly be held as guilty.'

An X-Jastuvian stood up from the bench, close to the Arlucian counsel and said, 'This court is considering the breaking of a law within the jurisdiction of the Union of Planets. The crime was committed here, breaking laws set here. Ignorance or non-recognition of the law is no defence.'

'Thank you both for your comments,' said the judge. 'Captain Destrom, did you or did you not deliver trunpis and sabcagbe to the planet Mepdetvis on the date in question?'

'Yes, as part of my normal trade. I committed no crime,' the captain said.

'Did you know that Arlucian had had sanctions applied by the Union of Planets?' asked the judge.

'No. If it is so, it is not general knowledge to the merchant shipping companies.'

'So, you are indeed claiming ignorance of the law as a defence,' said the judge.

'Call it what you will. If it helps, I'll take my ship and cargo away and deliver it to a planet which is not a member of the Union.'

'Counsellors, please come into my chambers,' said the judge.

The judge, the X-Jastuvian and the Arlucian followed the clerk out of the courtroom. Emily was left staring across the room. She supposed she could have chosen any of the four in a variation on the scenario if she wished, but right now she was the freighter captain and was experiencing his hopes and fears.

He thought he might be released with some sort of caution not to repeat the action but niggling away at the back of his mind was the possibility he might be made an example of. Emily was amazed at how she too was feeling the concern and worry.

The court officials returned about thirty minutes later, followed by the judge who settled herself into the specially shaped chair to allow her fish body to be adequately supported.

She spoke. 'In the absence of any additional witnesses for the defence and owing to the admission of guilt by the defendant, this court has been able to come to a decision.

'The defendant is of otherwise good character and we believe that the real cause of this crime being committed was the lack of direction from the administration of the planet Arlucian as full details of the introduction of the sanctions had not been provided to commercial operators.

'Captain Bral Destrom, you will receive a suspended sentence of two years lack of freedom. Should you repeat your crime, this will be added to any further sentence passed.

'Secondly, the Luedat Logistics Company, who are responsible for the ship and its contents, will have their vessel impounded in reparation for the lack of diligence and the contents will be sold on the open market. The revenue from the sale will be given to deserving charities. The defendant and his crew are free to return to Arlucian.

'Notice of this judgement has been sent to Arlucian and to President Boronic Feredic, the current general secretary of the Union of Planets, with a recommendation to implement the clause in the sanctions charter which permits security vessels to enforce sanctions in future.'

The judge rang a bell and left the courtroom. Everyone stood and the clerk announced, 'This court is no longer in session.'

The scenario faded through black and Emily found herself within President Drow Duf and sitting behind his oversized desk. The president shuffled himself in his seat. The Arlucian sitting opposite her was obviously a high ranking military man, judging by the blue and yellow braid adorning his uniform and, sitting in his lap, the peaked cap with the same braiding around its rim.

‘What is your plan of action, Admiral?’ asked the president.

‘There are sixteen ships, eight from X-Jastu, four from Garnth and another four from Pestoch. They have stopped eight freighters in the last twenty-four hours and instructed them to return to Arlucian,’ said the admiral.

‘Did none get through?’

‘Yes, one jumped into hyperspace when challenged. It was followed and we don’t know the outcome at this time, sir.’

‘And your plan, Admiral?’

‘We have a freighter due to leave shortly accompanied by five cruisers. I need your authority, sir, to permit them to open fire if any of the Union’s ships attempts to stop them.’

‘How sure are you about their firepower and ours?’

‘Well, sir, we know we can handle the Pestochian and Garnthian ships, but we don’t know about the X-Jastuvian fleet. We have no intelligence on their weaponry and firepower. We would be prepared with full shields, though, sir,’ said the admiral.

‘And my other request? The retaliation for the imposition of these sanctions in the first place.’

‘Yes, sir. We have the full fleet ready to move once we’ve seen how things have gone with the support of the freighter,’ said the admiral.

‘And the targets are as discussed?’

‘Yes, sir, with extra emphasis on X-Jastu.’

‘But all conventional weaponry?’ asked the president.

‘Yes, sir. Laser fire at communications centres and high explosive bombs for government buildings.’

‘Okay, Admiral. You have my permission to go ahead.’

‘Sir, what if they allow our freighters through and we do not need to attack their ships?’

‘Accompany more freighters until they do react with force.’

‘Yes, sir,’ said the admiral. He stood and left the office.

The scene faded to black and the room-bot was, once again, talking to Emily, reminding her to sit still for a while and not to return for forty-eight hours.

The delay was infuriating. She was desperate to know what happened. Would the Arlucians manage to bust the sanctions? She didn't like President Drow Duf. Too authoritarian. How on earth could a government put so much power into the hands of a single individual. Perhaps they hadn't. When she left the esponging centre, she went straight onto the Frame and looked up the constitution of 146,324 Arlucian. Surely there had to be a cabinet or something the president had to report to?

19 White House

Speechwriter, Heston Madison, FBI director, David Mendoza, General Walter Braun, General Donald Alexander, Admiral Alan Mann, President's advisor Matthew Brown and Vice President Erol Tucker sat in the oval office, all apparently very relaxed. The contents of a couple of trays of coffee cups and flasks with cream and milk jugs had now been distributed. The chair at the head of the famous Eagle rug was empty, awaiting the president's arrival.

'He seems to get later and later, these days,' said the vice president.

'He'll be here momentarily,' said Matthew Brown. 'If you have something else to do, I'll let him know.'

The sarcasm did not go unnoticed by anyone present. Brown's tentative position as economics advisor had been gradually morphing into some sort of unofficial right hand man to President Slimbridge. With increasing frequency, if a request were made directly to the president, he'd tell the person to see Matthew. In this way, Brown had been increasing his power and influence and it was now exclusively him, and his growing department of assistants, who negotiated with the aliens and administrator of the rest of the world. Horvat. How she'd gained power since the invasion, too.

President Slimbridge entered the room from his private office and the entire assembly jumped to their feet with numerous of them saying, 'Good morning, Mr President.'

'Okay, okay, okay. Sit,' the president said, waving them all back down.

Brown passed a coffee cup to the president, poured a sensible measure and offered cream. He knew how the president took his mid-morning coffee and he'd made a study of everything the commander-in-chief liked and disliked. Brown knew how the little things were important when one was dealing with a man who would be a dictator.

'Reports, please,' he said, sipping his coffee and looking around the table. 'Come on. One of you get the ball rolling!'

Mendoza opened a manila file. 'There is definite action beginning among the insurgents again, sir. General Beech is back in the country and, from what we understand, his right-hand man, Colonel Henderson, is recruiting extensively on the East Coast. Meanwhile, in California, those who supported independence are now forming a very influential group of politicians who want to make a second attempt.'

'That's right, sir,' said General Braun. 'We've been watching them carefully.'

Mendoza continued, 'Charles Mayne has again become the figurehead for the insurgents, and we understand that he is guaranteeing an election and referendum on the Federation if he can get into power. This has encouraged a number of Republicans to join with the Democrats in offering support. If there were to be no referendum, Mayne might have had even more Republican support.'

The president was about to react when Brown put a hand on his arm. He didn't say anything, but the president took it as a suggestion not to speak yet. The president relied on Matthew. Matthew was good. Matthew was loyal and Matthew took the pressure off him when it came to dealing with the aliens.

General Braun said, 'Mayne is working out of Washington and although we haven't pinpointed his HQ, we are able to monitor most of the activity of his supporters. Currently, they're not causing us concern.'

'Ensure it stays that way, Walter,' said the president.

'Where are the dangers then?' asked Matthew Brown.

'California,' said General Braun. 'We can control any rebellion there quickly enough though, better than in the east coast states.'

'How?' asked Matthew.

The general knew that any question from Brown was as if from his commander-in-chief. 'Since their attempted declaration of independence, we have troops stationed throughout the state. They can be activated into a policing function almost instantly and martial law could be quickly imposed if you thought it had become serious enough, sir,' he said, pointedly addressing his reply not to Brown, but to the president.

General Alexander added, 'All military base commanders are in possession of a dossier on what measures they may need to take if there is rebellion. Training on that is now ongoing, but the troops, below captain, have no idea of the reasons behind it.'

'Very well,' said the president. 'Madison, what are you doing at the moment?'

The speechwriter, lifted his tablet and said, 'You have rallies in Detroit, Chicago and Indianapolis later in the month. Mr Brown is looking at the logistics with General Braun. I'll let you know when the details are finalised, sir.'

'And I'll be safe at these?' The president looked to Brown, not the FBI director.

Brown nodded towards Mendoza, who said, 'Yes, we are prepared for all possibilities.' The president looked sceptically at the FBI director.

'Very well,' said President Slimbridge, standing and causing the others to jump to their feet. 'I leave this meeting in Matthew's capable hands.'

He left the room and the members of the meeting returned to their seats.

'I'd like to provide a round-up,' said Matthew Brown. The others all looked at him in anticipation. They knew this was to be the real thing. The president's presence had been nothing but theatre.

'As you will know from the news media,' said Brown, 'the airlines are causing serious problems. They have sacked tens of thousands of employees now that there are no longer international flights. Plane manufacturers are going out of business. All international orders have been cancelled and the home market is tiny as used planes have been arriving from all over the world. No one will require a new aircraft probably for decades.'

'What about compensation?' asked the vice president.

'Yes. I don't mean to imply that they are not being generous. They agreed to pay for all cancelled orders in full and, of course, are letting USA citizens travel free anywhere in the world on their shuttles. It is that which is so depressing. We can't buy the shuttles and, in a decade or two, when our planes are beginning to need replacing, our own factories will no longer exist.'

'Is it just the airlines?' asked Heston Madison.

'Not at all,' said the vice president. 'All heavy manufacturing is in similar trouble. No Federation countries want our goods. They can make everything better and less expensively. It's a disaster.'

'Again, they've compensated us,' said Brown, 'but the jobs are going. The compensation is allowing us time to create new jobs. Skills are being lost, though. The new jobs are in service industries and for the home market. The only thing which works in our favour is that they won't let us buy technology, but that doesn't stop industry taking Federation technology and backward engineering it. We have some good automatons now.'

'Ha, if you don't mind them stopping halfway through a production run because no one bothered to write the software properly. We're trying to learn a millennium of cybernetics in a few months,' said Mendoza.

'More than five hundred millennia,' said Brown.

'What's unemployment?' asked the vice president.

'Twelve per cent and growing. It is now the largest part of our annual budget,' said Brown.

'But we're saving a fortune on defence,' said General Alexander. 'What use are tanks, fighter planes and warships when we're constrained to our own borders. I can't imagine the president wanting to use tanks and heavy armaments on insurgents.'

‘We must be prepared for an invasion by the Federation,’ said General Braun.

‘We have no defence other than our nuclear arsenal. We can threaten that to ward them off,’ said General Alexander.

‘And you seriously think they would not have a way to counter any launches before the bombs met their targets?’ said Admiral Mann.

The meeting fell into silence for a short while.

‘We must remain as prepared as we can,’ said General Braun. ‘We put tanks on the streets in San Francisco and Los Angeles to end the rebellion there. Some weapons will always be needed.’

‘We’re not sitting back doing nothing about this,’ said Brown. ‘I have vast numbers of industrialists and manufacturers working out how they can adapt production and the economy to the new situation.’

‘There’s unrest among the unemployed,’ said Madison. ‘They are surviving on the generous benefits we can afford from the Federation compensation, but they hear and know about people everywhere else in the world earning much more than them. I get feedback that they are wishing they’d voted to join.’

‘Well, we need to show them that it can be rosy here too,’ said Brown. ‘You and I need to sit down together before these rallies and turn the negatives into apparent positives.’

Without giving the impression he was speaking to Brown, Mendoza said, ‘We haven’t made a decision on what we do about Beech and Mayne. They’re still fugitives. We could pick them up.’

‘No,’ said Brown. ‘Not yet. Just observe them and keep reporting back. As long as intel is good, it is better to know who we are dealing with rather than imprison them and have to find out who has taken their places.’

‘You want me to report back to you or to the president?’ Mendoza asked.

‘Of course, to the president,’ said Brown. ‘But ensure I know what is going on or the information could become, let me say, *confused.*’

20 Sanctions War

X-Jastu scenario three of five began after Emily had chosen the recommended two characters the room-bot had suggested. Firstly, she would be the captain of the lead Arlucian cruiser accompanying the freighter who was to bust the sanctions deliberately, and second, the admiral she'd met in the president's office during her last visit.

The first scene to appear was familiar to her from an early session in the Iasuqi scenarios. She remembered the layout of the Arlucian bridge before it was attacked by the Miiftians and she experienced dying in space. That time, she'd been one of the ship's officers. This time she was sitting in the captain's seat. Arlucian's moon was in view, just off to the right. In front of her were two ships. To her right she could see a freighter and two cruisers similar to her own. They were moving slowly forward, towards the two ships blocking their path.

'Transmit to the Pestochian ships,' she, or rather, the captain said.

'Channel open, sir,' said one of the crew.

'Pestochian ships. This is the cruiser Hedor of the Arlucian fleet. We are accompanying this freighter to Desfogg,' the captain said.

'Captain of the Hedor. What does the freighter you are accompanying contain?' came a voice over the radio.

'Machine parts.'

'Machine parts are included in the sanctions. You may pass, but the freighter must return to the planet.'

In an aside to one of the bridge officers, the captain said, 'Target both ships' main drives and be ready to fire on my command, then immediately raise the force field.' He then opened the radio channel again and said, 'Pestochian ships. Stand aside immediately and allow us to pass.'

'Arlucian ship Hedor, you are breaking sanctions and will not be permitted to pass.'

‘Fire!’ said the captain.

Six purple blobs with pink contrails headed towards each of the enemy ships. The first two heading towards the left ship exploded against some sort of force field or shield, but the other four reached their target. A similar event occurred with the second ship, only it was the first four which exploded prematurely and the remaining two which hit the ship.

Enormous explosions took place at the rear of each ship. Millions of gallons of water shot out into space, evaporating in seconds. Of course, thought Emily, Pestochian was a water world, and they probably carried plenty of water with them on missions, for relaxation or some other reason. Fire could be seen in the bridges of both of the Pestochian ships.

‘Helm. Take us through the ships and set course to Iasuqi.’

The flagship accelerated forward, between the two Pestochian wrecks. The scenario faded through black and Emily was now the admiral, standing in the bridge of a larger vessel with a fleet of more than a hundred ships spread out around it. This must be the same fleet which had attacked Miift and dropped the nuclear bombs.

Over to the left, Emily saw the explosion of the two Pestochian ships and immediately, the admiral said, ‘Target the remaining sanction ships and open fire at will!’

The fleet split into a number of squadrons and rapidly disappeared from view. The flagship and eight other ships banked left and accelerated. In the distance, three X-Jastuvian ships turned in their direction.

‘Open fire!’ said the admiral.

Once more, the purple torpedo objects left three of the ships en route to the X-Jastuvians but, this time, they seemed to impact a stronger forcefield and did not get through. Five more X-Jastuvian ships were arriving from somewhere to the left and opened fire on the Arlucian flagship and its flanking support vessels. Emily watched in horror as two of the fleet exploded as bright red laser-like rays hit them. One of the beams crossed the flagship's bow as it banked to the left, just missing by millimetres. Was this ship going to be destroyed as had been the Arlucian ship she'd been on at Miift. She remembered being an Arlucian and being thrown into space during an attack, gasping to try to breathe as the vacuum sucked the life from her. No! Not again. Should she shout out the safe words. She vowed to do so the moment the bridge exploded, but would hold on, hoping the flagship could be spared.

A message arrived, 'Sir, all Pestochian and Garnthian ships destroyed.'

'Get here quickly. We may need support,' said the admiral, then to his captain and fleet, 'Keep firing!'

Emily watched as dozens of the purple objects made contrails towards the enemy, and an equal number of red beams headed in the opposite direction. Another of the fleet blew up, close to her this time, and debris rattled against the hull and windows. More of the fleet appeared around the flagship and fired even more missiles or torpedoes, or whatever they were.

The force fields continued to protect the ships, but Emily saw the shape and size of them weakening with each strike and the Arlucian weapons began to get through. It took time, more than an hour, but eventually the last of the Union fleet vanished into hyperspace. All the remaining ships had been utterly destroyed.

'Set course to Pestochian,' said the admiral. 'How many casualties?'

'Course set, sir. Casualty reports still arriving, sir. Fourteen ships limping back to space base. Eight totally destroyed.'

All of a sudden, the ship entered hyperspace, the stars vanishing and space becoming an emerald green colour. Only seconds later, a beautiful world hung beneath them in the firmament. A water world with only small continents. Emily knew it must be Pestoch.

'You have the coordinates for their parliament?' asked the admiral.

'We do, sir,' said the captain.

'Single bombing run. Hit them and return. One clean strike. Understand?'

'Yes, sir. It's an underwater target, sir, so I've told both ships to attack.'

Orders were passed and two of the fleet peeled away from the rest and slanted down into and through the atmosphere.

Emily watched the surface of Pestoch in the direction they had taken. The anticipation on the bridge was palpable. Time ticked by and she noticed several of the officers checking timepieces.

'Approaching the city,' said the radio.

Everyone peered in the same direction. A puff of smoke arose from the ocean just off one of the continents. It wasn't smoke, it was a waterspout and a huge wave could be seen spreading out from the impact point, then a second bomb hit the target.

'Attack successful, target hit by both ships. Extent of damage unknown,' said the radio.

'Well done. Re-join the fleet,' said the admiral. 'Captain, any damage to the attack ships?'

'No, sir. There was minor flack, but to no real effect. We seem to have the beating of all their ships except the X-Jastuvian sanction vessels, sir.'

The two sleek cruisers emerged from the atmosphere and the fleet was complete again.

'Well, we destroyed them in the end. Hyperjump to Garnth,' said the admiral and, almost instantly, they were in hyperspace again.

'Yes, sir, but twenty-two of our ships seriously damaged or destroyed in the process,' said the captain.

Seconds later the flagship and fleet materialised above the third civilised planet in the Arlucian system. This world looked very much like Earth, perhaps more land than water, though.

The order was given for a similar attack to that on Pestoch. Ships again peeled away from the fleet and completed their mission without incident.

'Ready, Captain,' said the admiral. 'Jump to X-Jastu. As one of their ships escaped from orbit around Arlucian, be sure everyone is ready for a hot reception. When we arrive, I want five ships to carry out the attack on their parliament immediately we exit hyperspace.'

'Yes, sir.'

Emily got the distinct impression that this would be the main event. In the meantime, this was a longer journey and all that could be seen from the bridge was the speckly green of hyperspace.

∞∞∞∞∞∞∞∞

The green instantly changed to black and Emily grabbed her seat as the flagship twisted sharply to the left, faster than the artificial gravity could compensate. Then the ship turned nose up. A huge battlecruiser was bearing down on it, guns blazing. The skill of the captain meant that they managed to avoid the crimson killing beams and his officers were returning fire with the purple torpedoes. None got through the X-Jastuvian ship's defences.

Over to the right, dozens of the Arlucian ships buzzed like flies around two more of the huge ships. It was clear the Arlucians' weapons were occasionally getting through the force field shields, but for every shot which hit part of the gigantic vessels, several Arlucian fighters were being shot and destroyed. It reminded her of old film she'd seen of whaling when dozens of men in small boats used to try to bring down a huge whale with harpoons.

Twice Emily felt the flagship being hit by incoming fire and each time the artificial gravity failed momentarily, the crew being tossed around the bridge like beans in maracas.

The battle was going badly. A fourth gigantic X-Jastuvian battleship had arrived on the scene. Everywhere Emily looked, there were exploding Arlucian ships then a message came over the radio, ‘Bombs away! Four cruisers downed by anti-aircraft fire. Returning to orbit.’

‘Captain,’ said the admiral, ‘get us and the remaining fleet out of here and regroup at space base.’

Emily could feel the heat in the admiral’s face and knew it was not from the danger of the battle, but the fear of telling President Duf that the fleet had been routed. These X-Jastuvians had some incredible firepower. Their four giant battleships had torn through his fleet. Yes, they’d suffered some minor damage, but all of them seemed to still be intact and operational.

The green of hyperspace vanished, and Emily recognised that they were in orbit above Arlucian, with its ephemeral rings.

‘How many lost?’ barked the admiral.

‘At least fifty-eight plus the eight in our orbital attack here and there are over thirty with damage to some degree or another. We need repairs too,’ said the captain.

‘You’re telling me our fleet of over a hundred ships is down to just a handful?’

‘Sixteen undamaged. Early reports say that of the repairs, ten are minor, but the others will need some time at space base,’ said the captain.

‘And the flagship?’

‘We’re space-worthy but need a new shield generator before we can see more action.’

‘How long?’

‘I don’t know, sir. I’ll try to find out.’

The scene faded to black and Emily found herself, still in the admiral, waiting in the president’s office. He was dreadfully nervous and worried that the president had the habit of shooting messengers who brought bad news. Not literally, but the admiral could find his career ruined, in fact, he expected it to be so.

President Duf, entered the room and the admiral jumped to attention. The president didn’t sit.

'What happened?' he snapped.

'Sir, we broke the sanctions and took out four Pestochian and four Garnthian ships. The X-Jastuvians were much more of a problem. Their shields are better than ours. Eventually we did manage to destroy seven of the eight, but one jumped away, presumably back home. However, we lost eight in the battle and fourteen ships were damaged and are now being repaired at space base,' said the admiral.

'They lost seven and we lost *twenty-two*?'

'Yes, sir. Their firepower exceeded ours, but we got them in the end.'

'Except one?'

'Correct, sir. We then carried out bombing strikes on parliament buildings on Pestoch and Garnth without loss before jumping to X-Jastu.'

'And what happened there?' asked the president, already knowing from other sources that the battle had been a disaster.

'We successfully bombed the parliament building, or at least we think we did. Four of the five ships on the bombing run were shot down so there was no visual confirmation. The battle was another matter. X-Jastu, with just four gigantic battleships, routed us completely. We now have just sixteen remaining in our fleet of one hundred and eight. Thirty-one are being repaired including my flagship, sir.'

The president glared at the admiral. 'And what should I do with you after such an unmitigated disaster?'

'Sir, it was not a tactical error, it was strictly down to the enemy's incredible firepower. You need me, sir. There is no one better and I fear we are about to enter a war. You should keep your best people around you,' said the Admiral.

The president said nothing, just continued to glare at the officer. Emily was wondering if he was admiring the admiral. After all, he had the gall to tell him that he was still the best man for the job. Emily had those feelings about the admiral, anyway.

In her view he'd been sent to carry out a task without any intelligence about the strength of the enemy.

The president circled his desk and sat behind it. 'Admiral, get out of my sight and get the fleet ready for action. There will, no doubt, be repercussions. Go!'

'Thank you, sir,' the admiral said and left the room as fast as he was able. As he exited, he and Emily heard the president calling the defence minister and telling him to drop everything and get to his office.

The admiral guessed there was going to be a major drive to build fighting ships, but doubted there would be time and, when push came to shove, those X-Jastuvian battleships were more than a match for any fleet the Arlucians could put together.

The scene faded to black and the room-bot broke the silence, telling her she had experienced X-Jastu scenario three of five, with the usual warning to rest before leaving and to not return for forty-eight hours. How could she wait that long? She was so hung up on the story, she had to know what would happen next. She was binge-experiencing galactic history. Wonderful.

21 Lara Horvat

I arrived at the administrator's office and was greeted by Marcia Gray, with whom I chatted while waiting for the administrator's earlier appointment to end.

A number of aliens emerged from Lara Horvat's room accompanied by a very black, shiny-skinned human who reminded me of my visit to Nigeria. They said goodbye to Marcia and left the reception area.

A few minutes later, I was summoned.

The administrator was quickly up from her seat, around her desk and greeted me warmly. 'Let's sit over here, Professor,' she said, guiding me to lounging chairs beside the window. 'Would you like something to drink?'

'Thank you, administrator. I have grown rather fond of your orange juice,' I said.

'No problem. And call me Lara,' she said.

'And me, Rummy,' I said.

Marcia entered the room on some silent signal and took the order for freshly squeezed orange juice and a latte coffee.

'Now, Rummy, what would you like to know? By the way, did Paula get in touch?'

'Yes, she did. I'm seeing her next week. She lives in a place called Trinidad, which she tells me is very hot. She offered to meet me in London, but I like exploring so I'm going over there.'

'Excellent. Glad you made contact. You'll love the Caribbean.'

I materialised my secradarve, 'You don't mind me recording?'

'Not at all.'

'What I'm interested in is everything and anything which has changed, particularly for the better or worse. What about your own life?'

'It is easier to say what has not changed,' she said and laughed. 'I had a relatively senior UN position previously, but the atrocity in New York saw almost everyone having their positions reassessed and I was nominated to replace Perfect Okafor. I was unopposed.'

'You were elected to the office of secretary general?'

'Yes. Suddenly I was head of the United Nations organisation. That was a huge change, because not only were we trying to find our way through the mess caused by the UN bomb, but everything else we were doing in the world had to continue as seamlessly as possible. I have never been so busy as I was during that period before the Federation decided that the Earth could join without the United States of America.'

'I can imagine. What about since membership?'

'Our moving of the UN HQ to the Isle of Sheppey had to be managed and a UN document had to be produced which all nations had to sign, permitting me to temporarily become Earth administrator. I've never felt so proud in my life. My parents still can't believe it.'

'When's your re-election?'

'Next March. That will be for a five-year period.'

'What has the relationship been like with the various prime ministers, presidents and other leaders?'

'It was decided that each country would have a representative. Some leaders actually wanted to undertake the task for the same period as me, to see the job through, so to speak. Others couldn't wait to get out of office once they realised that there was no financial benefit. It was interesting, but not at all unsurprising, to observe which nations they were.'

'So, is your role more of a coordinator?'

'Yes, very much so and, let's face it, the automatons do the bulk of the actual organisation. That was the biggest surprise for me personally, discovering that many of the admin-bots were truly sentient, and following on from that, that they didn't want to throw the humans out of the loop.'

'How do you mean?'

'Well, if you are a sentient being who is looking after the management of the whole of England, wouldn't you be aggrieved to watch a less competent human being become your boss?'

'Ah, I see. You're anthropomorphising them and they don't have the ambition a human would have in the same role.'

'Yes. Why is that, Rummy?'

'It is built into their creation. They don't tolerate fools, though. If they considered the English administrator was making a mess of their duties, the automaton would soon discuss it with the person and help them resolve it, by improvement or replacement.'

'The robot would sack the human!'

'Not quite as brutal, but the application of logic usually brings the correct result,' I said. 'Are there any improvements in relation to the United States? You were telling me about various problems like air travel and cruise ships. I'd love it if you could expand upon what similar problems have arisen as this split-world situation has never occurred before.'

'We do know that they're having real problems with the industries which used to export to the rest of the world. Heavy industry, plane building, shipbuilding although that was not such a problem. Quality steel production, electronics etc. Suddenly, from Federation Day, we cancelled all the orders for American goods. Everything could be purchased cheaper and better from elsewhere in the Federation.'

'How was that handled financially?'

'That surprised me too, Rummy. The Federation authorised the payment of all contracts in full when they were cancelled. I know for a fact that British Airways had over fifty new jets on order, but the Federation paid for them in full.'

'That will only help in the short term,' I said.

'Yes, probably.'

'The jobs will never be recovered,' I said. 'The United States will need to redeploy all of those workers or give them some sort of unemployment benefit.'

'Oh, yes, I understand what you mean. That is happening currently, but I hear that even with the United States paying unemployment benefits which are more generous than normal, the unemployed people are hearing about the lives of those living in Federation Earth and are becoming dissatisfied. It can only lead to trouble.'

'And President Slimbridge. Has there been any change in his attitude?'

'No, none at all. Virtually all negotiation with me is done by Matthew Brown who also deals with the Federation directly through the ambassador to the United States.'

'What has caused you the most difficulties so far?'

'Areas of the world in poverty and strife. Let's take somewhere like Myanmar. Huge numbers of displaced persons and a tyrannical government within a government. People had nowhere to live, no food, no medical treatment and many had crossed the borders to get away from the regime. Many headed for Bangladesh which is almost as poor.'

'How was this dealt with?' I asked.

'Firstly, large numbers of robots went into Myanmar and they clamped down upon the Burmese military by placing everyone into stasis for increasing periods for the slightest infringements. This quickly put a stop to what was, quite frankly, bullying spurred by racial and religious hatred. At the same time food transports were arriving. Huge quantities of fresh food, supplied in thorbon packaging meaning that it could last for weeks without the need for refrigeration.

'Of course, alongside all of this was the distribution of afeds to every individual in the region. Suddenly this tide of humanity was no longer starving, and they wanted homes. The Myanmar administrator worked with me to ensure a section of the country was allocated back to the displaced people. Federation resources arrived to construct what we call "container towns".'

'Don't know the term,' I said.

'They are prefabricated structures, a little larger than commercial containers, which join together to provide temporary accommodation. They can be attached to separate infrastructure units which contain elevators and staircases so that the resultant buildings can be twenty or thirty storeys high.'

'What does temporary mean in that context?'

'Well,' said Lara, scrolling through some pages on her secradarve, 'Only a couple of days ago, Lianne Tau sent me an update.' She continued to scroll. 'Ah, here it is. Over thirty per cent of the emergency homes are now dismantled and Federation construction teams, all robotic, are building new homes for the displaced. Lianne says that they all have land which the residents can cultivate, if they wish, or provide to the robots to grow food for them.'

'This is all being done in conjunction with their own leaders?'

'Oh, yes. Communication and respect are the two most important weapons in the bringing together of peoples who were previously persecuting one another.'

'Will it take long to complete the transition?'

Lara scanned her tablet. 'Lianne is reporting that they hope to have removed all the temporary housing by the end of the year, so, yes, excellent progress and a worry out of my hair. Myanmar has been a headache for the UN since I first joined. I never expected that it would be teamwork, with me at its head, which would eventually solve it.'

'This has been happening elsewhere, I suppose?' I asked.

'Certainly,' she said.

'Anything in particular which stands out?'

'Yes. You said you'd been to Nigeria?' asked Lara.

'That's right, Kenya and Nigeria – to see how the inflow of Federation money was affecting day-to-day life.'

'You've heard of Jama'atu Ahlis Sunna Lidda'awati wal-Jihad?'

I entered the words into my secradarve, and it translated as "People Committed to the Propagation of the Prophet's Teachings and Jihad", with the Nigerian name of Boko Haram. I'd read that they were a fanatical patriarchal Islamic group against democracy, any wearing of western clothes, including trousers and any education for women, who were for breeding and looking after children. 'Yes, Boko Haram,' I said.

'That's right. They are an extremely violent group. Federation automatons, which the group have described as the devil's army, have been observing closely. Any activity or action which is against the Federation charter has been instantly stopped using stasis. At one point a huge section of the population of north-eastern Nigeria were in stasis. Gradually, teacher-bots explained how the charter allowed for the Islamic religion but not for fringe, fanatical groups who wished to impose their will upon others. The numbers in stasis have slowly reduced, but many have found themselves repeat offending, usually caused by their treatment of girls and women. There are, however, some of Boko Haram's leaders who are enduring months of stasis. Alternative concepts of punishment and education are currently under consideration. People whose beliefs are entirely contrary to common sense are almost impossible to educate.'

'So, the integration is not as successful as most peoples?'

'No. Boko Haram have been the worst to date.'

'Are they all followers of this Islamic belief system?'

'Boko Haram are, but there are others too. There have been several Christian sects which have fallen foul of the charter and many other fringe groups. The Federation is extremely tolerant of religious beliefs but will not allow them to be imposed upon others. Freedom is the key to it all.'

'Yes,' I agreed.

'Ordinary Christian groups have also found themselves falling foul of the Federation charter. It has always been an important part of the Christian religion in this country to ensure children are introduced to it at as young an age as possible. This falls under the charter section on indoctrination and there is currently a battle underway over the minimum age at which specific religious education can be given to children. This has upset millions of people. The Federation are taking a considered approach, ensuring that beliefs are given no more emphasis than factual science. No one knows how that might turn out, but it is at quite a fraught stage right now.

'Many asked how the charter rule that child education must always be factual fitted in with fictitious characters like Father Christmas, the tooth fairy, or Peter Pan. Those, and many other fairy tales, were allowed under the rules about fantasy children's stories which will one day be shown to have no basis in fact.

'What I find most frustrating, Rummy, is that the fundamentalists of these religions consider that the Federation is attacking them, when all they are doing is applying carefully thought out laws from being broken. Does this sort of situation occur everywhere in the galaxy?'

'Newer member worlds have the biggest problem,' I said. 'Daragnen, my world, has only been in the Federation for two hundred years. When we joined, there was one single religion that believed a god created us specifically in his image. Today the religion still survives, but it has changed and adapted. It is no longer supported by large numbers on our world and the "image" of god we are supposed to have been created in, has now become the fact that we are intelligent creatures. That way, the purveyors of the religion can now claim it represents all people in the galaxy who are intelligent. From my own study of religions within the Federation, I have become convinced that it is a harmless pursuit as long as it is not imposed. It is natural for new Federation members, such as Earth with its hundreds of different religious factions, to find adapting a slow and mentally painful process.'

'Thanks for that insight, Rummy.'

'You'll find many who don't agree. The beauty of the Federation is that you are allowed to disagree, but not allowed to persecute those who don't. Either way.'

My meeting with Lara Horvat, nominal leader of the world except for the United States, continued for almost two hours. We then sat with another coffee and orange juice to talk about ourselves and our families. I liked her. A very open individual.

22 Solidifying The Union

By the time Emily had spent some time on the moon with her parents, experiencing the new low-G holiday resort, it was nearly ten days before she was back at the esponging centre.

The moon had been an extraordinary experience, her first off-world journey. Her father kept telling her all about the first moon landing which he could hardly have remembered as he was two years old at the time, but it seemed to have been a fixture in his mind for his entire life. When the opportunity arose to be one of the first guests in Hotel Luna, he jumped at it, and as it was around the time of their golden wedding anniversary, it was only natural for them to invite her, her brother, and his wife to join in the excitement.

Most of their time was, of course, spent inside the hotel, looking out of the magnificent windows onto the lunar surface, and wining and dining in luxury. They took excursions in lunar vehicles on sightseeing tours to many fascinating scenic areas. One was an Apollo landing site, although it was given a wide berth as it was a site of protected historic interest, but the tourists were able to see the landing section of the lunar module, some of the experiments left on the surface, and one of the Apollo buggies.

Emily decided to blow a significant number of afeds to accompany her father on a guided spacesuit EVA. As part of a group of twelve visitors, they donned full pressure suits after instructions on safety, what not to do and how to use them. The safety lesson actually took five times the length of the spacewalk itself. Emily revelled in his enjoyment, as she stepped out onto the bright white regolith with her father. His grin was too silly for words.

The forty-five minute tour took them nearly two hundred metres from the hotel and into a deep, one hundred metre wide crater. Once within it, Hotel Luna disappeared below their visibility. The guide had them all form a circle looking away from the centre and, for a few seconds, they were able to imagine they were standing alone on Earth's satellite with the planet itself hovering high above. What on Earth would Neil Armstrong have thought of this? Tourists following in his footsteps.

All too soon, the guide took them back towards the hotel, Emily and her dad holding hands through their cumbersome gloves and she thrilling to his enjoyment of deliberately kicking up the dust and watching it fall in the moon's one sixth gravity. He told her he was planning a trip to Mars in the autumn. How wonderful for anyone in the world to be able take in such experiences. Emily heard from the guide that they were planning an orbital hotel at the rings of Saturn for the following year and she made a note to put her name down when she returned to London.

Back inside the hotel she asked the guide, 'How does that work, then? Where did you get the finance for the hotel?'

Simple, she said, 'We put forward a plan to New Developments and they asked us to come back with an indication of demand. We got thousands who wanted to come, so they began construction in November.'

'But who pays?'

'The Federation. We're talking to them about one at Io, too, in the Jupiter system.'

'They pay, just like that?'

'Once you show it is viable, they are happy to do it. It comes out of some sort of common good fund.'

'Wow!' said Emily and meant it.

The journey from the moon back to Earth took just fifty minutes. Emily returned to her apartment very late but was determined to be up at dawn and waiting for the esponging centre to open at nine o'clock.

ooooooooooooo

The room-bot advised Emily that she was about to partake of scenario four of five in the X-Jastu course. She made a cup of green tea and settled down in the deluxe chair, enjoying the images of alien wildlife showing on the giant monitor. Fascinating to see all of these diverse animals, some almost unbelievable and others amazingly similar to creatures on Earth, but exhibiting unexpected colours, patterns or numbers of legs. She'd always thought an octopus was weird, but some of the alien creatures made them look quite normal. The sequence so astounded her that it was over twenty-five minutes before she said, 'Begin' and the room faded to black. She quickly snatched up the cool blindfold as she became Boronic Feredic, sitting with Korodin Eveskreen and Coll Svertich either side of her. In front of them were another seventeen aliens plus an eighteenth on a video monitor to one side of the room.

Emily, or rather President Feredic of X-Jastu, opened the meeting, 'I call to order this fifth meeting of the Union of Planets and welcome our five new members. As you know, we are in a very serious situation. The behaviour of Arlucian has provided us with a dilemma. As both I and my deputy, First Minister Eveskreen of Pestoch, are involved in the situation, I am handing the chair to President Coll Svertich of Opwispitt.'

'Thank you, Boronic,' said President Svertich. 'Older members will be aware that it was I who first proposed some sort of confederation of worlds with common interests. I believed, by working together, it would provide us with strength. Mutual cooperation would also help each of our civilisations develop. My suggestion morphed into this Union of Planets.'

The humanoid Svertich took a sip of a turquoise coloured liquid in a glass before him. 'We are now faced with a conflict situation. One of the principles I suggested for the Union was that any attack by any world upon any of the planets in the Union, would be considered an attack on all. We would all respond collectively to put down the adversary. We are now in that situation.

'The Arlucians broke the sanctions we imposed upon them for their atrocity of the attempted genocide of the Miiftians whose planet was left uninhabitable. We then authorised the

Pestochians, the Garnthians and the X-Jastuvians to set up a sanctions block. That was done with sixteen light cruisers.

'The Arlucians broke the sanctions again and their huge fleet of over one hundred ships attacked the sanction patrol ships. Fifteen of the sixteen were destroyed and one escaped.

'Following that battle, the Arlucians jumped to Pestoch and Garnth in their own system and bombed their capitals. The historic and beautiful parliament building on Garnth was destroyed. On Pestoch, the bomb did little damage to their underwater administration centre, but the shockwave and tsunami killed more than sixty thousand residents.

'From there, the Arlucians jumped to X-Jastu who were better prepared because their patrol ship had returned with news of the sanction-busting attack. However, they were still caught by surprise by five bombers who attacked the capital city. Four were shot down, sadly exploding in residential areas and killing or maiming over three hundred people. The other cruiser managed to bomb some administration buildings which were, fortunately, empty of X-Jastuvians because it was a public holiday and only a few automatons were on duty.

'Four X-Jastuvian battleships attacked the Arlucians when they appeared out of hyperspace, destroying large numbers of them with hardly any damage to themselves. The Arlucians jumped away, presumably back to Arlucian. Two hundred and fifteen prisoners were taken from the wrecks of the Arlucian fleet. They are being held in prison on X-Jastu.

'That is what happened. Our meeting today is to consider our response,' said President Svertich who then sat down.

A feeler rose. 'Yes?' said President Svertich.

'Did they sign up to the Union?' asked a green creature in a vaguely human shape.

'No.'

'So, we don't have any jurisdiction over them?'

'No, but does that mean we should just allow them to be a pariah world, attacking and destroying whoever they wish for any purpose which suits them?' asked President Jovak of Mepdetvis.

'No, we can't allow that,' said the green creature. 'It is just that we've only just joined the Union and, frankly, I'm not sure if our first action as members should be to go to war.'

'One for all and all for one,' said President Nesofin of Desfogg.

'Something must be done,' said President Feredic. 'We X-Jastuvians cannot be left to do it all ourselves.'

'What would you like us to do?' said President Nesofin. 'We don't have much of a military force. It is why we joined the Union.'

'Yes,' said President Feredic, 'because there is strength in numbers. No one is suggesting planets should send fleets of ships which don't have shields or substantial firepower and sufficient manoeuvrability.'

'So, what *do* you suggest?' asked President Nesofin.

'Our cabinet has discussed and deliberated over this situation, and other related matters to do with the Union, for many days,' said President Feredic. 'We see everything as intimately connected. It would not be an overstatement to claim that our weaponry and shields are second to none in the Union. Other than seven of our lightly armed sanction cruisers, which were carrying out a police function, we did not lose a ship to the Arlucians whose fleet was decimated.

'We have a solution, but we need some time to prepare for it. We would like permission, when we are in a position to undertake the task, to imprison the Arlucian people on their own world for a period of time that will show them that they must never again attempt genocide or disobey the Union's rules. In return, we will throw open our technology to all Union planets, including our weapons, shields and automatons.'

'How exactly do you intend to imprison an entire planet?' asked President Trover of Garnth.

‘We still have work to do on that plan, and I would rather not give details until we are ready to act,’ replied President Feredic.

‘Then I don’t see how permission can be granted,’ said President Svertich. ‘You are asking for carte blanche.’

‘I am asking for time.’

‘How long?’

‘A year.’

‘A year! We do nothing for a year?’ asked President Svertich.

‘You maintain the sanctions while we prepare,’ said President Feredic.

‘I’ll second that,’ said First Minister Eveskreen. ‘With the help of the rest of you and Boronic’s weaponry and shields. We can enforce the sanctions.’

‘You’ll still have to come back to us for permission for your grander plan, when it is ready,’ said President Svertich.

‘Agreed,’ said President Feredic.

A show of hands, feelers and other body parts carried the motion almost unanimously.

The scene faded to black and the room-bot, as usual, warned Emily not to return for scenario five of five until at least forty-eight hours had elapsed.

23 Roberto Giordano

Sofia Lanzo left the booth in a far better mood. Now she had a plan and she'd be protected throughout. She returned to her apartment and cheerfully did some chores. She had believed she would have to leave Olzai and all her friends and family. Now she could stay.

What about Carlo? She knew he worked for the *family* and, although he was always loving and kind to her, she guessed he was not always so with others, with whom the *family* had taken offence. She wondered if Roberto had had him murder people or beat them up. She guessed it was so, because a big part of his job was collecting money.

If the Federation was able to help her, she could tell Carlo to go to the booth and they'd help him too.

It was two days before her phone rang and she saw the dreaded name Roberto on the screen. This time she had been told to answer it.

'Roberto, how are you?'

'I've missed you, Sofia. I was beginning to think you might be avoiding me. You haven't been, have you?' Just a hint of a threat in the tone of his question.

'Course not. You know I can't always answer my phone. Fact of life in my profession.'

'Why didn't you call me back?'

'Sorry, Roberto. You want me to come over now?'

'I'll send a car at eleven. Be there!' His words were a definite command.

Sofia didn't wear her normal work clothes, the slinky dress which hugged every curve or the miniskirt in which it was almost impossible to sit down without baring all. She dressed in her normal clothes. Pretty, knee-length skirt, flowery top, bag and summery pink panama.

The car was on time. A silver Mercedes and, oh no, it was Carlo driving. He'd think she'd given in to Roberto's demands.

'Hi, Carlo,' she said as she jumped into the front seat.

He turned to her and raised a finger before his lips and whispered, 'You look terrific.'

The vehicle must be bugged. She smiled back at him and sat with the panama on her lap. He reached over and ran his hand over her nearest leg, lifting the skirt and caressing her upper thigh. Sofia felt bad. He knew she was about to have sex with Roberto, or he thought he did, but he was treating her as if it didn't matter. Despite his declaration of love for her, how could he really love her and allow his boss to do this. Perhaps she was just a prostitute to Carlo too, but he was just a more caring client. There were loving clients, she'd had many who offered genuine affection over the years, but they were certainly a minority. Most just had their own personal needs and used her body to fulfil them in any way that suited their desires. Still, it was usually quick and had been very lucrative. People knew that she was a squillo girl to several local family members and that probably protected her from any violence.

They sat in silence, his hand finally finishing its exploration of her secret places, then sliding down her leg and back onto the steering wheel. He mouthed 'I love you,' as he swung the Mercedes around in the parking area and began the ten minute drive up into the mountains. Did he *really* mean it?

Nostra Palazzo sat majestically on the hillside, a solitary residence with uninterrupted views over the surrounding countryside. The sort of home that is owned by billionaires, famous actors, movie moguls and, of course, mafia bosses.

Three hairpin bends had to be negotiated once they departed the main road. The Mercedes' tyres squealed as it pulled away from each bend, the automatic gearbox not quite adjusting for each new punishing one-in-three slope. Finally, the car pulled in through a fine stone archway and emerged into a large parking area, partly hewn out of the cliffs. The Mercedes parked between Roberto's modern dark blue Bentley and his brilliant yellow Lamborghini. Sofia noted that Roberto's wife was out, the red Ferrari Testarossa was nowhere to be seen. If Carlo hadn't been sure that Sofia was arriving for sex before, he certainly knew now.

Carlo jumped out and ran around to the passenger side to open the door for Sofia. Roberto stood on the terrace, dressed in white trousers and a white, loose short-sleeved shirt which hid a bulging waistline. He shouted at Carlo, 'That's all, Carlo. I'll call you later.' Carlo waved back and returned to the driver's seat. 'Come up, Sofia, come up,' Roberto said, 'how lovely to see you. Join me on the terrace for a G and T.'

She forced a smile and climbed a flight of fifteen stone steps set into the terrace and emerged onto a flat area adorned with a white-painted circular table and half a dozen lounger chairs. A sky blue parasol covered the table which held a silver ice bucket with champagne plus a tray of other drinks and selection of glasses. Roberto walked up to her as she reached the terrace, gave her a short kiss on the lips, ran his hands up and down her sides, across her bust, feeling its shape and then guided her to the table. His hand fell to her behind, easing its way between her buttocks as he helped her along.

'Gin, Sofia? Or would you prefer some vodka, whisky or champagne?' he asked.

She could see it was Dom Perignon in the ice bucket. He always had the best. That he wanted her said a great deal about her skills in the bedroom.

'Whatever you're having,' Sofia said.

He poured two substantial measures of Harris gin. 'Lemonade or tonic?' he asked as he poured tonic into one glass while awaiting her answer.

'Tonic's fine,' she said.

He used a small silver scoop to add ice to both drinks and fished lime slices out of an attractive covered glass dish with ornate silver sugar tongs.

'Enjoy the view,' he said, patting the lounger next to his and sat heavily into the seat. Sofia walked around the back of him, feeling his hand on the back of her thigh as she reached the seat and sat delicately, crossing her legs decorously.

'So, Sofia, why have you been avoiding me? I have money again now. Sorry about last time. Here's the rest for last time,' he said and tossed a wad of afeds onto the table. A rubber band stopped them blowing away. Sofia thought it was at least a thousand. 'That's more than I owe you, dearest. How about two thousand today? Okay?' he asked.

How was he cheating the system to get all this cash? It had to be extortion from people's automatic Federation incomes. He was keeping them in poverty through threats and beatings.

'That's not necessary,' she said, looking at him and seeing a questioning expression crossing his face. 'I'm not doing it anymore, Roberto. I am no longer your squillo. I came to tell you in person.'

She watched his face harden, 'I want you, Sofia. I've been looking forward to this for a week, and you'd better behave, or you might find that life is no longer so good for you.'

'No, Roberto. It's finished.' She stood, ready to leave and began to walk around the table towards the steps.

For such a big man, he was quite agile. He jumped to his feet and ran around the opposite side of the table to cut off her escape. 'How dare you!' he said, grabbing the top of her arm in a vicelike grip, hurting her and, she was sure, bruising her flesh.

Two cop-bots materialised either side of him and he was instantly in stasis. His hand was forced to release its grip and he stood, looking at Sofia, powerless to move and seeing the two cop-bots walking from behind into his view.

'Yol Roberto Giordano. Nanobots have been observing you and the people who work for you for two days. Your people have been taking afeds with menaces from thirty-one individuals during that period. This young woman is under Federation protection.'

In stasis, it is impossible to speak, but the growing colour of Roberto's face showed that he was apoplectic with rage.

'As a gang leader, you are hereby sentenced to three months stasis. Your associates are sentenced to one month's stasis. You will have a Federation hearing which will determine how many of your assets and how much of your wealth is actually yours. If it is determined that any of it was obtained by illegal means it will be forfeit. Nanobots will continue to observe you and your associates. Any attempt at violence or verbal abuse or coercion will immediately be punished. Reoffending will attract twice the sentence length. Do you understand?'

The stasis field dropped, and Roberto almost fell over. He grabbed the table which caused the drinks to tumble and some glasses to break, as he recovered his balance.

'You can't do this!' he shouted, looking at Sofia and added, 'and I'll get you for this.'

'You have just added ten days stasis with that threat Yol Giordano. Do you understand my original statement, or do I need to repeat it?'

'How do I appeal? This is crazy!'

'You cannot appeal the three months and ten days stasis as you are guilty of the offences. At your hearing you can appeal any judgements against your wealth or assets. Do you understand?'

He looked around him. There was no one to help. Carlo was standing beside the Mercedes looking up at them. 'Carlo, do something. Call help!' Roberto shouted.

One of the cop-bots dematerialised and appeared beside Carlo. It said, 'Carlo Russo, you no longer have to work for this man. You will be protected, but I must also advise you that you're being investigated for past deeds.'

Roberto saw the bot standing beside Carlo and watched the man raise his arms in a gesture of helplessness. 'Damn you all!' the mafia boss shouted at the world in general.

'Do you understand the charges?' asked the cop-bot for the third time.

'I do,' he said and was immediately back in stasis.

'Sofia, you may now go home,' said the bot.

'Can I speak to Carlo?' she asked.

'You can do whatever you wish,' the bot said and promptly vanished.

Sofia looked around at Roberto. He was staring at her but could no longer intimidate her. 'You're an evil monster,' she said and turned to the steps, descending them and walking over to Carlo. The bot had gone.

'Are you okay, Sofia?'

'I am. Now drive me home.'

They both got into the Mercedes, which then swung around in the parking area and exited through the arched gateway. A cop-bot stood against one side of the entrance. Carlo's hand found its way under her dress and she whispered that she loved him too.

24 Reign of the Robots[2]

Emily's next visit to the esponging centre was forty-eight hours, on the dot, after the previous one. Rummy had told her this was where the automatons really came into their own and she couldn't wait to find out exactly how.

The room-bot told her she was about to view the X-Jastu course, scenario five of five and she asked for the room-bot to select appropriate characters to give her the best feel for the history.

Emily found herself, once again seeing through the eyes of Boronic as he slithered into his office where five visitors' chairs were occupied by four generals and an important manufacturer. They all stood as he entered.

The strange bulk of the Boronic/Emily body made its way around an ornate desk and manoeuvred itself into the bucket seat which made some sense of the fluid nature of the creature.

'Well?' he asked.

'We're ready,' said the senior general.

'How many automatons, Krishov?' Boronic asked.

'Close to a hundred million and over two hundred thousand coming off the production lines every day,' said the only civilian among the visitors.

Boronic looked back to the senior general. 'Is that enough. We cannot afford for this to fail. Arlucian mustn't realise what has hit them until it is way too late.'

'We're sure, sir.'

'Okay. I'll contact the council and get the final approval. Dismissed.'

---

[2] *It was while I was trying to come up with a name for this chapter, that I remembered the late Frank Hampson, to whom the trilogy is dedicated, who wrote amazing story titles including this chapter heading.*

The generals and the manufacturer oozed out of their seats and were soon exiting the office door. Boronic relaxed back into his seat. 'Deridid,' he called on the intercom, 'set up the Union videocon.'

'Yes, sir,' came the reply.

The right wall of the office comprised twelve video monitors, but on this occasion, only six came to life. The six other executive members of the Union of Planets.

'Good morning, gentlefolk,' said Boronic. 'We are ready to act and are seeking final permission.'

'Sounds good, Boronic,' said Korodin of Pestoch. 'Run us through the plan.'

'As you know,' said Boronic, 'factories on each of the Union worlds have been producing the policebots. We now have around a hundred million and feel that is enough to carry out the invasion.

'We have also built sixteen of our large battleships to support the robot transports.

'Our first action will be for those battleships to appear in Arlucian orbit. Fifteen over the planet and one over the moon which is also inhabited these days.

'The sequence is …'

The scenario faded through black and Emily found herself in one of the Arlucian people, living in the capital city, Oridin. She was a female who worked in one of the Arlucian government ministries, but at the beginning of the scene, she was at home with her family which comprised her husband, brother, and three children. Two were the equivalent of teenagers and one under ten. Emily could see that she was in a lounge area and the brother was bringing in a tray of mugs of some steaming beverage. Emily could smell something between chocolate and that strange Swiss-invented drink, Ovaltine. Emily found the latter unpleasant but managed to live with the combination which the female sipped.

They'd been watching a television drama, but suddenly, the programme was disrupted by a stark message. 'EMERGENCY TRANSMISSION. SWITCH TO CHANNEL ELEVEN.'

She scrabbled for the handset, punched in the digits and the screen showed five or six of the huge X-Jastuvian battleships in orbit, being attacked by the Arlucian fleet. The smaller cruisers were moving rapidly, trying to avoid the beams which emitted spasmodically from the enemy ships. Each time a beam was seen, an Arlucian cruiser was completely disabled, losing all power and floating off in whichever direction it had been heading at the time. The Arlucian purple torpedoes never got through the X-Jastuvian forcefields and exploded harmlessly. It was undoubtedly an overwhelming defeat, but one in which there had, so far, been no death or destruction.

The scene continued to show an increasing number of cruisers floating in disarray and the battleships using fewer and fewer beams as the enemy floundered.

A communicator buzzed. Emily saw her character grab it off the table.

'Vedriff,' she said.

'Minister Vedriff, can you get to the ministry urgently. The president is calling in the cabinet.'

'On my way,' said Vedriff, jumping up from the easy chair and, in seconds, she was out of the door. She shouted, 'See you later,' over her shoulder.

The street was strangely quiet. Perhaps people had stayed indoors to watch the newscast. Vedriff wondered what was happening. She recognised the battleships as X-Jastuvians, but why were they here now. All of the empty threats were nearly two years previous. It had seemed that there was to be no retaliation for the destruction of the Pestochian, Garnthian and X-Jastuvian administrative buildings and their sanction patrol cruisers. Most of the government felt that it had been just that, empty threats and posturing. This, however, was something tangible and very frightening. The Arlucian fleet was powerless against the enemy.

Vedriff's hover-vehicle was winding its way through what remained of the unusually quiet rush hour. The parliament building and her ministry were now visible ahead. Parliament was a dome-shaped structure with an ornate gilt roof and elaborate walls peppered with sculptures of famous Arlucians. The ministry was more utilitarian – a glass and concrete-like block on the opposite side of the road. Vedriff guided the vehicle to an adjacent layby, tossed the keys to a valet-bot and, with the strange gait of a short-legged Arlucian in full flight, she dashed up the steps to the glass doors of the building.

Her assistant was waiting in the corridor outside her office. 'Minister,' she said, 'you're wanted in the cabinet office.'

Vedriff changed direction in mid stride and was soon heading towards the eastern end of the building. 'Bring my secradarve, it's on my desk!'

'Will do,' replied the assistant, disappearing through her office and into the minister's.

Vedriff, somewhat out of breath, arrived in the cabinet room to find several of the cabinet already in situ and the president at the end of the table looking exceedingly glum. Everyone was looking at a monitor on the wall, where the admiral of the fleet was providing a report.

'… and we cannot get through their defences, sir,' the admiral said. 'Our flagship was hit a few minutes ago and we too are floating without any power, shields or weaponry. I fear our orbit is deteriorating, but I'll report for as long as I can.'

'Nothing gets through?' asked the president.

'Nothing, sir. We even tried the new blursters, but they were completely ineffective. We're trying to bring systems online, sir, but with no success so far.'

'Let us know if there is any change,' said President Duf.

'There are new ships arriving, sir. Not seen them before. They're even larger than the X-Jastuvian battleships but look more like gigantic freighters rather than military ships.'

'How many of those?'

'Unbelievable, sir. Too many to count and more popping out of hyperspace every second. Impossible numb…' The screen went dead, cutting off the admiral in mid-sentence.

Two more cabinet members had arrived, the cabinet secretary filling them in on what was happening. Everyone looked at everyone else. No one had anything to say. Their fleet had been wiped out, or at least made ineffective. The planet was wide open to invasion and there was nothing any of them could do about it.

No one could do anything about what happened next. The president and defence minister vanished from the room, slight plop sounds announcing that the space they'd so recently occupied had been filled by inrushing air.

Several of the cabinet jumped to their feet. An armed security detail rushed into the cabinet office. One of them, a colonel swung around looking at all parts of the room. 'Where is the president?' he asked.

'Vanished. Minister Gord vanished at the same time,' said one of the other ministers.

'What do you mean, "vanished"? How the hell can someone just vanish?' shouted the colonel.

Several of the ministers shrugged.

'He can't just have gone!'

'They did. There one minute, gone the next,' said Vedriff.

'It's madness!' said the colonel.

The madness multiplied a few seconds later when four robots materialised at the president's end of the cabinet table.

Each was humanoid in appearance, standing close to two metres in height with a square head on blocky, rectangular shoulders. Four arms were attached to the shoulders and chest.

There was a narrow waist and two powerful legs with rather oversized feet, out of proportion with the rest of the humanoid impression given.

'What the hell!' shouted the colonel and opened fire on the closest.

No sooner had his gun begun to fire its pellets than it disappeared from his hands. The five armed police became strangely motionless.

'What have you done to them?' asked Vedriff.

She was almost surprised when she received a reply. 'They have been put in what we call stasis. They are not dead, but they cannot cause any further harm.'

'Where is the president?' she asked.

'He and the minister responsible for defence, have been transported to another location where they too, are now in stasis.' The robot looked at the other ministers. 'Please sit. You will not be harmed.'

'What is going on? Why are you here?' asked Vedriff and one or two of the others.

'Please sit,' the robot repeated and this time, they all took their seats. 'I shall explain.'

'Please do. This is outrageous,' said the chancellor.

'We are robots of the Union of Planets enforcement division. Arlucian is being punished for its attempted genocide of the Miiftian people and the rendering of Miift as uninhabitable for hundreds of millennia; the attack on the sanction patrol ships two years ago; the destruction of the parliament building on Garnth; the attempted destruction of the administration sector of Pestoch, including the death of tens of thousands of Pestochians caused by tsunamis created by your weapons, plus the failed attempt to strike at the parliament of X-Jastu, in which your shot down ships caused the death of hundreds when they crashed.'

'This is ridiculous,' said the chancellor.

The robot looked at the minister but ignored him. 'The punishment is as follows. There is no appeal.

'One. All space vessels are grounded except for specific passenger transports and supply ships to and from your moon.

'Two. We shall rule your world until the period of punishment is complete. Millions of us are arriving throughout your world and a full explanation will be given later today on your visiscreens.

'Three. Any resistance will be negated by the use of stasis as you see being used here on the armed police.

'Four. When your species stops behaving in such an abhorrent manner, the Union of Planets will free you from your punishment and you will be allowed to become independent, worthwhile and productive members of the Union.'

'We must have some right to appeal,' said Vedriff.

'Sorry. No. However, those of you in this room will become part of a management committee to represent your people. Firstly, though, you will need to admit your crimes against Miift, Garnth, Pestoch and X-Jastu,' said the robot.

'Never,' said the chancellor and he promptly vanished.

'Where did he go?' asked Vedriff.

'Into stasis with the president. We will not tolerate dissent. Please read this,' said the robot and twenty sheets of paper appeared from a slot beneath his chest. Vedriff picked one off the table.

'This is a statement which each of you will be recorded reading. You will then contact the visiscreen stations and organise a worldwide broadcast tomorrow at prime time in which you will show the confessions of your government.'

'What are we supposed to call you?' asked Vedriff.

'I am A1,' said the robot.

'Well, A1, some of what is in this so-called confession may well be true, but not all of it.'

'You were a collective. You allowed this to take place,' said A1.

'Most of these decisions were taken by the president and defence minister. Not the full cabinet.'

'But, do you not see, Minister Vedriff, it was done in your name?' said A1.

'Our regime was more of a dictatorship than a democracy,' said Vedriff.

'That was your problem, minister. You allowed this to happen, and by not stepping in and protesting, you are equally guilty.'

'But if we had protested and stood up to President Duf, we'd have been dismissed. It always seemed better to try to change things from the inside, rather than lose our jobs and have no influence whatsoever.'

'You had the benefits of power, the wages of the powerful, the prestige of office. Your failure to act, to stop this megalomaniac from running roughshod over all common decency is as much your responsibility as his. President Duf committed genocide on Miift. Literally billions of people died, despite the best efforts of the Desfoggians to save them. The planet will lie, lifeless for half a million years. That is *your* responsibility.'

'Vedriff, it's right, you know,' said Zigruff, the environment minister.

Vedriff looked at him. 'How do the rest of you feel about this?'

Another two ministers said, 'Ashamed'.

Vedriff looked around the table, 'Perhaps you're right, but none of us meant any of this to happen.'

Zigruff said, 'No, we didn't, but we didn't stop it. We didn't even attempt to stop it. I'll read the confession.'

Several others agreed with Zigruff.

'Okay,' said Vedriff, 'I'll read it too.'

The scenario faded through black.

ᴑᴑᴑᴑᴑᴑᴑᴑᴑᴑ

A caption appeared on the blackness – 'TEN YEARS LATER'.

Gradually the lack of light gave way to a comfortable living room. An Arlucian female was comfortably seated in an armchair. Behind her was a large window with small panes which gave onto an exotic garden. Trees with palm-like fronds fringed the area and colourful tropical shrubs with bizarre and beautiful blooms graced the nearer elements.

The scene zoomed in to the ornate cover of a book, a little larger than the average textbook. It was propped up on a side table. The leather exhibited fancy scrolls and a frame around a title – Reign of the Robots, by Yis Hef.

The camera withdrew and the woman in the chair picked up the volume, tugged on a bookmark and it fell open part way through.

She cleared her throat.

'The president, his defence minister, admiral and vice admiral were held in a new form of imprisonment called stasis where they were unable to take part in normal life but were permitted to read from a selected list of novels and works on wildlife, astronomy and modern interplanetary politics. Their sentences were from ten to twenty-five years depending upon their culpability.

'Arlucian and its moon were administered by First Secretary Vedriff and her cabinet, under the watchful gaze of robots provided by the Union of Planets. There were over two hundred million of the automatons which provided all police functions and ensured the violent dictatorial politics of the Duf regime were no longer in circulation.

'All resistance by the ordinary people of Arlucian quickly evaporated as the robots demonstrated their abilities and powers. Gradually life settled down to a form of reluctant occupation. No Arlucians were allowed to travel into space and all interplanetary freight operations were closed down except between Arlucian and its moon. The system had been placed in lockdown.'

The woman closed the volume and chose another bookmark from later in the book. Emily could see that it was approaching the last few pages.

She read from the new section, 'The Union of Planet's occupation of Arlucian continued for forty-nine years. The whole generation of people who had been part of the Duf regime were gone, or at least no longer in power. Those who were now the administrators of the Arlucian government had almost forgotten their species' horrific past and were beginning to press the elite robots for permission to join the other planets in interplanetary cooperation. They wanted to become part of the growing Union of Planets.

'One day in that forty-ninth year, the committee of the Union broke into the Arlucian visinews and announced that the occupation was over. They further announced that there would be a conference of all of the now one hundred and four strong Union and it would be held in Oridin, Arlucian's capital city.

'Immediately following the worldwide broadcast, the robots stood down from their police role and transferred their allegiance to the Arlucian government.

'The Union of Planets' conference took place and new rules were added to their charter. Interplanetary conflicts were banned, all technologies were to be shared between all member planets and the seat of government would be Oridin on Arlucian to demonstrate that the Union of Planets had truly forgiven the atrocities committed by the Arlucian leadership more than half a century previously.

'As new planets of intelligent beings were being discovered almost on a daily basis, it was decided that Union of Planets was not an adequate name for such a growing assembly. The name was changed to the Galactic Empire.'

Emily saw a final caption appear as the scene faded into blackness – Reign of the Robots was read by its author.

She was back in the cubicle watching a video depicting honeybees inside a hive. The room-bot advised her that the X-Jastu course was now complete and reminded her to leave forty-eight hours before returning.

25 Paula Wilson

While en route to Trinidad to seek out Paula Wilson, I decided to visit one or two other islands. Jamaica was larger than I expected and much too busy for my liking. My favourite was St Lucia and I did some hiking into the rainforest. Trinidad was even nearer to the equator and, I must admit, I found it rather hot. My species doesn't sweat, so I had a need to regularly cool off in swimming pools. Very enjoyable and I surprised many of the humans who were staying at the hotels when they saw how loose skin on my feet and hands developed into paddles between my digits. It gave me a fair turn of speed compared to the average human swimmer.

I arrived at Paula's house by taxi. The road twisted and turned as we climbed away from Port of Spain into the mountains behind. Paula's house sat majestically overlooking the capital and the Caribbean Sea, its colourful timber structure adding a note of extra joyfulness to what was, indeed, a beautiful location.

We exchanged pleasantries and Paula guided me outside onto the veranda where a cool breeze swept across this corner of the island. We sat in comfy seats with low coffee tables. She'd brought out a whole jug of my favourite Earth drink and it was accompanied by lots of ice cubes.

Although I had read her biography of Perfect Okafor, which I'd found in Ambassador Trestogeen's files, I knew little about her. She was quite a small human with fair skin and short dark hair. I'd watched an old supernatural film called *Ghost* during my time in the USA and, as she sat in one of the loungers in her colourful T-shirt and shorts, Paula's face and hair reminded me of the actress in the film.

I asked about Perfect Okafor, of course, and it was obvious that the sadness was still there in Paula, even so long after the UN bomb. She told me that she'd only escaped death herself because she'd attended a wedding in the south of the United States. She was very angry and bitter about President Slimbridge and his administration. She'd been most glad to get out of the States when she was invited to assist Lara Horvat in London.

Although Paula tended to lean towards the Republican party when she'd lived in the USA, her anger with Slimbridge and his lack of compassion for human life was very apparent.

'The man murdered all of those heads of state to grab power,' she told me. 'He claimed it was to save America, but it was clearly nothing of the sort. Under his regime, there's been a clampdown on all opposition, and he has had people executed on live television. Horrible man.'

'Are you supporting any of the resistance groups?' I asked.

'I'm not in a position to do much, but I did enjoy watching Free America making Slimbridge look stupid. They actually sprayed the White House green! It would have been really funny if we hadn't known that members of the resistance were living in fear of exposure and dying regularly,' she explained. She looked at me seriously, 'Lara says I can trust you. How deep does that trust go?'

'How do you mean?' I asked. 'I won't tell anyone else what you are saying until I publish my book and that will be a few years away. I need to study Earth's transition over at least a decade.'

'If I tell you something about the resistance then, it won't go any further or cause them any problems?' she asked conspiratorially.

'No. I promise I'll be discreet, Paula,' I assured her.

'I have a cousin who was in the Free America group and he was telling me that they are beginning another campaign. This time it is centred on getting rid of Slimbridge by fair means or foul, and putting Charles Mayne in the White House – he's a Democrat, but he's promised an election within months of the coup and also a second Federation referendum.'

'Do you believe him?'

‘Oh, yes. Everything he’s ever told me has come to pass. I even knew about the Super Bowl players being sprayed green before it happened.’

‘Do you think they can do it?’

‘Yes, but it would happen much more quickly if the Federation provided some support,’ she complained.

‘I’m sure it would, but non-interference is a prime edict.’

‘They interfered to prevent the execution of Mayne, Beech and the others. Dropped a forcefield around them in the nick of time and beamed them to safety.’

‘Well, that was a life and death situation,’ I said.

‘They could do more to help, Rummy.’

We continued to talk about the resistance and the potential direction of their efforts. I wasn’t convinced that the uprising would succeed, but it certainly promised some interesting times ahead for me to record.

∞∞∞∞∞∞∞∞∞∞

When I returned to the coolness of London, my first task was to find Miles to discover how his recordings were coming along. In fact, he was in Rio de Janeiro, but when I gave him a call, he agreed to return for an afternoon to go through his interviews. We met up in his Edgeware Road flat with its extravagant claim of the view of Marble Arch.

I brought some John Smith’s ale with me, another beverage of which I was growing fond. We sat in his lounge and cracked open the beer.

‘Here’s an interesting one for you, Rummy,’ Miles said as he made a selection from his tablet.

The scene was a noisy family room. Miles entered and propped his camera up on the arm of his chair so that it recorded a general scene of the whole room. ‘You’re sure you don’t mind talking to me about this?’ he said to the woman ‘I really appreciate it.’

'No, it's fine,' she replied, sitting in an armchair opposite with one small child on her lap. 'What would you like to know?'

'I understand you were in an abusive relationship and that becoming part of the Federation changed that. Just give me a run through of what happened,' said Miles.

'And it is just for this alien author. It won't be seen by anyone else.'

'No. It's absolutely confidential,' Miles assured her.

'Okay. I suppose I was a fool. I was one of those women who love their man no matter what. He was always very sorry, but if he'd been drinking, I only had to say one thing out of place, and he'd slap me. On at least one occasion he gave me very obvious black eyes, but it wasn't just being hit.' She took a sip from a cup of tea or coffee.

'He kept me pinned down financially,' she continued. 'He insisted my pay was paid into his account and he only gave me enough money for the shopping and essentials for the children. I had to ask for everything – the money for a new skirt, top or shoes; to buy new household goods; even to buy things for the children. Meanwhile he spent more and more time at the pub and the British Legion Social Club and I wasn't allowed out at all to see friends or family. I was a virtual prisoner.'

'So, what happened after Federation Day?' asked Miles.

'Because we were a family, we had to set up three accounts. One for him, one for me and one for the children. It didn't take long for him to make me pay for all the household costs. I decided to complain to one of the Federation Information Booths. We were called in while one of the robots looked after the children. They wanted us to resolve our problems and come up with a plan which would be more equitable, but when we got home he started shouting and screaming at me, raised his hand to strike me and a cop-bot materialised out of thin air between us. What a shock it gave him. Well, and me too. He was given fifteen minutes stasis. When he came out of that, he started on at me again. Another cop-bot arrived and gave him thirty minutes stasis. That was it. He moved out and left me with the children.'

'That must have been difficult for you,' said Miles.

'Not at all. The kids and I had more money than we'd ever had before and our life, well, it became almost idyllic. My only regret is that I still love the man but can't ever invite him back. Shame they're not as good with solving people problems as they are with admin and money.'

'What do you mean?'

'If they could make him a better man somehow. He keeps asking if he can come back and he's on a course at the moment. He's hoping it will sort him out. I hope it does, but I'll believe it when I see it.'

'You'll take him back?'

'I must try. I love the damn man.'

The screen turned blue and Miles selected another scenario from his tablet. He held it on pause.

'This is a surprising one. She's an ex-girlfriend of mine who used to work in an advertising agency. With the coming of the Federation, all adverts died away, or at least they became more informative about products than trying to sell things. A new kettle for instance, would be shown with a list of positives and negatives. Anyway, her job was suddenly no longer needed. The agency shut down.

'I saw her a few weeks later and she was quite depressed, then she vanished. I wanted to film her for you, but my calls were never returned. I'd given up when she called me out of the blue and asked why I'd left so many messages for her. Anyway, here's the recording,' Miles said and pressed the play button.

The video started. 'So how have you been, Jean?' Miles asked.

'Brilliant,' she replied.

'Last time I saw you, you were pretty down.'

'Ah, yes, then I discovered travel.'

'You've been going around the world?'

'Wake up, Miles. We're in the Federation now!' She looked at a notebook. 'I've just returned from my twelfth planet.'

'Twelve?'

'Twelve, and all different and fascinating. A wonderful experience.'

'So not depressed anymore?'

'Not a chance. I'm planning another trip starting the week after next, but, I tell you what, that moon of Arlucian is definitely worth a second visit. Fabulous!'

Miles stopped the video. 'Another satisfied customer,' he said.

'Any who are still having a hard time?' I asked.

'Not in this latest batch. Want to watch them?'

I nodded.

'Okay,' he said, 'I'll crack another two beers.'

26 Ewoinusi Cybernetics Amalgam

Emily spent the next few hours trailing through the expanded Internet, the Frame, the aliens called it, following the early history of the Galactic Empire. Much as she enjoyed esponging the scenarios, she realised that life was not long enough for a human to follow all the twists and turns of the fortunes of the new Galactic Empire. The Internet still contained all things to do with Earth and its knowledge, but the Frame used quantum technology to be updated instantly, whether the information was entered by someone living in a remote village in Finland or an alien living on a planet 30,000 light years away.

Rummy had hinted that there was quite a gap between Arlucian being conquered by the X-Jastuvians in the name of the Union and the improvement in the automatons to reach the point where they were able to carry out almost all human functions and had certainly given that occurrence a great deal of emphasis.

Emily discovered that a huge amount of development work was occurring on an empire planet called Ewoinusi close to the galactic centre, or at least as close as you could get without being frazzled by gamma rays from the giant black hole at the Milky Way's centre. She decided that she'd like to drop in on that period. A scientist called Jon Sokut seemed to rise to great fame in the year 201,015 NE, over 50,000 years after the formation of the original Union of Planets.

At the esponging centre, she asked the room-bot if there was anything on Sokut.

'There is considerable information on Professor Jon Sokut, the founder of the Ewoinusi Cybernetics Amalgam. He appears in several courses as a character. Do you know which aspect of his work you would like to study?' asked the room-bot.

Oh, dear. How could she make such a choice? 'Can I see his major breakthrough in robot production? Is there a scenario for that?' asked Emily.

'Yes, Emily. Scenario three of nineteen in the ECA course should be quite illuminating. If you wish to go straight into that,

I can provide course notes on the background before it begins. Would you like that? You can always exit the course if it is not what you are looking for,' said the room-bot.

'That sounds ideal,' said Emily.

'Make yourself comfortable, put on the mask and say "Begin" to start the scenario.'

Emily hurriedly made herself a coffee and became totally absorbed by the notes the room-bot had printed out for her. She gulped the remainder of her drink, which she'd allow to grow cold, and said, 'Begin.'

The scenario opened with her looking at herself, or rather the character of Jon Sokut, staring into a mirror and carefully positioning a garment, a sort of delicate scarf, around his neck so that a corner pointed downwards beneath a bristly chin. His face was a dull greenish-brown. The mouth was relatively normal, above the chin, but the rest of the face was puffy, with two deep-set eyes. Beneath them was an organ of an unknown nature which, perhaps, provided a sense of smell or even hearing, for Emily could see no ears on the bald head.

Professor Sokut turned away from the mirror, made his way through the hallway of what was, presumably, his home, and climbed into a vehicle. It was quite low-lying with three wheels and an aerodynamic shape.

'Laboratory,' the professor said.

The motor pulled away and joined traffic as it negotiated its way into the fast lane of a six-lane highway, heading towards a city of skyscrapers a few miles in the distance. High in the sky above the city, Emily could see the huge lens-like shape of the galactic core. Amazing that it was so clear in such bright daylight. It must dominate the sky at night. As the vehicle continued along its way, Emily wondered why the scenario had all this detail of the professor's journey.

As the vehicle approached the city, it pulled across to the left side of the carriageway and took an off ramp.

'Why the change of route?' asked the professor.

‘There will shortly be slow traffic ahead and this will get us to the laboratory faster,’ said the car.

They continued their journey through the quieter streets of a suburb of the city, following the line of the main highway, which Emily/Jon kept an eye on to the right. ‘I still don’t see why you took this route. The traffic on the highway is still moving much faster.’

All of a sudden there was the cacophony of horns blaring and Jon saw a truck sideways on to the flow of the highway traffic. The traffic backed up immediately and Jon realised the decision to get off the highway had been correct after all.

Beyond the blockage, it was quite clear the traffic was moving at normal speeds. The car-bot could not possibly have known about the truck blocking the traffic. It hadn’t happened until after they’d pulled off.

It left the professor perplexed as the vehicle pulled into the industrial complex and parked itself in the professor’s space.

‘Car, send me a log of that journey,’ said the professor.

‘Yes, sir,’ said the car.

The scene faded through black.

∞∞∞∞∞∞∞

A laboratory gradually materialised. Emily, or rather Jon, worked his way through the car’s log and discovered that the car-bot had worked out that there was about to be an accident through logic and statistics. It didn’t seem possible and the professor soon had a team of eight cybernetic experts working on the problem. How had his car-bot foreseen this accident, but none of the other vehicles had?

‘Professor, we cannot find anything to explain the incident. That section of road often gets blocked, but we don’t see how it could have been predicted. Marl has been in touch with the truck’s bot and there is nothing untoward there. I suspect that we’re wasting our time on this,’ said Duryl, a senior cybernetic engineer. ‘However, we have learned something interesting from the spread of your car’s decision making.’

‘Explain,’ said Jon.

‘Immediately prior to the vehicle deciding to turn off the highway, there was a rush of alternative scenarios being analysed. During that, it appears to have accessed your own personal memory and backup systems.’

‘But nothing has access to them without my knowledge,’ said the professor, immediately opening his private computing system and studying various files and reports.

‘I can only tell you what we found,’ said Duryl.

‘Yes. Yes, I’ve found it. All of my CPUs ran at one hundred per cent for six seconds at six minutes past nine this morning. Does that tie in with your timeline?’

‘Spot on, Professor, and your car left the highway at seven minutes past nine.’

‘Okay, Duryl. Call in your four most trusted cybernetics geniuses and we’ll work on this together,’ said the professor.

The scene shimmied and reappeared with Jon, Duryl and four other white-coated figures sitting in the professor’s office.

‘I cannot emphasise strongly enough how confidential this project is,’ said the professor.

‘We all understand, sir,’ said Duryl. The others nodded.

‘This,’ the professor said, holding up a black box about five inches square, ‘is a new Quantum Memory System which I’ve been working on for almost a year. It’s a bit of a breakthrough. It can handle six million, trillion calculations a second. My car-bot somehow got access to it while I had my communicator open during the journey. I don’t use the QMS with my communicator as it would be too slow to benefit, but it was connected. The car-bot must have accessed the QMS through the communicator.’

‘The number of alternatives it was looking at during that six seconds is no longer impossible if it had access to that memory,’ said Duryl.

‘Thought that at the time we were analysing it,’ said Edyl, another of the elite cybernetics team. ‘It had to have access to some other source.’

‘I want all of the work on this done in this laboratory. No electronic equipment is to be taken out of the lab once this project has begun. Do you all understand?’

There were a number of positive responses.

‘That means you must not bring your own communicators, computers or other devices in here during the project. That is vital. I don’t want the rumour mill to explode with this.’

They all agreed.

‘Right. Too late to start today. Back here at nine tomorrow and remember that everything is to be left outside the lab.’

‘Smartwatches?’ asked Bureel.

‘Absolutely,’ said the professor. ‘Nothing electronic.’

The group stood to leave, and the scene faded through black once more.

∞∞∞∞∞∞∞∞∞∞∞

The following morning, Jon was into the laboratory before any of the others and began to put the lab’s main computer through its decision making processes while connected to the QMS. Usually its decisions were standard, but when asked something complex, the QMS became very active as alternative possibilities were investigated.

Gradually the rest of the team arrived.

‘I’ve been doing some tests,’ said Jon. ‘Our lab computer is now connected to the QMS but I noticed that it very rarely accessed it, then I gave it some decisions to make which were not black and white. Decisions where it had to weigh up alternative possible answers. The QMS was instantly accessed to assist with the answers.’

The professor tossed a coin. ‘I put this coin into the vacuum flask over there and allowed an automatic lever I rigged up to toss it. I asked the computer to predict the outcome.’

The rest of the team leaned forward, becoming really attentive. 'The first sequence of five tosses were poorly predicted, not better than pure chance, but it suddenly changed. Four of the next five were correctly predicted and, after the tenth toss, it was right every time. No error in more than sixty tests. What is fascinating is that I added some air to the chamber and the next three results were random before its analysis returned to one hundred per cent.'

'So,' said Bureel, 'it is examining the force of the toss, the coin's initial position, its interaction with the air or lack of it in the flask and gravity.'

'Exactly!' shouted Jon. 'It is the decision making capability we've needed for thousands of years.'

The team each looked at each other. 'This is astounding,' said Edyl.

'Okay, sir, how do we proceed?' asked Duryl.

'Firstly, we need to find a way to mass-produce the QMS blocks and try to miniaturise down to, say one centimetre cubed. Secondly, we need to work with some production robots. See if they access the QMS blocks when available and how differently that makes them behave. Will it allow one type of automaton to carry out the function of others?'

'I see,' said Edyl. 'Can a packing robot become a cleaning robot just by working out how to use its existing tools to change function.'

'Spot on, Edyl!' said Jon. 'Now let's get busy!'

Emily saw the scene fading and it rematerialised in another part of the room.

∞∞∞∞∞∞∞

A caption hovered in mid-air. "FOUR WEEKS LATER".

Edyl, Duryl and Jon hard-wired a QMS into a utility housekeeping robot. They moved clear, Duryl switched on the automaton and they watched it rise into an upright position.

‘Robot, dust the lab bench please and be careful to reposition everything accurately afterwards,’ said Edyl.

The automaton stood about two metres tall on three legs, with four arms. The two upmost arms were substantial with large hands. The smaller arms below emerged from the chest area and were for finer work. On the command it sprang into action, extracting a duster and chemical spray from a hip compartment and began to clean the bench, lifting each item, carefully dusting it and putting it back exactly where it had been previously.

In front of the scientists, a monitor showed the activity of the robot’s central processing unit and also that of the QMS. Initially CPU usage rose and fell extensively. When it began lifting and moving objects the graph spiked several times and the QMS showed minor activity.

‘It’s storing location data and re-accessing it as needed,’ said Jon.

‘It’s approaching the test,’ said Edyl.

The robot lifted a tubular item about the size of a cotton reel off the top of a cube and, instantly, a trapdoor panel in the bench flipped open, sending the cube skidding along the table. The spring within the trapdoor shot into the air, rebounded off a light fitting and fell to the floor where it rolled under the bench.

The QMS activity rose sharply. The robot walked to the end of the bench and collected the cube. It then got down onto the floor and extracted the spring, stood up and put it onto the bench near the trapdoor.

‘That’s how the control robot, with no QMS access, left it last time,’ said Edyl.

‘Right,’ said Duryl.

The automaton lifted the spring and examined it, compressing it and releasing the compression. The QMS activity sky-rocketed. It looked into the hole in the bench, lifting the trapdoor and seeing how it sat naturally in position. The QMS graph hit one hundred per cent as it opened the trapdoor, placed the spring into its socket, closed the trapdoor, compressing the spring and kept one hand on it. Next it picked up the cube and placed it on the trapdoor where it had been sitting originally before setting the tubular object, a heavy lump of titanium, on top of the cube. Tentatively it released the pressure on the objects. Neither moved. The titanium was heavy enough, with the cube, to hold the trapdoor in place.

'Look at that,' said Jon. The QMS activity dropped to zero and the robot continued cleaning the rest of the bench.

'Brilliant!' said Duryl. 'Amazing,' said Edyl.

The scenario froze and the room-bot began to speak. Emily had not encountered this before in these courses and guessed it had to do with her only looking at part of a course this time.

'This was the first time an automaton had made such complex decisions in a scenario it had never previously encountered,' said the room-bot. 'Jon, Duryl and Edyl went on to form the Ewoinusi Cybernetics Amalgam, which became the second largest manufacturer of intelligent automatons in the Galactic Empire.'

The scene faded to black and when Emily removed the blindfold, she was watching video from the surface of Pluto.

'What do you suggest next, room-bot?' she asked.

'From what you've told me,' said the room-bot, 'the results of Jon Sokut's automaton breakthrough would be logical. Return in forty-eight hours. The room-bot you encounter will read this conversation from your chip.'

Emily relaxed with another cup of coffee then exited to brave torrential rain in the Bayswater Road.

27 Freedom Army

Colonel Mike Henderson put the platoon through its paces in the football stadium. Congressman Charles Mayne, General Dick Beech and two other colonels were looking on. Mike shouted a few further instructions to his officers and walked up to the other four. He gave a smart salute.

'Thanks for laying this on for us, Colonel,' said Dick. 'You know Colonel Geoffrey Thomason, but you might not have met Colonel Kirsty Wall.'

Mike shook hands with both. 'Pleased to meet you, Kirsty.'

'Geoffrey will be forming a similar platoon just north of Washington, and Kirsty the same on the coast. The plan is to have around three hundred soldiers armed and ready to fight. Are you happy with the way these soldiers are performing.

'Yes, sir,' said Mike. 'Some lack of general fitness, which you can see we're working upon. They're not ready to pass muster yet, but I have a good team training them.'

'Secure here?' asked Geoffrey.

'Yes. We have another twenty soldiers who you might have noticed on the way into the stadium. No one they don't personally know will be allowed to see what is going on here and we have a signal system if we need to stop training and scatter in a hurry. It's working okay at the moment.'

'Very well, Colonel,' said the general. 'After our meeting, I'd like you to allocate a major and captain to Colonels Thomason and Wall to assist them to establish a similar routine.'

'Yes, sir. How long will the meeting last?' asked Mike. 'This training session will end at sixteen hundred hours.'

'You'll have plenty of time to get back here after the meeting, Colonel,' said the general, turning to the soldier standing behind him. 'Private, bring the Jeep around to the main entrance.'

The soldier snapped a salute and smartly marched towards the exit.

'Any timescale yet, sir?' asked Geoffrey.

‘That is partly the reason for the meeting. I wouldn’t normally like so many of us to be in a single place at the same time, but planning is now becoming critical. Let’s go,’ said the general and the four of them ambled slowly out of the ground. Behind them, majors and captains were barking orders at the troops who were now running and throwing themselves onto the ground on each command, then rising and running again. It was obvious that this was not easy for some of those who had not been in the military for several years.

Outside the stadium, a dark green Jeep pulled up and the senior officers jumped on board. The windows were extremely dark to protect the identity of individuals. The Jeep made a right out of the parking area and headed towards the centre of Washington.

∞∞∞∞∞∞

The green Jeep turned into a driveway, and passed through a pair of stone pillars crowned by eagles, the gates to which automatically closed behind it. The vehicle continued for another fifty metres and approached a large detached house which looked as if it had been built in the grand tradition of mansions of the early twentieth century. In front of the limestone edifice was a roundabout. The Jeep came to a halt beside a stone canopy supported by four columns, two of which were built into the front of the house. A sergeant in uniform opened the door and stood to one side.

The colonels entered the door.

Charles gripped the general’s arm and held him back. ‘I don’t see why you are training hundreds of troops, Dick.’

‘That’s because you know the plan, Charles. The enemy does not know the plan. The troops will blindside them. They’ll be dashing around like blue-assed flies, trying to get intel on how we’re going to use them.’

‘Right,’ said Charles and they both followed the colonels inside.

Bob Nixon rushed up to the general and shook his hand. 'Come this way, gentlemen, ma'am,' he said, guiding the party along a corridor which led from the grand entrance hall towards one of the ground floor rooms at the back. 'A surprise visitor has arrived to see you too, Charles.'

The ornateness of the room was rather unexpected, but it had obviously received some tender loving care over the decades. It might have been an area to play billiards, table tennis or pool, but was now a classy lounge which would easily have passed for a gentlemen's club in the UK.

Jim Collins jumped to his feet and Charles strode forward to give him a genuine hug of friendship. He said, 'Wondered if we'd ever meet again after the last time, Jim.'

'Yes, facing that firing-squad was an experience I don't ever want to repeat.'

The general turned towards the colonels and said, 'You know Mike. This is Colonel Kirsty Wall, late of the California uprising, and this is Colonel Geoffrey Thomason. The four of us will be the high command of the insurrection.'

Handshakes took place all around, flasks of coffee, tea and some pastries arrived, and they all took their seats.

The general began proceedings. 'Kirsty, Geoffrey, Congressman Charles Mayne is our nominal leader. He has committed to calling a new election once he's in the White House and will also offer a second opportunity for the people of the United States to choose whether or not to join the Federation. Charles is a Democrat as is his right-hand man, Jim Collins, but this other gentleman, Bob Nixon has strong Republican roots, including being White House chief of staff for President Spence. Bob has agreed to temporarily take the role of vice president for Charles.'

'Pleased to have each of you on the team,' said Charles. 'Bob and I will be controls on each other during the period when I'm acting president. He will also be ideal to take over from me should I be incapacitated in any way. Jim will be my chief of staff when we walk into the White House.'

'You sound very confident, sir,' said Colonel Thomason.

'I am… it is because I have Dick, you, Kirsty and Mike batting for my side. We're far better organised than we were as Free America. This time we *will* defeat the usurper. You just need to get your troops up to muster.'

'Now,' said the general. 'Colonel Henderson, please take Colonels Thomason and Wall to your HQ, show them the plan and then sort out their majors and captains. Meanwhile, we'll get Peter Stone on the videophone and run through exactly how we're going to overthrow Slimbridge.'

28 Economic Collapse

It was almost four weeks before Emily returned to the esponging centre to continue her exploration of the early Federation. Part of that was owing to her mother becoming unwell, but mostly it was because her mother's illness led to her meeting a rather dashing surgeon. He became her first serious love affair, which in turn led to her normal routines being turned upside down.

The surgeon, Dr Allan Cutler, lived in Welwyn Garden City, about twenty miles north of London. Emily was spending an increasing amount of time in the once experimental new town and on weekends he stayed with her in her London flat, taking in shows and sporting events together.

This Monday morning, Allan was taking part in a medical seminar in Grimsby, so Emily saw him off and was determined to get back to the course on the Ewoinusi Cybernetics Amalgam. This time, the room-bot was suggesting she jump to scenario seven of nineteen to learn about the repercussions of the arrival of intelligent automatons. Emily told the room-bot to choose appropriate characters for her and then she poured a coffee. She enjoyed five minutes of watching video of the raging surface of the sun and then felt ready to start.

'Begin,' she said.

The blackness descended then fragmented to reveal a factory setting. Emily didn't know the species; it was like nothing she'd encountered so far. She was on all fours, or rather it wasn't four legs, but six! She stopped walking and sat up, her four rear legs supporting her while the front of her torso bent almost at right angles, in the manner of a centaur. She read some figures off a machine display. Her front legs were now hands and made notes before pressing a couple of buttons. She dropped to all six and scampered across the factory, stopping at another machine, adopted the centaurian posture again, tapped a gauge and, this time, recorded the reading on a smartphone-like gadget strapped to her/his side. If this were the size of a human cell phone, then the creature must be the size of a basset hound – very low slung.

'Come up, Tedray!' shouted a voice from above. Emily looked up and saw another of the creatures looking down at her from a gantry walkway.

She dropped back onto her six legs, ran across the open decking and climbed vertically up a ladder device which was obviously made specially for her species. She was amazed how swiftly she reached the top level where she ran along the balcony and entered an office. The creature who'd shouted for her was seated at a desk which was littered with papers and various tools.

'You wanted me, Indron?'

'Yes, Tedray. Take a seat. Would you like a drink?'

This was unusual. Emily could tell that Indron did not usually offer drinks to his employees. She sensed her character wondering what was going on.

'I have unj or vilter,' said Indron.

'Thank you. I'll take unj, please.'

Indron took two bottles from the cupboard behind him and a couple of strange-looking containers – a little like a ceramic petri dish with a lip at one end. He poured some brown liquid into one of the dishes, yellow liquid into the other and slid the latter across the table. 'Good health, Tedray,' he said and slurped the brown liquid from the dish.

Tedray leaned forward and lapped up the yellow liquid. Emily wanted to recoil. It was disgusting, smelled of urine and tasted exceedingly bitter! 'And good health to you, Indron. Why did you want to see me?'

'The time has come, my friend. You and Eildit are my last two Bireenian workers. I have to let you go. We're going one hundred per cent autonomous,' said Indron.

Emily felt the total shock which went through her character's mind and body. The empty feeling of desperation sank into her stomach. Tedray stopped drinking, 'But we've worked on this business for a lifetime, Indron.'

‘Yes, and you’ve been a good employee. I’m putting you on a pension of thirty per cent of your wage for the remainder of your life. The same with Eildit.’

‘What am I going to do? I have a family to support and elderly parents in care. As you know, Baran lost his job last week. Mistil is starting university next month and I can’t afford the fees on that drop in income. It’s not right. There is no work available anywhere for females.’

‘I understand, Tedray, but it is no longer economic to keep people as employees. You know how efficient the new robots are. They don’t need to be overseen. I don’t have a choice.’

‘There is always a choice, Idron. I know you own the company, but we built it together. It was *our* business. I’ve put my heart and soul into it for fifteen years. You couldn’t have done it without me. What you’ll save on our salaries will just boost your own income.’

‘But you were well paid with bonuses for all of your improvements and design ideas. Sometimes you and Eilit earned more than me, you know.’

‘Idron, you are a millionaire. I helped make you those millions – now you just cast me off in the prime of my life. You know what is happening out there,’ Tedray said, throwing an arm in a leftward direction. ‘There are no new jobs. This is criminal!’

Idron stood up and said, ‘Well, I’m sorry you feel like that, but what’s done is done. You can leave immediately. You’re on full pay until the next pay day, then the pension will kick in. This letter contains the details.’ He handed a thick envelope to Tedray.

The scene faded through black.

ooooooooooooo

In her next scene Emily was a male of a very solidly built furry animal, sitting at a table. Around her, she could see a slim and more delicate version of herself which Emily guessed was a female. Also at the table, were three smaller versions. Children, she guessed.

'It's horrible!' yelled Baronu, the smallest.

'Add some more of the sauce you like. Here it is,' the female said and slid a container across the table.

It was intercepted by one of the other children, a male, who squirted the red sauce over his dinner and passed it to the youngest child. 'It *is* gross, Mum,' said the older male child.

'You should be more like Dinda,' the mother said. 'She eats what she's given like a good girl.'

'I don't like it though, Mum,' said the female child.

'It's not the best, Hind. What is it?' Emily heard herself, the father apparently, saying almost in a whisper to his wife.

Hind cupped her hand around her mouth and whispered back, 'It's a skrat. Berint down the road is selling them.'

'What? Has it come to eating…' he lowered his voice, 'skrats?'

'We've nothing left to trade with, Brune.'

'What about the vegetable crop?'

'That's the problem. No one wants to take promised payments and a lot of crops are being stolen as they reach maturity.'

'Won't happen to ours,' said Brune confidently. 'Our alarm will alert us if anyone crosses the boundary.'

'And how long will that last anyway, dear,' Hind said. 'Say we eat thirty per cent ourselves over the winter. The remainder won't buy us much.'

'It'll buy us better than this,' the older son said, holding up a piece of gristly meat he'd skewered with his knife.

'I'm worried about promising the crop before harvest. People ask for more than their goods are worth. When is it due for harvest?' asked Hind.

Two weeks. We can't eat skrat for the next two weeks,' Brune said.

The younger creature heard the word. 'Ugh! It's not skrat!' he shouted, pushing his plate violently away and spilling some of the watery gravy onto the table.

'Behave yourself!' shouted Brune, and his wife said, 'Eat your dinner. There's nothing else.'

Emily could hear Brune's thoughts. Two months earlier he'd been a top managing editor at a paperback publisher. Now the work was all done by robots. They could scan manuscripts in seconds, picking out all of the grammatical and punctuation errors, but also making suggestions on how the stories could be improved. Authors were some of the few people who had not suffered during the reign of the robots. Brune wondered how long it would be before the automatons were writing better stories than Hegrudon authors. Brune's brother was a writer and he still earned a fabulous income from his books. He wasn't aware of the struggle of his brother's family. Brune resolved to pay him a visit. Perhaps he could borrow to buy some meckets. At least that would provide some ongoing eggs to eat or trade.

Emily smelled the rancid odour of the piece of meat she found in her mouth. Could she vomit through someone else in these scenarios? She didn't want to find out and shouted, 'End course!' also pulling off the blindfold. Ugh! What a horrible dish! No wonder the children were rebelling.

The room-bot said, 'You ended that scenario just two minutes prematurely. Would you like to continue to the next character?

'I'll make myself a tea first,' Emily said. 'What's a skrat?'

'Here's some video,' said the room-bot.

Emily was looking at a riverbank on the giant television monitor. Water bubbled through grasses and other plants. She saw a hole in the bank and a head appeared, looking up and down the river. It slithered into the water. Emily had nothing from which to measure scale, but it looked to her like a furry snake. She saw no legs and it swam sinuously along the surface. The next scene showed it catching a fish. The skrat held it crossways in its mouth, surfaced and swam back up the river. It stopped by a ledge beside its hole, curled itself up, exactly as would a snake, then began to tear the fish apart.

'Okay, room-bot. Enough. I'll get my tea and be back in a moment,' said Emily.

∞∞∞∞∞∞∞

When the next scenario commenced, Emily found herself still in the Hegrudon called Brune. She was out of breath and peddling hard on a quad-cycle. Rather ancient, it made noises of rust against rust. The pedals drove a chain which passed the power to the front pair of wheels while the rider sat upright. Handlebars, arising from behind the driver, then passed by each side of him where his hands held them. He controlled direction by turning the back set of wheels. It seemed an awkward layout to Emily. Each side of the driver's seat were smaller seats, slightly lower in the structure, where two children sat, his young daughter and the smaller male child.

It was tiring. Emily was out of breath. How far were they travelling?

'How long now, Dad?' asked Baronu with the whiney voice of all bored children taking a journey when they could be playing.

'We're halfway, son. Another eight miles to go.'

'Nooo! It's taking forever,' the youngster replied.

'Perhaps you'd like to pedal, then?'

The grumbling ceased. Emily noticed that every few minutes the scenario darkened, and the quad-cycle was further along its journey. She guessed the room-bot wanted her to feel the effort involved in this sixteen mile journey by Brune to visit his brother.

After a last, extremely steep, section of road, the quad-cycle made a right turn into an impressively large detached house with two gleaming cars standing in the driveway. Emily's, or rather Brune's chest was still heaving from the exertion and the children ran off to ring their uncle's doorbell.

Emily couldn't tell whether these creatures were smiling or serious, but there was no missing the obvious joy the two adults at the door were experiencing as the visiting children were being cuddled and mussed. Two other youngsters emerged from the house and the four kids dashed off around the side of the house to play.

'Brune, how lovely to see you,' said the brother as he walked over to the visitor and they exchanged hugs. 'Don't tell me you rode this thing all of the way.'

'Yes,' said Brune. 'I needed the exercise, Yarold.'

'Come on, Brune. Come on in and we'll fix you a cold drink or a hot cup of cland. Which would you like? Come inside.'

At the door, Brune hugged Yarold's wife and entered a lovely, cool, air-conditioned hallway which led through to a well-equipped, modern kitchen.

'Cland or fruit juice, Brune?' asked Tirrin.

'A mug of cland would go down a treat,' Brune said and Tirrin switched on a squat coloured device which appeared to Emily to be some form of kettle.

'How have you been?' asked Tirrin. 'Didn't Hind come with you?'

'No, she's fine, though.'

'He came on that rusty old quad-cycle of Dad's,' said Yarold. 'Why is that?'

They all sat around the kitchen table. Emily still felt puffed after the cycle ride. 'The car went six weeks ago, brother,' said Brune.

'It's that bad. No work at all?'

'None. No publishing house needs editors anymore and I can't find anything else. We've dug up the lawn and are trying to grow some vegetables,' said Brune, then he lowered his voice in shame. 'Last night we had to eat a couple of skrats.'

'No!' cried Tirrin, 'really?'

'Yes. It was the last straw honestly. Our crop will be ready in a few weeks and Hind doesn't want us to pre-sell it otherwise it won't last the winter. I didn't want to come.' Emily felt tears welling up in Brune's eyes. 'But we're desperate.'

'My God,' said Yarold, as two robots brought the cland, biscuits and cake to the table. 'I had no idea it had gotten so bad.'

'Grund-a, go and set some cland and cakes up in the parlour and ask the children whether they'd like that or cold drinks,' said Tirrin and one of the robots dashed out to find the children while the other prepared a tray.

Brune demolished a large slab of cake. 'First cake I've eaten for weeks. We ran out of flour.' He dried his eyes and looked at the remaining slices.

'Damn it! Take it, Brune. Eat your fill,' said his brother.

'Wait,' said Tirrin. 'Would you like something more? How about a nice piece of skirrit, yeen and katrolos?'

Brune's face lit up. 'Is that okay, Tirrin? I don't want to be any trouble.'

'Grund-b, message Grund-a and ask him to ask the children what they'd like for an early lunch then get some skirrit out. Brune is having skirrit, yeen and katrolos,' said Tirrin.

'Certainly, Tirrin,' said the robot and busied himself.

'You're broke, then? Hence the quad-cycle,' said Yarold.

Brune hung his head, 'Yes.'

'Damn, you should have called me,' said Yarold. 'I'd have sent a car. You're *not* going back on that thing. I'll call up a pick-up and it will take you all, and the cycle back later. I can't believe this. You were always the clever one.'

'It doesn't matter how clever you are. If you don't own an important business or if a robot can do your job, that's it. So far, they can't write good fiction so think yourself lucky.'

'They're trying to do that, but still not very well. The plots are too formulaic.'

‘Save up, brother, while you can, or invest in an automaton manufacturing business. You remember Gistik?’

‘Yes, owned a chain of bakeries, nice man. Great bread,’ said Tirrin.

‘Committed suicide. One of the larger nearby bakeries was taken over by Gu Harone. He put robots to work and they’ve put all the small bakeries out of business. Same quality, cheaper. Gistik didn’t stand a chance, especially with sales falling off a cliff anyway as unemployment rose. Now there’s only one bakery in the region, Gu Harone’s and he lives in luxury.’

‘I know him,’ said Yarold. ‘We’ve played dimplert together. He’s grumbling about sales being bad, so even he’s suffering.’

‘Well, that’s easy explained. No one can afford to buy anything. I had to sell my car for just six hundred. It was worth several thousand. People either have money or they have no money. There’s no middle ground,’ said Brune.

‘Didn’t realise it was that bad,’ said Yarold.

Grund-b delivered a sizzling skirrit steak with golden yeen and crispy katrolos to Brune, who tucked in with gusto.

‘Wow, Tirrin. This is wonderful. Not had skirrit steak for months.’

Emily was apprehensive about the first mouthful, remembering the rancid flavour of skrat. Perhaps all Hegrudon food tasted terrible to humans, but no, the skirrit steak was incredible. A little more like lamb than beef and then the yeen, like mashed potato, but with the subtle flavour of asparagus. Emily saw herself cutting into the katrolos. Brune scooped some gravy onto the blue coloured vegetable and ate it. Wonderful. If you could forget the colour it was like eating deep-fried sweet potato wedges.

All the time, Brune’s brother and sister-in-law were telling him about their lives, his latest novel and where they were going on holiday this year. To Brune, it all seemed like dreams. He couldn’t see any way he could ever afford to take his family away again.

Between mouthfuls, he said, 'I've a plan to get fifty meckets, set up that paddock at the end of the garden for them and trade the eggs for produce others are growing.' He swallowed another juicy piece of steak. 'If we keep some of the eggs, we could maybe build up the numbers to a hundred over a year or two.'

'I can't believe you'd need to be doing that.'

'No other way, brother.'

'Sounds a nice idea,' said Tirrin. 'I've always loved watching meckets burrowing. You'll have to watch they don't escape.'

'The burrowing is just for food, Tirrin. They never dig very deep and it keeps the ground turned over. We can swap the garden for the paddock every couple of years. Meckets make good fertiliser too. I've been reading up on them.'

'You think it'll work?' asked Yarold. 'Will it let you live better. I still can't believe you ate skrat.'

Brune put his fork down. 'There's a problem. I'm short four hundred desos to buy the meckets.' He continued to eat.

'You want a loan?' asked Yarold.

'Well,' said Brune, looking his brother in the eye. 'It might take years to pay it back. You might have to take it in eggs.' He laughed. 'But I won't be offering a quad-cycle delivery service.' Tirrin and Yarold began laughing too.

'Don't want it back, brother. Not unless things change. And if the damn robots learn to concoct and deliver a proper plot, I'll take it in eggs then!' They all laughed again. 'What's the cost? Is four hundred enough?'

'The meckets are four hundred. An extra hundred to keep us going until our crop is ready and the meckets start laying wouldn't go amiss. Hind is at her wits end with feeding us all.'

'That's a done deal, then Brune. Call it a straight thousand.'

'No, no, I can't take that much.'

'Well I never loan less than a round thousand, brother. Makes the paperwork less tricky, and I'll expect five or ten eggs every now and then as interest, but only if you can do that without having to resort to eating skrat again.'

Brune stood up, pulled his brother off his seat and gave him a huge hug, tears rolling down his cheeks, leaving damp areas on his facial fur.

Tirrin joined in the hug and said, 'You should have come to us much earlier. We had no idea things were so bad.'

'It's very general,' said Brune. 'We know many in a worse state than us. People with small crops like ours or a few animals have had them stolen. I guess people are that desperate.'

'The government needs to do something,' said Yarold.

'But what? The way I see it,' said Brune, 'only a rich handful of people like you and business owners are buying anything, and what they do buy is provided by other rich people.'

'We're not rich, Brune. Just comfortable,' said Yarold.

'Not any longer, brother. No one is "just comfortable" anymore. You either still have an income or you are in abject poverty. To more than ninety-five per cent of the population you are stinking rich.'

'It's as bad as that?' asked Tirrin.

'It is. People who own the businesses are living a life of luxury, so are the people who invested in them, but when you see what happened to Gistik and his successful bakery, it seems to me that the millionaires who own the automaton companies will eventually take over everything else. The Gu Harone bakery is just one step from being put out of business by something bigger and better. Robots can even produce niche products. Nothing is beyond them, these days and, Yarold, their owners *will* be after your income sooner than you might think.'

'I had no idea. Hadn't thought of it like that,' said Tirrin.

'It is only when it happens to you that you realise the extent of the problem. Even if the government does do something, it will still leave Hegrudon with two classes. The people who can still earn money and those who live in poverty. Such a system can only work when the number of unemployed is relatively small and relatively stable. Once almost everyone is in that situation, the system breaks down.'

'But won't lots of small businesses like your mecket project fill the gap? If you do well, won't you try to get more land and expand?'

'That is *exactly* the problem. If I do have some success and begin to expand, I'll soon acquire robots and expand more and each time I do that, other mecket egg producers will be squeezed out, because, with my lower overheads after using robots for a while, I'll undercut the other producers and start, perhaps, to bridge the gap with the wealthy, until, that is, one of the big egg producing robot-run companies sees my expansion as a threat and they'll wipe me out. Back to square one.'

'So, what *is* the answer?' asked Yarold.

'I have no idea,' said Brune.

'Give me your account details and I'll transfer the cash,' said Yarold.

'No good. I'm overdrawn and they've closed my account.'

'Really? That's diabolical,' said Tirrin.

'All part of the problem, I'm afraid,' said Brune.

'How much overdrawn? You'll need a bank account.'

'Too much. Thousands and most of us are trading items rather than money now. If you can give me cash, that'll get me up and running and I might try to open a new account with the remainder but can never go back to our bank. We're lucky we paid off our mortgage two years ago.'

'I was going to ask about that,' said Yarold. 'At least your home is safe. But won't the bank come after it as an asset. What do you owe them?'

'Eight thousand.'

'Phew!'

'We could do that, darling,' said Tirrin.

'We certainly could, but I hate to think of a bank taking all that money for doing nothing,' said Yarold. 'Brune, speak to them and ask them how much they'd settle for to write off the debt. If there are these sorts of debts throughout the world, they might take an offer. Tell them your brother has offered you two thousand if they'll write the whole debt off. Worth a try.'

'You're so kind,' said Brune. 'Can you get me the cash?'

'I'll get it tomorrow and bring it over to you, and that two grand is sitting there if you need it. More if necessary, if the bank won't play ball.'

'Thank you, Yarold, Tirrin. You have no idea how much this means to me.'

'You want to get back? I'll call a pick-up to take you and the cycle home,' said Yarold.

'And I'm going to give you a basket of goodies. I'll put in a couple of frozen meckets, half a leg of skirrit and some vegetables,' said Tirrin.

'No. Nothing frozen. We've no power.'

Tirrin and Yarold looked at him aghast. 'No power? Have you got water?' asked his brother, most taken aback with the news of the lack of power.

'Water, yes. But it's okay, with that extra money I can get power put back on,' said Brune, 'but it'll take a couple of days.'

'How much is owed?' asked Yarold.

'You can't do any more for me.'

'How much!' said Yarold severely.

'Three hundred.'

'You're sure? Is there anything else likely to cause a problem?'

'No, brother. That's it.'

'Okay. I'll bring thirteen hundred over tomorrow and *no* arguments. I'll call that pick-up.'

‘I’ll still give you one of the frozen meckets. Hind can cook it tomorrow. I’ve also got half a mecket pie here, so I’ll put that in the box too,’ said Tirrin. ‘That’ll do you for tonight.’

‘You’re too kind. I hate needing charity,’ said Brune who began weeping again. Emily was sure she was crying too.

The blanket of blackness descended once more.

∞∞∞∞∞∞∞∞∞∞

As the veil lifted, Emily found herself seated at a polished wooden table, some fifteen feet long, surrounded by people of yet another species. They were not too “odd” from the human perspective, about two metres tall, slender and had the colour and shininess of a ripe rhubarb stick. Their features were human-like with a central mouth, two eyes above and ears on the side of their heads. Under the mouth, where a human chin would be, she saw four flared nostrils. She noticed that the nostrils were in almost permanent movement, as if continually sampling the air, like a rabbit or guinea pig. She found herself regularly sniffing and she could sense no end of complex odours. Some were being emitted by her neighbouring creatures. Usually pleasant, but occasionally slightly pungent. She wasn’t sure that she liked the idea of continually being aware of the odour of her two neighbours and the three sitting opposite.

She snapped herself back to the matter in hand and realised that, because of the distraction of the smells, she’d missed some of the conversation, or debate, or whatever this meeting entailed.

‘But there is nothing for people to do,’ said one of the creatures, further along the table.

‘We can’t do anything about that. We’re hardly going to shut automatons down so that some Fapfiian can have something to do!’

‘It isn’t that so much as the fact that people are no longer earning any money, and that they’re not spending anything either, and what they do spend is on absolute necessities, like food,’ said another.

‘And bartering is increasing,’ said yet another.

'But while they're not buying things, my business is producing fewer and fewer items. My income's suffering from the fall in sales, but also because of the drop in profits it's affecting dividends. It's not just my business. It's most of us in the same boat.'

'It's what I was saying, Prime Minister,' said another near the centre of one side of the grand table. 'All the income is now being generated by the companies who own the rights to the robots, and some large organisations who've weathered the storm, but even they are finding demand falling as the industries which employ the robots are finding their sales crashing too. The ordinary people are broke. It's a downward spiral.'

'Well, Chancellor,' said the creature at the centre of one side of the table – Emily guessed that it was the Fapfiian prime minister. 'What do we do about it?'

'Get rid of the damn things,' said the creature next to me.'

The prime minister snapped back at him, 'And I suppose, Onry, you are quite happy to return to doing your own lawnmowing, washing, cleaning, driving and managing your communicator production?'

'Might as well, if I'm not earning anything much from it!'

'Whatever you're earning, it's way in excess of the pay your ex-employees now receive,' said another. 'They can't even afford food!'

'There's nothing for it, Prime Minister, we'll have to pay people for being unemployed. A small sum, just enough for them to buy food and fuel,' said the chancellor.

'And where are you going to find *that* money?' asked another member of the cabinet.

'We'll have to tax people who do earn money more, won't we?' the chancellor retorted. 'The introduction of an income for the poor might stimulate the economy a little.'

One of the other ministers threw up his hands in horror. 'What you're suggesting is socialism. It doesn't work… ever. Just let things find their own level.'

'*What?*' said the chancellor loudly. 'Don't you understand? The people are starving. We must do something, or we'll be out on our snouts at the next election. A small increase in tax should do it.'

'I don't agree to that,' said a louder voice from Emily's left. 'We've invested heavily in the production of electronic components. Increasing tax on my business will necessitate putting up the prices and we'll be in the same downward spiral loop all over again.'

'Ahem,' accompanied a cough from an individual to Emily's right. 'I have been doing some quite detailed analysis.'

'Statistics never helped anyone,' said the protesting person at the left end of the table.

'Quiet. Let's hear what he has to say,' said the prime minister. 'We agreed this would be a no-holds-barred meeting.'

The statistician started again. 'The brutal figures show us that the number of people earning over one hundred thousand per annum has been growing rapidly. Four years ago it was four per cent, then five, seven and ten per cent. However, the number of people earning under ten thousand has been growing even more rapidly. Four years ago it was only five per cent. The last three years have shown it grow to eleven, eighteen and thirty per cent. These are people living in abject poverty. Automatons were supposed to improve life for everyone, but thirty per cent are now starving. Even more surprising is that the percentage earning between ten and one hundred thousand has fallen even more rapidly. Ninety-one per cent, then eighty-five, seventy-seven and now sixty per cent and that sixty is crowding at the bottom end of the scale, sliding over the ten thousand barrier, hence the continual rise in the ultra-poor. If the statistics maintain their current direction, we'll have ninety-nine per cent of the population with nothing and one per cent living in absolute luxury. How do you all feel about that?'

'But I don't see how my wealth is growing in that way when sales are continually tumbling,' said the protesting voice.

'I'm sorry,' said the statistician, 'that you were not educated in mathematics, but it is obvious. The income pot is falling so there is less to go around. Even worse poverty for the poor, but fewer riches for the wealthy. We're in an economic depression and we need to do something about it, before the people themselves do.'

'How do you mean, "before the people themselves do"?' asked the prime minister.

'If they can't wait to vote us out of office, they might revolt!' said the statistician.

Several ministers laughed.

'You think I'm joking? I assure you that I'm not. This same problem is being faced on countless worlds in the empire. If nothing is done about it, people will, most certainly, revolt. We could all end up as very wealthy dead people!'

The scene faded to black and Emily removed her mask. She was sad to be told to wait forty-eight hours for the next scenario as she felt fine. She'd have to fit another session in before Allan returned from Grimsby on Thursday. She couldn't wait.

29 Mass March

Peter Stone, the computer guru who had helped Free America achieve many of their most spectacular attacks upon the Slimbridge regime, had not been idle while time had passed after the near-miss execution of Mayne, Beech and co. He'd been gradually building up an enormous online army, recruiting people who had realised that Slimbridge had been lying and that the Federation, although with a strangely anti-American economic policy, were actually an improvement upon what they had now.

Through social media, Stone circulated information films, explaining the true difference between Federation economics and socialism or communism which had been so hated by many of the American population since the fifties. One of his interviews went viral and swung a lot of support behind the Federation.

'Mr Stone, you are a supporter of the Federation system, can you explain why? As a billionaire, why would you want to see communism replace the American system where you can live in luxury?' asked the journalist.

'Firstly, I think it is important for people to realise that having a huge fortune is not an overriding desire for many businessmen. Many of us, and I include myself in this number, are quite happy to give the money away if it is going to provide a better life for others, elsewhere in the world. Until the Federation took over the rest of the world, I was paying more money into African and Far Eastern charities than I was earning.'

'I can understand that, but to give so much away that you end up with no more than the people you're supporting is crazy, surely? Your personal fortune has been estimated at four hundred *billion* dollars!'

'It all depends how it is done. There are charities in America who help the homeless, the disabled, and the poor, but they are ineffective, throwing money at temporary relief which, in most cases, fails to raise the living standards of the beneficiaries. In Africa, it was different, but also a failure. Over forty per cent of the money I ploughed into giving help to African nations, was either stolen or taken by corrupt officials, including many within the charities.'

'Exactly,' said the journalist. 'It doesn't work, just like socialism and communism. Great idea, but not practicable.'

'That is because it relies on distorted systems within the great nations, but before dealing with that I want to correct you. Almost every European country works on a form of socialism. Free health care, adequate social services, substantial state pensions, free education, and so on. So *don't* tell me socialism doesn't work; there are billions in Europe who will tell you it works just fine. Communism is a different matter, but I get really annoyed at the misrepresentation of socialism in the US.

'Anyway, back to charities. Many people give money to charities because they can see that people are worse off than them. It is a great trait in humankind, to want to help others, but while it might give them a good feeling to give five dollars to prevent starvation in Sudan, that represents less than one per cent of their income. To the people they are helping it is a lot because they only earn a dollar a day. Now, if you can feel good about helping someone earn a dollar a day, while you earn two hundred dollars a day, something is badly wrong with your individual scale of justice.'

'But it is better than doing nothing,' said the journalist.

'Is it? Throwing five dollars at the problem and knowing that half of that will be stolen by corrupt officials, is *not* a good situation. Really wealthy people like me and others I know, want to do more than that, but our incomes are so huge that we can rarely put a dent in our fortunes. Ask Bill Gates. Surely there must be a better way?'

'So, what is different about what the Federation does and the old communist regimes like the USSR and China.'

'Everything is different. Absolutely everything!'

'Explain.'

‘Communism works by the state owning most of the industries and evening out the pay packets of all of the workers, except that it doesn’t work. Most communist leaders corruptly acquired enormous fortunes. They and their immediate colleagues saw nothing wrong with buying themselves second and third homes and the finest cars and they stashed huge wealth in investments in capitalist countries. Even worse, these people were not like me, with my wealth. They were actually incompetent and ran the state businesses so badly that they stagnated. That filtered downwards, causing a poor proletariat class who found their living standard spiralling into poverty. With people like me at the top, the businesses are run efficiently and profitably and that provides the great American drip-down system, gradually improving the lot of those at the bottom of the food chain.’

‘So, what happens in the United States is better. Let me ask again,’ said the journalist, ‘what makes the Federation system different to such a degree that you’d throw away an economic structure which has worked well for two hundred years?’

‘In the Federation system, where everyone in the galaxy earns exactly the same income, the leaders are drawn from the people who want the very best for everybody. There is no other reason to be a leader. Corruption is impossible. Nanobots watch everyone and every afed. Literally, every penny of currency is traced, ensuring it is used only for valid purposes. It is not possible to be corrupt. If you have too much money, the bots will find it, work out where it came from and you will be charged with corruption. If you don’t overdo the corruption, as the ownership of afeds is traced, you’ll be taxed for reaching the threshold of wealth each year. The key to the whole system is the automatons. They grow food, they manufacture widgets, they account for government costs and income, they look after you, they care for the elderly, the sick, they are better surgeons than humans. They do everything. Humans are not needed.’

‘And?’

'This is not like, say America, where there are always low paid jobs at the bottom. Those jobs are gone. The robots do them. Even skilled jobs are gone. A brilliant electrician or mechanic, can never be as good as a robot and because robots are cheaply produced, they do everything we could ever need a person to do. Even your job is likely to go in Federation territories and certainly the jobs of these camera and sound system operators!' he said, pointing at the recording team.

'Now, if the robots are taking away not just some of the jobs, as they do in America today, but *all* of the jobs, something needs to be done. The Federation didn't see how to do it at first. They made a great mess of it.'

'How do you mean?'

'They allowed a free market to develop. Billions of people were dying of starvation and unless you were born into one of the families who owned everything, particularly the companies which built robots, you could never have a decent life. Can you imagine what that led to?'

'Friction? Unrest?'

'Exactly. There was a revolution and the wealthy and powerful were wiped out in many of the worlds. Literally, put up against the wall and shot. It was just like the Soviet revolution.'

'So, what happened?'

'The revolution happened! A charter was created which stated that everyone owns everything. Everyone would be given their actual share of every penny generated throughout the galaxy and the robots would ensure there was no corruption. The most altruistic of people became the leaders, running their planets and groups of planets for no more income than the man who does nothing but sit in the park all day feeding ducks.'

'But that's unfair!'

'*Why* is it unfair? Once you accept that the problem is *you* and *your* jealousy the unfairness vanishes. You have one life. You can do with it exactly what you will. You can invent things, write books, paint paintings, run governments or feed the ducks!

Everyone earns the same. Once you overcome the paranoid tendency to be jealous of someone getting something for nothing, and find you can ignore them, you find the system works. In fact, once it is up and working, you find that the good-for-nothing layabout no longer wants to sit all day watching television but starts to learn things or make things or help other people. It is a remarkable fact about intelligent creatures, that we would all like to help others. If there is no one to steal what you have or defraud you, and governments are no longer in it for what they can get out if it, you can relax and enjoy life yourself.'

Peter Stone sat back in his seat, 'The Federation wants everyone to be able to do exactly what they want and provides everyone with the means to do so. Feed the ducks if you wish, or run a region or country. You still have to be capable, of course, but nothing else need hold you back. Which side of the tracks you are born on is no longer relevant. Shame on us all that it once was!'

Not everyone believed the message, of course, but a substantial number did. It was that interview which began the accumulation of supporters which Peter Stone needed. When he called for a mass march on Washington they were only too happy to oblige.

The day arrived and his Internet army took to the roads, parking as close as they could get to the city and beginning to march from there. Several hundred of General Beech's freedom army concealed themselves within their ranks.

∞∞∞∞∞∞

'It has begun, sir,' said General Braun. 'We have several people who have infiltrated the group. The call went out yesterday to march on Washington this morning. We're getting reports of tens of thousands on the move. Free America has two or three hundred of their troops in among the protestors.'

'What will the troops do? Can't you go and stop the marchers? This isn't right. Tell them they're breaking the law,' said President Slimbridge.

Matthew Brown sighed to himself and said, 'Mr President, if you remember, we all discussed our course of action last week and agreed that we would let it happen. Spies have told us nothing violent is planned. We know about the troops, so we will monitor them. Intelligence is half the battle. They intend to form a sea of people around the White House and chant. We're going to ignore it.'

'I don't like it, Matthew. What if there's another faction within this march who are intent on attacking me? The Free America troops?'

'Then they'll have my men to deal with, sir,' said General Braun, 'but we're fairly sure this is a dry run. When they intend to activate their army, we'll know about it. As far as we're aware, they'll not even be carrying weapons today.'

'How many men are protecting us?' asked the president.

'More than enough, sir. You have no need to worry. When Free America do think the time has arrived to really attack, we'll ensure you are moved to safety. They are infiltrated by many of our own men. The intel is good,' said the general. 'We know their plans.'

ooooooooooo

News helicopters were soon on the scene as the morning progressed. One live reporter was describing the event as it took place.

'It is wall-to-wall people. Every street leading towards the White House is full of people, moving in a very orderly way. Every inch of space from the Lincoln Memorial to the Washington Memorial and beyond is flooded by a sea of humanity.

'The army were holding a line at Constitution Avenue Northwest, but we're seeing that they are gradually pulling back towards the White House. Jack Riley is down there right now. Over to you, Jack.'

Jack's voice came over continual video coverage from the helicopter. 'It is all very easy going at the moment. The army is pulling back and, frankly, they're chatting with the protestors. I haven't seen such a well-behaved crowd since this president came to office.

'I can see a firmer line of soldiers on E Street Northwest. That looks to me like the line in the sand. Back to you, Pete.'

'That's right, it seems as if they are going to hold the crowd along the south edge of the President's Park. Everything north of there on 15th and 17th streets is full of troops. We're flying north beyond the White House now.

'I'm told we're getting commands to not fly over the White House, so we're skirting around behind the Eisenhower building.

'Oh, yes. We can see many troops completely filling 15th and 17th streets right up to H Street, which is also occupied, providing cover to the north. This is like a siege, folks. The White House is surrounded by troops and they will, in turn, soon be surrounded by this enormous, yet apparently good natured crowd.

'We've had counting technology at work and have now got an estimate of the extent of the crowd. I can tell you that we are seeing in excess of one and a half million people in the streets. Police are keeping order in areas not under the military's control. How's it going down there, Jack?'

'We're squeezed between the Ellipse and E Street. There is a substantial line of troops on E street and reinforcements in the President's Park. The pressure of people south of me, that's behind me, is growing. There was an immediate rush to fill the Ellipse after the troops backed off. Hold on, I'm hearing megaphones from the army.

'Okay, they are trying to prevent crowd injuries. Roughly the message is "Avoid crushing. Do not push anyone in front of you. Remain orderly. Peaceful protestation is welcome. Don't crush. Injuries can be caused in crushes. Hold still. Don't push anyone." They're obviously concerned. I don't suppose there has ever been a crowd of this size anywhere in the world.'

'Stay safe, Jack,' said Pete.

‘I am as best as possible. The pressure eased after the bullhorn announcement. They’re continuing to put out safety messages. I can hear them from either side as well. Back to you, Pete.’

CNN had choppers off in the wings and the huge crowd now filled every green space within a mile of the White House. A sight never before seen in Washington. As the morning progressed, more people arrived. An unbelievable mass crowd which now filled every available space from Union Station across to 23rd Street.

∞∞∞∞∞∞

‘What’s happening, Matthew?’ asked the president nervously.

‘It’s okay, sir. The crowd is very orderly,’ said Matthew.

‘Intelligence tells us, sir, that at midday, they will chant in support of the Federation for fifteen minutes and then it should break up and disperse,’ said General Braun.

‘We must keep this away from the media,’ said the president.

Matthew Brown turned away and rolled his eyes at the general. ‘Sir,’ he said, ‘we cannot stop the media from filming and showing this. Madison is writing a great speech for you to put out either this evening or tomorrow. Don’t worry. We’ll handle it.’

∞∞∞∞∞∞

Midday came and the crowd hushed. It took a minute or two for the eerie silence to become complete, then a small group just south of the Ellipse began to chant, ‘Slimbridge out! Slimbridge a murderer! Remember New York! Not in our name!’

By the time it was repeated four or five times, the crowd started to pick it up and join in. Within a couple of minutes some two million voices joined the chant against President Slimbridge. ‘Slimbridge out! Slimbridge a murderer! Remember New York! Not in our name!’

‘I thought you said it was going to be about the Federation!’ shouted the president angrily.

‘We thought it was,’ said Matthew, glancing worriedly at General Braun.

‘That’s what intelligence said, sir. “When midday arrives, you are to become silent. Wait for the chant to begin and follow on.” There was nothing about it being a chant against the president,’ said the general.

‘Very clever,’ said Matthew. ‘They knew the crowd would chant whatever the lead group shouted.’

‘Slimbridge out! Slimbridge a murderer! Remember New York! Not in our name!’

‘Stop it!’ shouted the president. ‘Get it stopped, or heads will roll. Braun – do something!’ He turned and left the Oval Office.

The general looked towards Matthew, who shook his head just enough to indicate that it would not be possible to satisfy the president’s wishes.

‘Slimbridge out! Slimbridge a murderer! Remember New York! Not in our name!’

30 Smash and Grab

Looking back, now that I have returned to Dinbelay University and to my wife and children, and am trying to finish my trilogy on the experiences of the Federation's interaction with Earth, there is one aspect of the situation in the United States which was obviously going to occur, even if it was officially not allowed.

Humans are very clever creatures. It might not always seem to be so, but when you look at their behaviour in recent centuries, it is easy to see how their intelligence and life skills have improved by leaps and bounds. By the time the Federation discovered Earth, humans were approaching their peak levels of innovation.

It is only natural, therefore, that some humans within the United States, used their wealth to be able to finance Federation citizens in nearby territories to buy technology which was normally too expensive for individuals and of little use to them too. The wealthy, habitually getting their own way on a pre-Federation world, were naturally going to try to apply their old techniques to a new problem. That Peter Stone was a Federation citizen, but controlled billions of dollars in the USA, was ideal.

Inadvertently, the Federation brought about the situation whereby the founders of Free America and the Freedom Army, were able to circumnavigate rules and regulations to pursue their objectives tangentially and there is no species better at being devious than humankind.

I am, of course, assuming that it was not "allowed" by the Federation, "accidentally on purpose". Perhaps therein lies a future work for one of my students. I think I might have had my fill of the chaos of two systems on one planet and so I'll leave that joy to others.

Peter Stone's vast wealth, held in United States businesses he owned, could never be transferred to him once he'd become a Federation citizen in Canada. If it had been, then it would have been taxed away. Keeping his Federation citizenship separate from his corporate wealth in the USA allowed him to use those resources to acquire the equipment, technology and hardware, to bridge Free America's gap between its needs and actual capability.

∞∞∞∞∞∞∞

Starships come in all shapes and sizes. Some Federation ships can be several miles in length, especially some of the cruise liners which visit spectacular locations purely for fun. The Pleiades star cluster is one of the most popular among visitors, closely followed by the Veil Nebula and the Pillars of Creation. Large starships are almost exclusively Federation owned, but smaller vessels are sometimes purchased by groups of explorers wanting to study less popular parts of the Federation section of the galaxy. There are countless millions of planets which are uninhabited, or have no intelligent species living upon them. What better way to spend a lifetime than in visiting them and enjoying the wonderment of new places, never before visited by sentient beings.

Small starships tend to be few and far between as most inhabited locations are linked by regular routes. They do exist though and General Dick Beech, financed by Peter Stone's US wealth, had managed to obtain one. Only Federation citizens could own their technology, so Beech couldn't own it himself as he was back in the USA and had relinquished the Federation citizenship which had been offered to him, but Stone *could* own a starship. Hundreds of millions of US dollars found their way through the back alleys of financial wizardry and the starship arrived in orbit. Peter Stone beamed aboard where he met the crew who, in order to be coerced into this illegal plan, had been offered hundreds of thousands of US dollars each to provide their services for this one operation. This shows just how difficult it is to rid worlds of corruption, but, in the Federation's defence, this was the unique case of a divided world. Although not US citizens, Stone had secretly opened US accounts for them all through his corporate empire. They could never take their wealth out of the country, but they could certainly vacation within the US borders and enjoy spending their ill-gotten money.

Meantime, a Free America supporter, Rob Herbert, had been working in the offices of Ambassador Yol Lorel Distern, Federation Ambassador to the United States of America, and had acquired the secret coordinates for the White House meeting room which the ambassador was allowed to enter directly for meetings with the administration.

When the starship came into orbit around Earth, Charles Mayne, Dick Beech, Bob Nixon and Jim Collins were among the first to come aboard. They were much impressed by its size and facilities. A further group arrived consisting of Colonel Mike Henderson and a small elite squad of Marines. They all moved through the ship and gathered in a room approximately thirty metres by twenty, containing chairs laid out theatre style with two tables opposite and facing them. It could pass as a courtroom.

'You ready?' asked General Beech of Colonel Henderson.

'Yes, sir,' he said, standing at the head of his twenty Marines.

'Okay, Peter?' asked the general. 'Are the crowd still chanting?'

'They are, General. Yol Twedin, please transport them,' Peter Stone said to the alien standing beside a console to one side of the room.

Mike Henderson and his Marines vanished.

31 Revolutionary Wars

Emily's next visit to the esponging centre saw her partaking of scenario fourteen of nineteen, so she guessed a lot of time must have passed since her seeing the loss of Tedray's job and the poverty the family of Brune were experiencing. Then that cabinet meeting on yet another planet. The room-bot had warned her that there were some distressing scenes in what she was going to see today. She steeled herself for what was to come and said, 'Begin.'

Another new species. Emily found all the unusual varieties of aliens in these scenarios most fascinating. Today she appeared to be a large multilegged, yellow and black striped being. The scenario didn't last long. This was yet another family on the absolute breadline despite having been wealthy industrialists only a few years previously.

After another curtain call, she was in a more upright well-built creature which she recognised. It was an Arlucian. It took only seconds to absorb the poverty of these creatures, some wearing rags, gaunt expressions and with obviously emaciated torsos. They were starving. Eight sat around a bare table except for a jug of water.

'Where is he?' Emily heard herself saying.

'He said he'd be here at eight,' said another

'We're wasting our time,' moaned a third.

'What can we do if the government won't even listen to our representatives?' asked a fourth.

The door opened, blasting the room with what seemed like an artic gale.

'Shut the door!' they all called out, some adding colourful adjectives to the noun.

It slammed and another Arlucian pulled off his outer cloak, shaking snow onto the rough stone floor. He walked to the fireplace and held his hands out to the naked flames which provided the only heat in the room.

'Well, Vrist? What did they say?'

'Nothing,' said the newcomer. 'They're not interested in the plight of the people. Offered me a glass of forol, they did, as if hearing my complaint warranted some sort of celebration. They all sat around, fat as pigs with their robots bringing them snacks and drinks as if there was no end to their self-indulgence and wantonness. And me having nothing but a slice of stale pie in two days.'

'That's it then. Do we do it or not?' said another.

A cry of 'Yes' reverberated around the room.

The scene flickered into darkness and then immediately metamorphosed into a bright, but cold day in a large city square. Policebots were marshalling the crowd as it forced its way towards the Arlucian parliament building in the centre of Oridin. Clearly the numbers were in the tens of thousands, all moving and progressing as best they could with placards and lyrical chants. 'We want food! Food! Food now! Want it now, now, now!' and various combinations. The signs, frequently being buffeted by the cold winter wind, contained equally pointed messages to tell the government about their hunger, of children starving, of the elderly dying, of dissatisfaction.

They got to the parliament building. High on one side, an ornate balcony jutted forward from the white marble façade. The chanting increased in ferocity and loudness. Finally, the doors to the ornate platform opened. Through them came the prime minister, the chancellor and another minister.

The chants and cries faded, the silence winding its way outwards from the leading pack until you could have heard an afed drop.

'Go home,' said the prime minister. 'There is nothing for you here.'

'No,' was the reply, starting from the front and being echoed continually as the word worked its way back through the square and into the packed feeding side streets. 'No!' The message was one word and only one. Its clarity could not have been more eloquently presented.

'We have nothing for you,' said the third person on the terrace and the three of them turned to return inside.

The façade of the building above the balcony began to shatter as machine gun fire rattled from somewhere within the crowd. Robots flashed into action, barging through the tide of Arlucians to reach those with the weapons. People were grabbed by their shoulders and vanished into some holding area away from the square. Some handed over weapons and the firing continued, turning windows into gaping maws, but the noise of the firing gradually reduced as the robots found the perpetrators and eliminated them and their guns from the crowd.

The crowd noise ceased in an instant. A field of stasis held everyone within sight of the parliament building. They could no longer move. The protest was finished, the voice of the starving masses silenced. Emily was literally frozen solid. She could not move a muscle and the biting cold wind was chilling her whole body.

'Now, listen,' sounded a disembodied mechanical voice. 'You are all held in stasis. We will release the stasis, but you must immediately leave this area and go home. If you do not leave, you will be placed back into stasis for a period of twenty-four hours. Given the temperature today, many of you will not survive. It is your choice. Leave immediately or risk dying where you stand.

The stasis field vanished as quickly as it had come, and the crowd began, reluctantly, to disperse. The protest was truly ended now.

The black veil fell over the scene, Emily found herself in darkness until a new scene appeared before her. She was an Ewoinusivian. She recognised the dull, greenish-brown skin colour. Last time she'd been a native of Ewoinusi, she'd been in the body of Jon Sokut, the inventor of the first truly intelligent robot. This time, however, she was with a family in an apartment, high in a skyscraper. The television was blaring a warning.

'If you live within twenty miles of the Ewoinusi Cybernetics Amalgam factory, please leave now or take cover in the cellar or basement of your building.'

The television continued, 'Get out now! The protestors claim that they have placed a nuclear bomb in the factory. We cannot be certain whether or not it is a genuine claim. Stasis fields have been placed over the entire facility, but they may have no effect if it is a fission bomb. Get out now!'

Emily looked around. There was a frail elderly female in one of the chairs. 'Leave. Leave now!' the old one pleaded.

'We're not leaving you, you're our mother. We'll take our chances with you. We're twelve miles from the factory.'

Emily felt herself putting her arm around the elderly female as she looked at the other male in the apartment. 'We don't both need to stay,' her character said.

'Life's not worth living, anyway, Nril' said the other male. 'I'll take my chances here.'

Emily's character stood and pulled the old woman's chair away from the window and positioned it with its back towards the scene. Emily looked around at the view. She wondered where the factory was. She could see, a long way away, a huge industrial complex. She knew this factory was one of the biggest automaton manufacturing businesses in the empire. Perhaps it occupied the entire industrial complex.

The last of the twilight from the sun was fading, but the rising galactic lens provided the equivalent of half normal daylight. The city was still clearly visible.

Then it happened. A brilliant flash in the far distance. Nril's eyes were instantly blinded, leaving Emily seeing nothing but brilliant white. It was probably a good thing that she could no longer see, because it took away some of the terror she'd have experienced a few seconds later when the blast wave hit the skyscraper. It swayed three times, she heard Nril scream, and the concrete structure collapsed with her inside it. The scenario ended moments later with Nril's death. Emily's white blindness became jet black.

Now the scenes flashed by. Emily was lying beside a swimming pool outside a luxurious mountain top villa with a drink in her hand. A few friends were gathered around, drinking and eating while robots dealt with filling glasses, finding more food and picking up the debris which was left behind on tables and around the pool. She didn't recognise the species, but watched in horror as three more creatures appeared over the edge of the patio, their automatic weapons cutting everyone down, while robots threw themselves into the line of fire to try to protect their owners, all in vain.

And now inside a terrorist, another unknown species in a small spaceship, approaching a starship with hieroglyphs on its side. A caption flashed up that it said, 'Juranda Automaton Corporation.' The small ship faced the side of the luxury vessel and opened fire. It exploded into the vacuum, with people and possessions being flung far and wide.

Another scene, with creatures inside a luxurious saloon vehicle, passing between two ornate gates of a factory compound. The car exploded, killing all. A caption showed, 'Mepdetvis Cyber Company.'

Emily marched into a lavishly furnished boardroom. She was a large, lumbering creature not unlike the size of a grizzly bear, but smooth skinned, most of its body clothed and a face which did not have a bear's muzzle.

'We've been given an ultimatum, Mr President,' Emily heard her character saying.

A dozen similar creatures looked around at the newcomer. On the wall at one end of the room, a huge television monitor was showing scenes of thousands of protestors being held back by squads of robots.

'And what is it?' asked the president.

'Surrender and we'll be spared. Resist and no mercy will be shown.'

'Barrul,' said the president to the defence minister, 'why aren't the robots taking action?'

'They cannot hurt the protesters, sir. They can only hold them back.'

'Put them in stasis!' the president said.

'Can't, sir,' said the defence minister. 'The large field generator has been sabotaged and the others aren't able to do much. The robots can only freeze half a dozen at a time.'

Emily's character, still standing just inside the doorway, said, 'Sir, they gave me ten minutes to respond.'

'Tell them no, goddamnit!' the president responded.

'Hold on, sir,' said another minister. 'I'd rather surrender than die.'

Emily heard a communicator singing a discordant jangle. Her alter ego touched a button and held it to his ear. 'Sir, they've broken through. They've got weapons and are destroying the robots.'

Everyone looked around at the monitor where a large group had pushed by the robot guards; weight of numbers saw the gates tumble and the front group disappeared towards the cabinet offices above which the camera was mounted.

'I'm not dying in here!' shouted another minister, and he bolted for the door. Three more deserted the president who now sat with his head in his hands, staring at the desk.

Emily's character turned and followed the deserting cabinet members. In seconds they came out into a grand hallway. Protesters were charging against the doors, carrying park benches to use as battering rams. Eventually, there was a sharp crack. Bullet proof glass split as one of the doors twisted on its hinges and the crowd was inside. Emily held her arms out wide as did the others. She guessed it was a sign of surrender on this world. Ten or fifteen of the crowd pressed up against them, searching for weapons. Some spat in their faces as they were pushed back against a wall. Emily felt the fear of death flood through her character as the ministers' arms were cuffed. The remainder of the crowd charged the doors to the cabinet office. Shots were fired. They returned to the grand hallway. One of them, perhaps one of the leaders, told the others, 'Take them away, don't harm them. They'll go on trial.'

A television crew entered the hallway, squeezing through the crowd, past the rebel leader and into the cabinet office. Film of the carnage within was taken and the crew began interviewing the rebels.

That was the last of the inside of the building that Emily saw as she was manhandled across a courtyard. Another group of protesters made a concerted effort to destroy a section of ornate railings, broke into the courtyard and charged at the captive ministers. Emily felt a blow on her face and saw a cudgel falling away to her right. *What was that?* She felt a sharp pain in her chest. Blood was everywhere. She was dizzy. Unsteady. She fell into blackness.

The next scene broke into her vision. It was daylight. A caption to tell her she was on X-Jastu, looking at the empire's largest robot manufacturing company crossed her vision. She recognised the strange liquid-filled aliens as X-Jastuvians, rushing away from the huge cluster of buildings. Her character also turned to run, dropping a television camera. She was one of a media team, trying to film the action.

As she ran towards an alley between two glass skyscrapers, she became aware of a brilliant flash, reflected in the glass as she was lifted bodily off the ground, and thrown into and along the alleyway. Her globular structure did not stand a chance of survival during the impacts, which saved her experiencing death from the atomic weapon's deadly fireball.

As the darkness lifted, Emily was now in an enormous domed meeting room, a hundred metres in diameter with hundreds upon hundreds of desks and seats all facing towards a raised dais upon which sat fifteen aliens, none resembling the others in the slightest. This was different. Calmer. More orderly. In front of her was a desk with a half-metre monitor. She could see her reflection in the monitor – she was one of those large blue gorillas. She believed they were from Purrs and one of the fifteen on the stage was also her species, but slimmer and more delicate. Emily guessed her character was a male and the other was female. She looked around herself and saw that each table had a different type of alien with one or two assistants. Her character turned towards an assistant on her left, and said, 'I think they're about to start.'

A bell chimed together with a bright light for those who did not normally use sound, plus vibrations for still other species. Emily saw and heard it on the monitor in front of her which also resonated with the pulsing tremors.

'I call this first full meeting of the assembly to order,' said a Pestochian in the centre of the table on the dais. 'My name is Parral Joroldasteen from Pestoch, and I have been duly elected president by the council of members. My vice president, here, Ya Eloo Vlorofirt from Purrs, has also been duly elected. Either side of me are the executive cabinet and their names appear on your screen.

'I take great pleasure in welcoming two hundred and one delegates representing the three hundred and seventy-four planets which currently form what was the Galactic Empire.

'It was felt that the word empire had connotations of emperors and excessive power, and so, from this day forth, our collection of trading planets shall be known as the Galactic Federation, or just Federation for short.

'The administration is run by the people, for the people. Sections of this cabinet of fifteen shall resign on different years so that the entire cabinet is replaced every ten years and that no time is given for factions to become dominant.

'As the Federation grows, the number of delegates will also rise, but the cabinet will never exceed fifteen so that we can run a tight and efficient administration.

‘A Federation charter is currently being prepared by a special committee of delegates and it will guide us along the following broad principles.

‘Number one – Every citizen of the Federation is considered equal to every other. All planets agreed to this except fourteen who have not agreed to join. Those planets are listed on your screens now.

‘Number two – With robots producing almost all goods and services, the value of the profit from said goods and services will be taken by the government and distributed equally to each Federation citizen.

‘Number three – No citizen shall receive more than any other citizen except for small amounts paid for inventions and occasional special services. For the purpose of this regulation, it should be noted that all delegates and cabinet members are ordinary citizens and receive no more than any others. Robots will monitor legitimate expenses and pay them accurately.

‘Number four – The currency shall be the afed.

‘Number five – The Federation shall be policed by robots and fleets of nanobots who will detect crimes, any corruption, and set punishments as decreed by the council of members.

‘Number six – No planet will be allowed to join the Federation unless they accept the entire charter once it is prepared and circulated.

‘Number seven – Each year, the council will set a maximum number of afeds for any individual to own. As each afed is individually monitored by automatons, keeping track of people’s individual holdings is relatively simple. Excess afeds held will be removed from the individuals on a graduated taxation basis and returned to the general pot of resources.

‘Number eight – All planetary armies, navies, air force and space fleets will be controlled by a central ministry and will be used to assist during and after natural disasters. A small Federation Enforcement Unit will deal with any crimes and will recruit as necessary to deal with any enemies of the Federation.

The council will always try to negotiate with potential members and the Federation has a principle of expansion only through total agreement with the applying planets.

'I should add that the revolution we have all just suffered has not left many wealthy citizens. The Federation is now primarily ordinary people who will share the wealth and resources of the entire Federation. While the full charter will take some time to be published, I can tell you that we have agreed the first section as follows.

'Sentient beings born on Federation territory are entitled to an equal share of the resources of said Federation, the gross product of said Federation and equal representation within said Federation. This applies whether or not such beings are more or less valuable producers, have more or less valuable intellects, are more or less able bodied or mentally able. The care and protection of all Federation beings is the ultimate responsibility of all fellow Federation beings.'

Emily realised that she was witnessing the first assembly of the new Federation, and that it had arisen out of the greed and selfishness of those in power previously. Three hundred and seventy-four planets at this meeting would swell to nearly a quarter of a million over the six hundred thousand years before Earth's encounter. The delegates would grow from two hundred and one to four hundred and thirteen and the charter had held strong throughout those millennia.

'End course,' said Emily, removing her blindfold.

The scenario disappeared and Emily found herself watching young alien animals at play on some unknown planet.

'What do you recommend next, room-bot?' she asked.

32 Spangled Banner

Inside the small meeting room in the White House, which had been designated as the arrival point for ambassadorial visits, a fully armed squad of Marines had materialised, with Colonel Mike Henderson at its head.

Mike had studied detailed plans of the White House. His first task was to wave his squad off in various directions. Each person encountered was irradiated with a marker beam which caused them to be transported up to the starship. They were held in two specially prepared rooms with locked doors and had no idea that they were in orbit.

So far, there had been no time for any person the Marines encountered to resist. Each person who so much as glanced at Mike's force had themselves immediately transported away. It was going well. The plan was to not have any casualties. After eliminating armed security men outside the Oval Office, Mike and two Marines burst into the hallowed room. Matthew Brown, General Braun, Vice President Tucker and Admiral Mann looked around in shock at the intrusion.

'Don't move,' said Mike as the four men turned towards them.

'What is this?' asked the admiral.

'This, sir, is an invitation to come quietly to a meeting,' said Mike, 'but first we need to find the president.'

At that moment, a side door into the Oval Office from the president's study opened, and two Marines entered with President Slimbridge between them. 'Found him, sir,' said one of the Marines.

'I insist you free me!' shouted President Slimbridge. 'Damn it, I'm your commander in chief!'

'Sorry, sir,' said Mike. 'You're coming with us.' He irradiated all of them and touched a chest microphone. 'Beam us up too, Yol Twedin.'

The West Wing and Oval Office were suddenly emptied of those in power.

The chant was no longer heard by those who mattered. 'Slimbridge out! Slimbridge a murderer! Remember New York! Not in our name!'

∞∞∞∞∞∞∞∞∞∞

As each of the kidnapped people from the White House arrived on board the ship, they were scanned for weapons and sorted into categories. Those who were of no major importance were held in a separate part of the ship where they had some food and leisure facilities – pool, dartboard, table tennis etc.

The more senior people were re-transported into the starship's theatre. General Braun, Admiral Mann, Matthew Brown and Vice President Tucker, escorted by the Marines, were seated behind a balustrade on the left of the room. They protested loudly but were ignored. President Slimbridge was transported directly into a glass booth on the opposite side of the theatre. It was reminiscent of the courtroom containers at Nuremburg.

Mayne, Beech, Nixon, Collins and Stone sat behind a large central table under the projector screen. The theatre seats were occupied by a couple of dozen Free America supporters, thirty senators and thirty members of Congress. The senators and members of Congress were split equally into Democrats and Republicans. They had all been contacted individually and had agreed to come to the meeting, not knowing its actual nature or location. The names Mayne, Nixon and Beech were enough to pique their curiosity. Many asked where they were but were not told. Three aliens also sat in the theatre seats. Towards the back of each side of the theatre were four television crews – CNN, FOX, BBC and Euronews who had volunteered to record the event, despite not knowing its actual nature. It had all been well organised over the previous week.

General Dick Beech, in his full four-star general's uniform, stood when everyone was present.

'Welcome to the Free America starship – Spangled Banner,' he said and there was an immediate buzz of conversation among those sitting in the audience. On each side of the room, steel shutters withdrew, and windows showed the heavens on one side and the curve of the beautiful planet Earth on the other. Gasps came from most of those who were on board. They'd had no idea that they'd been taken into space. More protests came from those kidnapped from the White House, except the president, who was held in stasis within his glass cage as he'd been disruptive from the moment he arrived.

'Please settle down so that I can explain why you have been invited or brought here,' said the general.

Gradually the hubbub eased, but most still looked in awe at the view of the Earth, gradually rotating beneath them.

'I am General Dick Beech. The four with me on the front bench are Presidential Candidate and Congressman Charles Mayne; Vice Presidential Candidate Robert Nixon; Congressman Mayne's Chief of Staff James Collins; and Peter Stone a supporter from Federation Canada.

'In the cage on my left, of course, is President John Silvester Slimbridge. On my right are members of President Slimbridge's administration. Vice President Erol Tucker, General Walter Braun, Admiral Alan Mann and Matthew Brown, the president's executive advisor. Beside them, but seated separately is the director of the FBI, David Mendoza, who has been invited as an observer.

'Finally, we are joined today by the Terotonian, Ya Zo Unsela, and the Clueb, Yol Teron Estorne who has one hundred per cent recall. The other alien is Yol Twedin, the captain of Free America's starship, the Spangled Banner.

'Let me explain why we have gathered you all here.'

Some more chatter rose and fell among the audience.

'This is not a trial,' said the general. 'We have no legal method whereby to call this a trial. It is, however, a hearing to demonstrate the requirement for proper judicial action. I want to start the hearing rolling, so, firstly, President Slimbridge, we will release you from stasis for as long as you remain quiet during proceedings. You will be allowed a statement when you are released, lasting not longer than one minute.' The general nodded to Yol Twedin and President Slimbridge steadied himself in the cage as the stasis field was released.

'You will pay for this kidnapping,' said President Slimbridge, then turned to the main assembly. 'I am President of the United States of America and do not recognise the authority of anything or anyone in this room. I demand to be released and returned with others from my administration to the White House. I see before me five wanted traitors to the people of the USA, of whom four were previously tried and sentenced to death, only having been rescued by illegal alien intervention. The United States of America is not under the jurisdiction of the Federation and I object, in the strongest possible terms, to them assisting in setting up this kangaroo court.' He sat down.

'Thank you, Mr President,' said General Beech. 'As a matter of record, this is not a Federation starship. The Spangled Banner is wholly owned by Federation citizen, Peter Stone, in the name of Free America and the aliens who are crewing the ship are doing so voluntarily. Robots on board are also owned by Free America. We've had no Federation assistance in setting up this meeting. We'll now hear from Vice Presidential Candidate, Robert Nixon who will present important evidence which led to the reasons for our calling this assembly.'

Bob Nixon got to his feet. He began, 'Some of you will know me. I was White House Chief of Staff for President Spence. I must say that he was a good man, who always had our country at heart. He was honourable, too, and did not take the decision to support the Federation lightly. More importantly, I need to impart some information about the day of the UN bombing. I was inside the White House that day and clearly saw General Burko and Vice President Slimbridge arrive in the vice president's office. General Braun, Admiral Mann and Matthew Brown entered shortly afterwards. This was a good hour *before* the bomb was exploded. John Slimbridge has always claimed that he was still being held in prison at the time of the UN atrocity. He is lying about this.'

'Lies,' shouted Slimbridge.

Dick Beech stood again. 'Thank you, Mr Nixon and Mr President, for your statements and comments. It is only right and proper that we investigate the president's claim that Mr Nixon is being untruthful. We are fortunate to have with us today, Ya Zo Unsela who is a Terotone. Terotonians have some extraordinary abilities. They can heal mental problems, calm down trauma victims and also tell whether a person is being truthful or lying. Ya Unsela, please tell us if Robert Nixon is lying or telling the truth.'

The strange alien continually phased in and out of reality, which made it very difficult to observe her. She got to her feet. 'Yol Beech, I can tell you as a matter of certainty, that Yol Nixon was speaking truthfully.'

'Thank you, Ya Unsela.

'The president is correct that this court has no official recognition,' said the general, 'but getting to the truth is its only objective. Now, General Braun, you claimed that a rogue anti-Federation faction within the military stole a nuclear bomb from the armed forces and placed it within the UN basement. Knowing that Ya Unsela is listening to you, would you like to repeat that claim now. Before you speak, Walter, can I plead with you on a personal level, as past colleagues, to do the honourable thing for your country and tell the absolute truth? Is it not time for this farce of an administration to be brought to an end?'

General Braun didn't move. It was clear that he was considering his position.

'Tell the truth, Walter. It will go better for you,' said Bob Nixon.

The general rose to his feet and looked around himself at his co-accused, the television crews, the senators, congressmen and

President Slimbridge. He shook his head several times. Was it in anguish or just that he was not going to speak? He looked at Admiral Mann. The two men exchanged glances and the admiral nodded to him.

'All right. It's time,' he said.

'Shut up, man!' shouted Slimbridge. 'They're just trying to browbeat you. This court has no power.'

General Braun looked straight at the president. 'I'm sorry, sir. This has gone on too long. Under orders from Vice President Slimbridge and knowing that President Spence was accused of treason, by planning to hand control to the aliens, we arranged for a bomb to be placed in the United Nations basement. Admiral Mann and General Burko countersigned my instructions. The vice president had convinced us it was the only way to save the country from alien invasion.' He crumpled back into his seat and gazed silently at the floor. Was he weeping?

'Ya Unsela,' said General Beech, 'was that a true statement?'

'Indeed, it was,' said the Terotonian.

'Admiral Mann, will you confirm General Braun's statement?'

He stood, said, 'I will,' and promptly sat again.

General Beech took the floor again. 'Yol Estorne, you were at the trial of General Buck Burko, who is now serving fourteen years in stasis at The Hague in the Netherlands. Does General Braun's statement match that of General Burko?'

The Clueb flew into the air and took a position in front of the main desk. 'I can confirm that General Burko admitted that, with a squad of his men, he placed the bomb in the UN building and personally set the timer on the specific instructions of President Slimbridge.'

'Thank you, Yol Estorne,' said the general. 'We come now to Vice President Tucker. What is your involvement in this immoral and illegitimate regime?'

The vice president, tall and rangy, got to his feet, ran his hand through his hair and said, 'I played no part in the UN bombing and, in fact, this is the first time I've become aware of it being anything other than a rogue anti-Federation group.'

'Ya Unsela?'

'True, but he had suspicions,' said the Terotonian.

'I'd like to say something else,' said the vice president.

'Go ahead,' said General Beech.

'When I became vice president, I had no idea of what Braun, Burko and Mann had done for the president. I tried to be a force for good in the White House, and a calming influence. I am ashamed that I did not believe my own suspicions. I have done nothing illegal but feel great shame to be associated with President Slimbridge and resign forthwith.'

'Fool!' shouted the president. 'You'll regret that when this farcical trial is over.'

'President Slimbridge. Do you wish to make a statement yourself to explain the circumstances? Ya Unsela will then advise of its truthfulness,' said General Beech.

The president returned to his seat. 'I have nothing to say to this illegal so-called hearing.'

'Mr Brown, do you have anything to say?' asked the general.

'I plead the fifth, but I had nothing to do with the UN explosion,' said Matthew Brown.

'Ya Unsela?' said Dick Beech.

'True,' said the flimsy being, 'but I sense that he knew the bomb had been organised and planted by the generals and the president.'

'Okay,' said Dick Beech. 'Let me outline the options here.

'We have two admissions of guilt. General Braun and Admiral Mann. You have a simple choice. These news cameras will show what has taken place here when they return to Earth. You can, if you wish, return to the USA. It will, no doubt, result in charges of murder, treason against President Spence's administration and crimes against humanity. A life sentence or worse.

'Alternatively, you could be handed over to the Federation for trial at The Hague which would result in Federation punishment. Which would you prefer? Choose now. We can transport you to either location.'

The general and admiral briefly discussed the situation, while President Slimbridge hurled insults across the room which became so bad that he was returned to stasis.

The admiral said, 'We'll go to the Federation.'

'Vice President Tucker,' said Beech. 'You have resigned, and we will return you to your residence in Washington. Whether or not you will be pursued for other crimes against the people, will be up to the people themselves once they've seen the recordings. Matthew Brown, the same applies to you.

'Yol Twedin, release the president's stasis. President Slimbridge, you do not have a choice. You will be returned to the USA in the custody of the director of the FBI and will stand trial for your crimes. It could possibly go easier for you if you resigned as president right now, thus allowing the speaker to become the acting president.'

'Fuck off, Beech!'

'As you wish. It is only right for the American people to decide your fate.'

General Beech turned to the audience. 'Members of Congress and the Senate,' said General Beech, 'you have seen what has happened here and the news media at the back of this theatre will show the whole event tonight. We have a proposal to put to you.

'Among you here are the Senate and House majority and minority leaders and the Speaker of the House of Representatives. If President Slimbridge had resigned, the Speaker would have become acting president. We are proposing to you that you call full meetings of both houses and appoint Democrat Charles Mayne as temporary president. He is prepared to step into the presidency for a period of six months with Robert

Nixon, a Republican, as his vice president and James Collins as chief of White House staff. At the end of that six month period there will be a new presidential election and a repeat of the Federation referendum. Would you be prepared to support such a temporary regime and put it before the members?'

There was considerable chatter among both the members of Congress and the senators. Eventually the Speaker stood up. He said, 'In principle, we would agree with this, but we would like Congressman Mayne and Robert Nixon to stand up and make statements to the effect that they will stand down in six months. We would then like the Terotonian to confirm that they are being truthful.'

'Gentlemen?' said General Beech, looking at Charles and Bob.

Charles stood, 'We have no problem doing that; however, I'd like it to be known that I might wish to stand again in six months' time in the new election.'

'Sounds good to us,' said the Speaker. 'Let's hear the statements.'

33 Looking Back

When I returned to Federation Earth, eight years later, with my wife and family, it was to enjoy a fortnight's scuba diving in Trinidad as guests of Paula Wilson. We hired a sailboat and I finally did get to sail some of the Earth's seas as I'd dreamed of that first time I saw the planet from orbit. As I was putting the finishing touches to my book, it would have been unnatural to not investigate the changes which had happened since the abduction of President Slimbridge.

President Mayne was good to his word, standing for a second term after his six-month stint in the White House, but it was not to be. He lost the election. A human unknown to me, President Derek Colclough, had taken office with Matthew Brown as his vice president – it seems that the economist hadn't been too tarnished by his time with the disgraced and imprisoned John Slimbridge, who was unlikely to ever be released. I am thankful to President Colclough for permitting me access to White House tapes recorded during the Spence and Slimbridge period.

Charles Mayne blamed his loss on his support for a yes vote in the Federation referendum. It had been much closer than the previous manipulated occasion, but Matthew Brown had provided very convincing arguments on independence, freedom and the right for Americans to live their lives in the way they wanted.

The United States had always had a very vocal and active religious right. It was natural for them to have a great fear that the Federation, being what they called ultra-socialist or communist, might take away their rights to live as they wished, bear arms and control their own destinies. Their influence, plus the gut feelings of many other ordinary Americans who had similar beliefs, to a lesser or greater degree, had caused the referendum to flounder. The United States was to remain independent.

In the years since the referendum there had been a gradual emigration of Americans who liked the concept of full equality of people. Many remained because the principles of honest hard work and even hardship were ingrained into their childhoods and youth. They preferred that to what some called luxurious slavery under the robots. Often their decisions were taken through lack of knowledge of what Federation life really comprised, but for many it was a matter of principle and the American way.

I must, in fairness, point out that a small number of people did move the opposite way, into the United States, but they were exceptions, moving because they believed their human rights were being infringed by the Federation. Quite a number of aliens followed their lead and were growing into a substantial population of people who did not like what they called the Federation's surveillance culture.

I said, once before, that humans were clever creatures. Scientists in the United States managed to backward engineer much of the Federation technology. Within five years, home-made shuttles replaced aeroplanes and they were also back in orbit with a new space station and plans to obtain their share of the moon's resources. The Federation cooperated whenever they could. It had no intention of stopping the USA from space exploration. The original ban had been on pre-Federation Earth after the New York atrocity. How long would it be before the United States had starship technology and roamed the galaxy as proud independent people? Only time would tell.

In the rest of the world, Federation Earth, it is now called, things had settled down. As in the other quarter of a million worlds, each and every being had the same opportunity as any other. Nothing was more important than health and health was guaranteed to be the top priority and provided without favour. Whatever was needed to improve the lives of individuals was undertaken in the best possible manner. Gone were the charities – there was no longer a need for a charity if the government's sole responsibility was looking after the people. A few still existed to support religions, but if anything else needed support, such as endangered species, the government stepped in, called upon the experts and resolved the problem. No longer would paraplegics or amputees have to live less well than able-bodied beings. Whatever they needed was provided as a matter of course.

Some fringe civil rights organisations would have still preferred a chaotic world as long as it was free, but the cries of communism or socialism no longer rang out among the populace, except in one place, where standards of living were soon lagging noticeably behind the Federation. But enough of the interminable waste of time worrying about politics – it no longer mattered except in America.

When we first arrived on Earth, we spent a few days in London and, while the family visited museums and art galleries, I looked up Emily Fraser, or Emily Fraser-Cutler as she now was. She lived in Welwyn Garden City and was happily married with two children. We met up for afternoon tea and I discovered she'd become quite a buff on Federation history, giving regular talks to school groups on how the Federation came into being. It was enjoyable to meet up and I promised her a signed copy of my book.

As for others, Lara Horvat was somewhere off-world, Miles had become a great crime writer with his books set on a violent and crime-ridden pre-Federation Earth. One person who had been a great influence on my book, but whom I never had the pleasure to meet, was Perfect Okafor. I think I'll dedicate my book to her and also to Jack Spence as, together, although they never saw it themselves, they paved the way for Earth's eventual joining of the Federation.

I plan to return at some point, perhaps after my book is published, or when I eventually retire, to discover if anything more has changed. For now, though, the family is enjoying the mesmerising colours of the fish and invertebrates which inhabit the Caribbean Sea, the place I first heard of while I was on Mars and finding out about the Earth from David Attenborough's wonderful *Blue Planet* documentary.

So long, fellow sentient beings. Look me up on Daragnen some time.

Rummy Blin Breganin

745,811 New Era (Earth date 2037)

END

Tony's Books

Thank you for reading ***HIDDEN FEDERATION.*** Reviews are very important for authors and I wonder if I could ask you to say a few words on the review page where you purchased the book. Every review, even if it is only a few words with a star rating, helps the book move up the rankings.

Currently, I have written nine science fiction stories. ***Federation*** and ***Federation and Earth*** were the first two books in my ***Federation Trilogy***. ***Moonscape*** is the first in a series about astronaut, Mark Noble. The second book, ***Moonstruck***, was launched at the end of January and ***Trappist-1*** is the third. The fourth book in the series, ***The Spolding Conundrum*** is due for release on 20th December 2020. My other books are all stand-alone novels.

More detail about each of the books can be found at **Harmsworth.net**.

THE DOOR: Henry Mackay and his dog regularly walk alongside an ancient convent wall. Today, as he passes the door, he glances at its peeling paint. Moments later he stops dead in his tracks. He returns to the spot, and all he sees is an ivy-covered wall. The door has vanished!

FEDERATION takes close encounters to a whole new level. A galactic empire of a quarter of a million worlds stumbles across the Earth. With elements of a political thriller, there is an intriguing storyline which addresses the environmental and social problems faced by the world today.

The ***FEDERATION AUDIOBOOK*** is due for release at the end of June 2020. Not just read, but Marni Penning, aka The Lady Hamlet, but dramatised through her many voices.

FEDERATION & EARTH. Book two in the Federation trilogy.

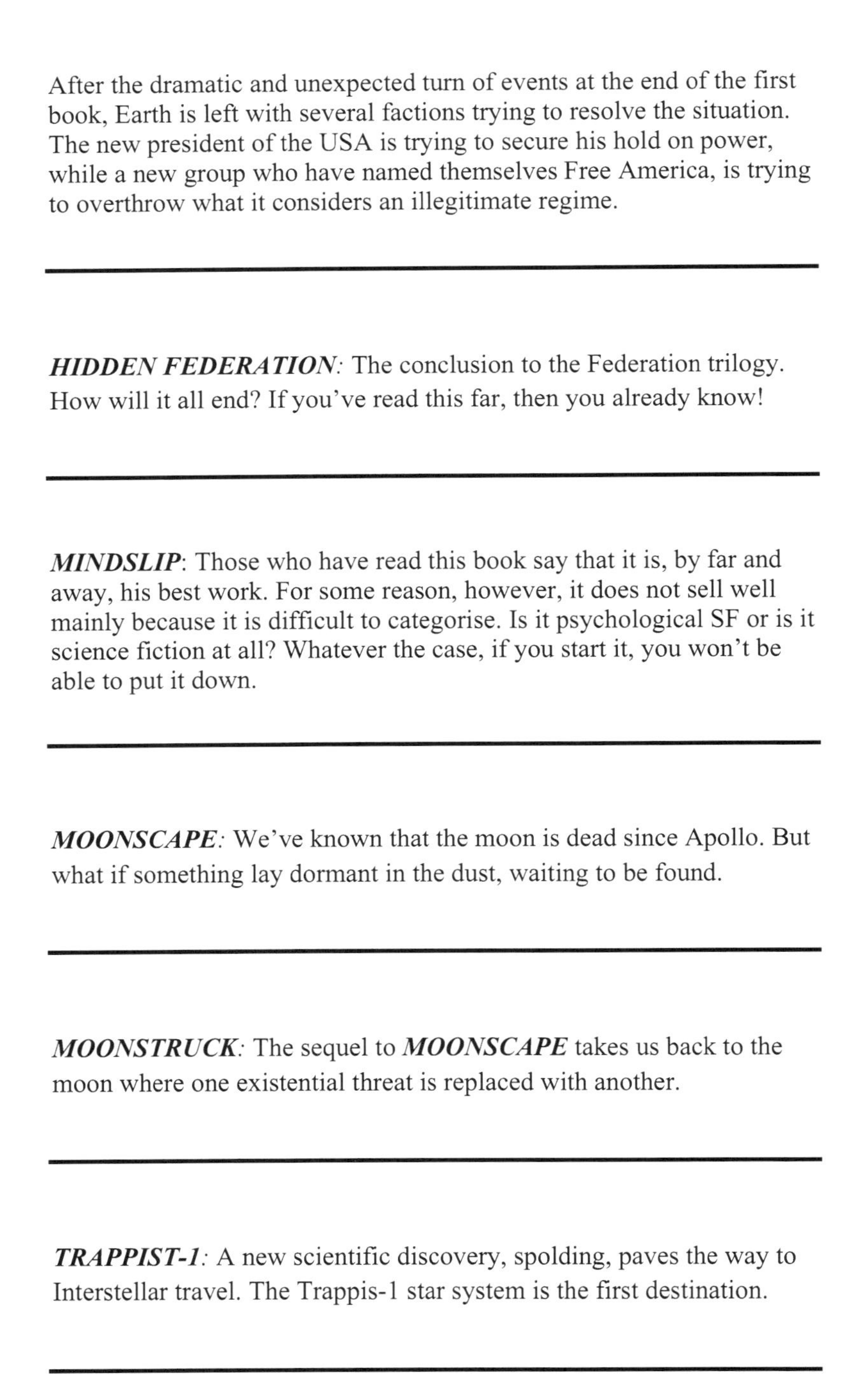

After the dramatic and unexpected turn of events at the end of the first book, Earth is left with several factions trying to resolve the situation. The new president of the USA is trying to secure his hold on power, while a new group who have named themselves Free America, is trying to overthrow what it considers an illegitimate regime.

***HIDDEN FEDERATION**:* The conclusion to the Federation trilogy. How will it all end? If you've read this far, then you already know!

MINDSLIP: Those who have read this book say that it is, by far and away, his best work. For some reason, however, it does not sell well mainly because it is difficult to categorise. Is it psychological SF or is it science fiction at all? Whatever the case, if you start it, you won't be able to put it down.

***MOONSCAPE**:* We've known that the moon is dead since Apollo. But what if something lay dormant in the dust, waiting to be found.

MOONSTRUCK**:* The sequel to ***MOONSCAPE takes us back to the moon where one existential threat is replaced with another.

***TRAPPIST-1**:* A new scientific discovery, spolding, paves the way to Interstellar travel. The Trappis-1 star system is the first destination.

THE SPOLDING CONNUNDRUM: The fourth book in the Mark Noble series of space adventures. Something went wrong at the end of Trappist-1 and the team must find a solution before time runs out. Due for release on 20th December 2020.

MARK NOBLE SPACE ADVENTURES ANTHOLOGY 1: Three books in one volume offering a money saving discount. Includes ***Moonscape***, ***Moonstruck*** and ***Trappist-1***.

THE VISITOR: Specialist astronaut Evelyn Slater encounters a small, badly damaged, ancient, alien artefact on the first ever space-junk elimination mission. Where was it from? Who sent it?

THE VISITOR is now an exciting audiobook beautifully read by Marni Penning, aka The Lady Hamlet.

Non-Fiction by Tony Harmsworth

LOCH NESS, NESSIE & ME: Almost everyone, at some point in their lives, has wondered if there was any truth in the stories of monsters in Loch Ness? ***LOCH NESS, NESSIE & ME*** answers all the questions you have ever wanted to ask about the loch and its legendary beast.

SCOTLAND'S BLOODY HISTORY: Ever been confused about Scotland's history – all the relationships between kings and queens, both Scottish and English? Why all the battles, massacres and disputes? ***SCOTLAND'S BLOODY HISTORY*** simplifies it all.

Reader Club

Building a relationship with my readers is the very best thing about being a novelist. In these days of the Internet and email, the opportunities to interact with you is unprecedented. I send occasional newsletters which include special offers and information on how the series are developing. You can keep in touch by signing up for my no-spam mailing list. It also gives you the opportunity to assist with future releases by becoming a VIP Beta Reader.

Sign up at my webpage: Harmsworth.net or on my Facebook page and I will send you a free copy of the first Mark Noble adventure – ***MOONSCAPE***.

If you have questions, don't hesitate to write to me at Tony@Harmsworth.net.

Printed in Great Britain
by Amazon